Mackenzie McKade

THE Game ECSTASY

ELLORA'S CAVE
ROMANTICA PUBLISHING

An Ellora's Cave Romantica Publication

www.ellorascave.com

The Game

ISBN # 1419952943
ALL RIGHTS RESERVED.
The Game Copyright© 2005 Mackenzie McKade
Edited by: Heather Osborn
Cover art by: Syneca

Electronic book Publication: May, 2005
Trade paperback Publication: November, 2005

Warning:

The following material contains graphic sexual content meant for mature readers. *The Game* has been rated *E-rotic* by a minimum of three independent reviewers.

Ellora's Cave Publishing offers three levels of Romantica™ reading entertainment: S (S-ensuous), E (E-rotic), and X (X-treme).

S-*ensuous* love scenes are explicit and leave nothing to the imagination.

E-*rotic* love scenes are explicit, leave nothing to the imagination, and are high in volume per the overall word count. In addition, some E-rated titles might contain fantasy material that some readers find objectionable, such as bondage, submission, same sex encounters, forced seductions, etc. E-rated titles are the most graphic titles we carry; it is common, for instance, for an author to use words such as "fucking", "cock", "pussy", etc., within their work of literature.

X-*treme* titles differ from E-rated titles only in plot premise and storyline execution. Unlike E-rated titles, stories designated with the letter X tend to contain controversial subject matter not for the faint of heart.

The Game
Ecstasy

Dedication

To Bill, Tia, Samantha, Ashley, and Dusty, thanks for believing and never giving up on me. And to Debbie, a wonderful friend and mentor, I owe you my deepest gratitude. Hugs to you all.

Trademarks Acknowledgement

The author acknowledges the trademarked status and trademark owners of the following wordmarks mentioned in this work of fiction:

Twilight Zone: CBS Broadcasting, Inc.

Chapter One

If paybacks were a bitch, Chastity Ambrose was about to be hit by two-hundred pounds of solid retribution.

Frozen to the stage, camera lights glaring, she strained to see clearly. Starbursts and black spots blurred the man's features. Nevertheless, his stormy gait said it all. Seth Allen was mad and ready to wreak vengeance.

A thunderclap of female and male appreciation filled the air. It was always that way with each personal appearance of the 2104 Astral-ball Champion. Men envied him for his virile masculinity and prowess. Women loved him for his more elemental aspects — sexy good looks and a to-die-for bod. Six feet two inches of honed muscle and dark charisma.

And he had been all hers two years ago.

"*Seth Allen!*" Monty Jamison, the game host of the Voyeur II series, announced him once again, clearly in awe. Any minute Chastity expected the man in the tan designer suit to fall to his knees and cry, "I'm not worthy!"

Okay, so she wasn't the greatest athlete of all time or worth over a billion dollars. Nevertheless, she had her own notoriety. A recognized figure in the modeling circuit, she was known as the only woman who had ever brought the great Seth Allen to his knees.

Fact was, she needed the prize this contest promised. Failure was not an option. She had to win. If not for the money, she wouldn't be caught dead participating in a sexually explicit game show like Voyeur II. There was never a hint as to what kind of situation or feat you might be asked to perform. It was simply icing on the cake that her opposition was her ex-fiancé. The man she had left at the altar two years ago.

"2104 Astral-ball Champion and the *new* owner of the Los Angeles Annihilators!" The stage shook as the crowd roared hanging on to each of the announcer's words.

So Seth had done it. Purchased the very team he played for. Her heart swelled with pride. It had been his dream and she was happy for him. And she wasn't the only one.

Vibrant faces beamed admiration. Many lunged to their feet, the applause deafening. Still, it didn't drown out the rapid heartbeat pounding in her ears. The audience adored Seth Allen. He was a man's hero, a woman's fantasy.

Chastity watched the play of muscles beneath his soft, transparent shirt as he approached. The chameleon material was a favorite of hers. In fact, Seth had purchased her several outfits made of the mesmerizing cloth that changed colors and hues with every movement, defining the mounds and curves of her anatomy. Body heat made the cloth glow. And judging by the fiber optics radiating enough energy to cause a power surge, the man was hot.

Yet it was the bulge between his thighs that quickly caught her eye. His jeans were a perfect fit, outlining an extremely generous package.

He was magnificent.

No one could make her pussy weep like him. No one else could bring her off the bed with an orgasm that shattered all threads of reality.

Regret squeezed her heart. If only they could forget the past. If only he'd forgive her, she would willingly spend this night with her legs wrapped around him, his cock buried deep within her wet core. If…if…if…

As always, Seth was gracious and humble to his fans. He bowed and his shoulder-length hair fell, flashing blue-black as light filtered through it. She swallowed the knot in her throat. Even now, she could feel the silky strands glide through her fingers. Feel its coolness slide over her naked breasts, down her stomach, pooling at the apex of her thighs. Her nipples tingled and her crotch ached with the need to once again feel his touch. A tremor caught her unaware as she inhaled a ragged breath.

Four large cinema-plasmic screens suspended in the air narrowed in on his handsome face. Now everyone was up close and personal with his piercing blue eyes and dark features. Even without his combat uniform, he appeared like a gladiator torn from the pages of the Roman days. And she had always loved his sexy Van Dyke goatee and mustache. Not only did it give him that strong, dangerous mien, but it was a helluva ride.

Spellbound, she watched as his sensual lashes lowered lazily to shadow even more sensual eyes. Then he winked, sending half the women to their feet and scrambling toward the stage. A barrage of bodyguards fought back the onslaught of lust swamping the platform.

Rich, thick laughter spilled from his lips like honey. A heady aphrodisiac that made every woman in the theater this October evening crave a taste of him.

Acoustics in the building amplified the soft moans of appreciation. A sliver of jealousy crawled beneath Chastity's skin. Over the years, she had heard rumors of his prowess. A boldly sensuous lover whose name women whispered like a prayer. But she knew the real truth. None of the tittle-tattle had even come close to his virile masculinity.

The scent of raw desire seeped into the air. Flung from somewhere in the back of the theater, a pair of black silk panties soared through the air and landed at Seth's feet. He stood for a pregnant moment, and then he stooped to retrieve the lingerie. Pressing the material to his nose, he closed his eyes, an expression of rapture crossing his face.

The audience went deathly still.

He inhaled.

The roar was deafening as the crowd came alive. Through heavy bedroom eyes he mouthed "thank you" and slipped the lacy thing into his pocket. As if on cue the room filled with womanly sighs and several deep-throated "yeah, babys".

Chastity's stomach churned. She was going to be sick. Seeing Seth again was excruciating. Assuming he was here to wreak havoc was too much to bear. She looked toward the stage exit and briefly considered a quick getaway. Only the thought of how badly she needed the money held her in place.

I can do this, Chastity quietly assured herself. But when Seth's heated glare glanced her way, her confidence took flight like a flock of skittish *henna-henna* birds.

Emanating effortless power and a strength held under control, Chastity knew he was about to detonate. The man was the essence of the quiet before the storm. On the outside people saw what he wanted them to see. On the inside he was preparing for battle.

And she was his enemy.

Tension vibrated between them as he stalked toward her. A demeaning gaze raked over her, coolly appraising. Slowly his lips curled and a flash of pearly white teeth smiled a predator's grin. She felt her heart fall to her feet.

"Chastity." Her name was rancid on his tongue. Sapphire blue eyes that had once looked at her with love were black with fury. His chest expanded before her, a sign that he was ready to attack.

God, Seth, don't do this. It was a silent plea—she knew even if he heard her it would go unheeded. Clearly, he despised her.

Why then, if he hated her so much, hadn't he exiled her to the moon? He had the money and the connections. Instead, here he stood ready to finish what she had set into motion two years ago—the total devastation of any love or feelings left between them. At least if she was banished to the moon she'd be with...

Chastity shook her head. She had to focus. Too much was riding on this contest. A quick assessment revealed nothing had changed. He was gorgeous. And that earthy scent he always wore was a sexual assault upon her senses.

She pulled at the neckline of her silk blouse. *Whew*! Had someone turned up the weather regulator? Judging by the desert that had just teleported into her mouth, the room felt as hot as a cruise around Mars.

Damn the man. He knew what she liked, and by the gleam in his eyes he had worn the cologne purposely.

Chastity squared her shoulders and let determination settle the tide of emotions begging for release. She forced her mouth into a smile.

"*Seth*." A whisper? That's all she could manage? A weak, tell-the-world-she-was-still-in-love-with-Seth-Allen whisper.

Devilish laughter broke out beside her. "So, you two know each other?" The not-so-inconspicuous game host's eyes flashed a conspiratorial glance toward Seth. "That's right, Chastity, it's your ex-fiancé." He turned and with an exaggerated wave of his hand he pointed toward the audience. "And right after this message, I'll reveal what's in store for these two reunited lovebirds."

The disgusting smell of a setup assaulted her. Had the show been fixed, arranged so that Seth could have his revenge?

An eruption of heat streaked up Chastity's neck and stormed across her cheeks. Fingers curled into fists. Through a red haze she faced the man who had haunted her dreams.

Before she could utter a single defamatory word, she was swarmed by a team of women. Female chatter filled her ears, their words inaudible in her muddled brain. It felt like a thousand hands tugged and pulled as they whisked her from the stage and into a small room just behind the curtains.

The enclosure was a cross between a dressing room and a costume storage closet. Everyone had their part to play — as one woman began to refresh her makeup, another set out to look at shoes, while still more fluttered around the room.

A blonde woman scrutinized her. Her identity chip glowed "Bitty". *How apropos*, thought Chastity. The female was itty-bitty, small of height and physique. Her own five-foot-ten frame towered over the woman.

"Yellow?" Bitty asked the redhead tearing through a chest of jewelry like she had lost a family heirloom. "No, red," the other woman replied.

Bitty cocked an appraising eye. "Silk?" She tugged at Chastity's skirt until the strips of Glootium—a substance discovered in the mid-twenty-first century that replaced buttons and zippers—gave way. The material slipped off her hips, pooling around her ankles. "No, leather."

Chastity turned her head and looked at the stout redhead who held a golden chain with something connected to both ends. "Leather?"

Blouse, shoes, and undergarments quickly followed the skirt, until Chastity stood before the assemblage stark naked. Hopefully Bitty would decide on an outfit soon.

A silence descended over the room. Bitty and the redhead scanned her from head to toe, each giving an appreciative nod.

"Red to match the fire in those beautiful sky-blue eyes of yours. Leather..." the redhead chuckled. "He'll never know what hit him." She placed the piece of jewelry on a satin pillow, while the blonde continued riffling through racks and racks of clothing.

Chastity shook her head. "I don't want him—"

"Is this what you're thinking?" interrupted Bitty.

Chastity's breath left her lungs in a single whoosh. The blonde was holding up a red leather contraption that looked vaguely like baby-doll pajamas, except instead of silk and lace, it was edged with gold chains and thin, black satin ropes.

"Yes. Release her hair," the redhead said.

Bitty waved a magnetic retractor over Chastity's head. She felt the familiar tingle as the transparent pins began to dislodge, and the wisp of electricity as they gathered in the middle of the retractor. Piles of brunette ringlets slid down her shoulders, resting at her elbows.

"Beautiful," both women chimed in unison. "Look at all those golden highlights," one said.

A rapid series of head-shaking was all she could manage. There was no way she would prance around the stage wearing *that*. Not to mention the obvious holes right where her nipples would peak. And, by the looks of the thong—a patch of material and a mere thread that would disappear into her crack—only her pubic hair would be covered.

A nervous laugh escaped Chastity's lips. "You're kidding, right?"

Bitty's brows dipped. The woman stared at Chastity as if she couldn't possibly understand her discomfort. "No ma'am. Why, this is normal attire for a sub."

Chastity shook her head in confusion, forehead furrowing. "Sub?"

The redhead's green eyes flashed a warning. "Hush your mouth, Bitty. Never mind her. Just slip it on."

Cautiously, Chastity took a step backwards. Her voice rose in protest. "I can't possibly wear something like tha—"

"Miss Ambrose, I believe your contract states that you agree to wear, eat or perform any deed as long as it does not do bodily harm to your person."

"Yes, but—"

"But, what?" A finely arched brow lifted. "Have you changed your mind about the money?" The redhead's eyes narrowed as she dangled Chastity's Achilles' heel in front of her like a carrot to a pika. Even the fur of the short-legged mammal with rounded ears would cover more than that piece of material they referred to as an ensemble.

"Are you afraid of Mr. Allen's reaction?"

A disgruntled huff pushed through taut lips. "Mr. Allen has seen all there is to see of me. Inside and out," Chastity added. "No, I'd say it was the billion plus pairs of eyes that puts me a little on edge." In reality it *was* a single pair of eyes that set her heart aflutter and knotted her stomach. Would the outfit turn him on, or would he publicly spurn her? And what feat must she perform to win the one hundred million dollars?

"Oh!" Red curls bounced on a single nod of understanding. She pressed the costume to Chastity's body. Chastity struggled, worming her way into the leather that adhered to her skin like glue. "Just pretend they're not there."

"Easier said than done." Chastity looked down at her perky nipples showing through the peepholes. Then she glanced over her shoulder, down her back.

Well, there's no reason to ask if the outfit makes my ass looked big.

Chastity wasn't shy. An ad agency had paid big bucks to plaster her cinema-effigy over every galactic placard from Earth to the edge of the Milky Way, wearing nothing but Glimmer Diamonds.

For the evening she could withstand a little display of "T" and "A", even in front of Seth Allen.

Surrendering, she slipped her feet into knee-high red leather boots that automatically shrank to the right size. She inhaled a deep breath. It was now or never. The time for reckoning had arrived.

The redheaded woman took a step back and eyed Chastity as if she had created a masterpiece. "Honey, you'll never even know the audience exists. Not when you're caught up in the moment." Chastity didn't like the Cheshire cat smile the woman gifted her with.

Before she could ask for clarification, Bitty draped a long velveteen robe over Chastity's shoulders, covering that damn leather outfit, and pushed her out of the dressing room door and toward the stage.

Seth flashed his don't-mess-with-me look as the stage-woman pulled a brush through his hair…again. It was only hair. How many times did it have to be brushed before she understood the tangles were gone?

But, *ohhhh*, she said, it was *soooo* soft.

Chastity had loved his hair. The thought sent him into a fury.

"Enough!" He stood in an abrupt movement, sending his chair backwards and the woman scrambling toward the door. "Shit!" The stage-woman wasn't his target. She didn't deserve his anger.

"I'm sor—" His apology was issued too late as she rushed through the open door past Monty, an old college pal, almost knocking the man on his ass. Monty gave him a "what's-up-with-that-woman?" look and then grinned.

"Ready for a little revenge?" He tipped his long nose into the air. "*Ahhhh*, you can almost smell it."

Seth frowned. Was it revenge? All he wanted was to humiliate Chastity like she had him. Okay, by definition he guessed it was revenge.

"Hey, buddy, you never told me she was a piece of eye candy."

"Huh?" Seth looked around the dressing room. Costumes of every shape and size hung on a rack. His own attire was a pair of black leather pants and boots. No shirt, no jacket, just tight—really tight—fitting pants. Butter-soft to the touch, they clung to every muscle and curve of his body. Lying on a table was a cat-o'-nine-tails, the handle wrapped in black leather, each braid a silvery wisp of a material he couldn't identify. Included in the accessories were a set of velvet handcuffs and a black leather collar with an inset of diamonds and rubies—and it was attached to a leash.

"Da-yum, those legs." Appreciation showed in Monty's eyes. "Didn't you say her legs were insured for several million?"

Chastity was a model, or used to be. The last couple of years Seth had lost track of what she was, where she was, or who she was with. In fact, the last thing he remembered was seeing her backside move through the church door, arm in arm with Josh Allen, his cousin.

"Yeah, five million." But it was her full, rounded breasts that Seth loved, every succulent inch of them. And her laugh. She had the greatest laugh.

"Man, wait 'til you see what I've arranged for you." His friend's mischievous grin made Seth pause. *Whips...handcuffs?* "Monty, what have you done?"

"A week of pure torture, or pleasure, whichever you choose to make it. Plus I've added a couple of surprises." His brows wagged knowingly.

"A week! I can't spend a week with her. Besides, I have several business meetings scheduled." Six nights and seven days with Chastity Ambrose would kill him. Even now he was rock-hard, wondering how to get the boy down before he had to face her again. When he'd walked on stage and saw her for the first time in two years he'd thought of two things—fucking her or strangling her. He'd give anything to get his first choice.

"Now, Seth—" Monty's tone was patronizing, "—you left the details to my discretion. Remember I'm balancing two balls here." He stopped to laugh at his own crude joke. "Your retaliation and the ratings. Your presence has already attracted more viewers than the time I had the delegate from Pluto and his alien girlfriend with three breasts. You know he could suck one breast while fondling the other two at the same time?" The man shook his head as if it had been an amazing feat.

"Monty, you're an intergalactic slimeball."

His friend's arm went around his shoulders. "Yeah, but you still like me."

Seth gave him a heartfelt shove. "That remains to be seen."

"Okay, I can live with that. Now let's get this show on the road."

Monty led Seth on stage in front of fifty thousand cheering fans. Seth flinched at the glaring lights that caused his eyes to squint. No wonder Chastity had reacted like she hadn't recognized him when he'd first entered. He wouldn't recognize his own father in this lighting. And the heat of the lamps was enough to entice him to strip down to his birthday suit.

When the crowd roared anew he turned to see Chastity enter. Glorious brunette curls framed her nonplussed face as she stumbled over a red robe covering her delicious body. The stiff, hesitant movement clearly showed that this was not her idea of a good time. For a moment he felt sorry for her. Well, almost.

"Ladies and gentlemen, our contestants." Monty guided Chastity to Seth's side. Forced footsteps revealed her resistance to being near him.

"Isn't she a beauty?"

Seth wanted to hurt Monty as the man threaded his fingers through Chastity's hair and waited for the applause to die down. "Would you like to see more?" he teased the audience, tugging at her robe.

Chastity's cheeks flushed scarlet. Clutching the robe, she drew away from the game host, which caused her to crash into Seth's side.

"Awww, she's shy. Come on, Miss Ambrose, won't you show us what you have hidden beneath there?"

When her wide eyes met his, Seth felt a moment of regret. A flicker of what might be fear appeared in them and just as quickly was replaced with cold detachment. She pushed away from him. Backbone ramrod-straight, she let the robe slip from her shoulders.

Everyone in the building caught their breath, including Seth. In fact, he might never breathe again. She was glorious. Those dusky rose nipples he had loved to suck, tease and bite called to him, jutting out, pleading for his attention. God, he could almost taste their sweetness, feel the weight of each breast in his hands. An instant hard-on was the result of his reverie. And he wasn't the only one. The bulge in Monty's pants told the story.

Seth wanted to kill him.

Chastity was a temptress, a dangerous siren bewitching every man that held her in his sights.

Legs slightly parted, she stood like a warrior—proud, daring. She needed no weapons to bring down a man. Her body had always been enough.

The silence broke when Monty's clapping sent the room into chaos. Men clamored toward the stage. Bodyguards appeared out of nowhere to restrain the crowd. A zap of electricity from a deadening gun felled several men. Momentarily stunned, they'd live, but wake up with a hell of a headache.

In all the confusion Chastity didn't move or flinch. Even when a young man dressed as a seventeenth-century servant arrived with the cat-o'-nine-tails, velvet handcuffs and a collar. It was as if she had separated herself from her surroundings.

"Seth Allen, it is your challenge to tame the warrior." Even Monty had recognized her likeness to a fighter. "You must break her will. Make her your subservient slave." He paused, expecting a reaction from the woman. A reaction that Seth would lay bets on would never come. Then he added, "Chastity, if you can last a period of seven days, six nights, under Master Seth's bondage, you will win one hundred million dollars."

Like a statue coming to life, she pivoted on her knee-high leather boots. Panic was evident in her wide eyes and flushed face. "What?"

"For your challenge, you must cater to the needs of Master Seth. You will be given a period of time to learn your role as his slave. You are required to complete each command and task given you. Your endurance and limits will be tested, of course." Monty released a taunting laugh before his voice lowered and he continued, "In the end you must display total submission to your Master." Then he jutted his finger toward the ground. "Now, kneel before him," the game host demanded firmly.

Her gaze whipped from to him. "Seth?" Her shaky voice reached out to him. Moisture gathered in her sky-blue eyes.

Eyes, he had to remember deceived him once before. But never again.

Square-shouldered, he raised his head, refusing to show compassion or leniency. He wasn't here to console her or strike up a new acquaintance. Time for clemency was over. He had waited in vain two years for her explanation. When Monty had mentioned she was appearing on his show, Seth decided to seek his own peace in revenge.

He took a dominant stance, legs parted, hands behind his back. "Kneel before me, *wench*." Monty's mouth gaped. Even Seth was surprised at the resentment and command in his voice.

Chastity's brows shot up so quickly he expected them to touch her hairline. Then slowly her eyes narrowed and she looked away. Feet planted to the floor. It was clear she would not submit.

"Miss Ambrose, do you refuse the challenge?" Monty asked in a formidable tone. "I'm sure there's a lady in the audience who would die to be where you are right now, even if there were no prize money." An onslaught of female confirmation rang in Seth's ears.

What would she say? What would she do? She was a proud woman, one that didn't acquiesce easily. He watched her jaw tense, the play in her throat as she swallowed, her chest rising, lifting her breasts.

Without a word she faced him. Her chin raised a fraction, shoulders erect, the gesture of a soldier yielding for the moment, but never considering surrender. To his surprise, she kneeled before him, head bowed, as if waiting for the axe to fall.

Triumph sparked in Monty's eyes. Triumph Seth should've felt.

But all he could think of was grabbing her by the arms and shaking her, before leading her from this mockery and making love to her all night long. No, not *love*, never love again. Just fucking her mouth and pussy until she screamed and begged him to take her back. Then he'd walk out on her without ever looking back.

Monty nodded and the servant boy rushed to Seth, bowed and handed him the collar and leash. Seth felt Chastity tremble when he fastened the cool leather around her slender neck. Funny, for two years he had thought of getting his hands around her neck. Now he could only think about ensuring the collar wasn't too tight.

Next the boy handed him the handcuffs and hurried from the stage.

Pinching her chin, Seth jerked her head up until their gazes met. A shadow crossed her eyes with an array of emotions he refused to comprehend. He helped her to stand. Seth grasped her arms and brought her hands before her, then clasped the handcuffs on her wrists. The expression on her face was priceless. Her blue eyes darted from him to the handcuffs and then back to him. But now there was fire in the depths of her gaze. Chastity was furious. She actually had the unmitigated *gall* to be angry.

Oh, I'll give you something to be angry about. He reached out and twisted her nipple hard enough to force a gasp from her taut lips. Her reaction was immediate. Fingers interwoven, she uppercut her cuffed hands, aiming straight for his groin. Anticipating her response, he hastened aside. The momentum of her attack threw her forward. She twisted in midair, trying to regain her footing but continuing to fall. Thankfully, he caught her before she hit the ground.

Buried beneath a cloud of brunette curls he heard her growl of frustration. "Let me go!"

So he did.

A dull thud and a breathy groan followed, when her ass hit the floor hard.

The stage shook as the crowd roared their approval. Excitement shimmered over the audience as if the weather regulator was pumping out ecstasy powder. Several women had shed their clothing and were attempting to break through the line of security guards. More than one man's cock was throat-deep in his partner's mouth. The scent of sex filled the air. Monty would have an all-out orgy on intergalactic cinema if he wasn't careful.

The gleam in Seth's friend's eyes flashed dollar signs. Then Monty nodded again and the servant boy arrived carrying a small cushion. On top of the satiny pillow lay two golden bands connected by a chain.

The boy knelt before Seth offering him the jewelry.

"Now for a treat. Especially made for you, Chastity, your own nipple clamps, each guaranteed to give Seth great enjoyment. Will you place your ownership jewelry on your slave, Master Seth?" Monty was having way too much fun. "Of course, you may need to stimulate the areolas before applying the clamps."

Seth was seriously considering wringing the man's neck.

The heat in the room raised ten notches. More clothes were tossed into the air.

Bloodlust seared Seth's veins like acid. Erection stretched to the hilt, throbbing painfully against his leather pants, it would be so easy to take her. She'd fight him. The enticing thought made him inwardly moan. Whenever she was mad, tense, she liked it rough, liked it fast, liked it hard. And by the looks of her she was ready to implode.

Fuck! He ran a shaky hand through his hair. If he touched Chastity in any sexual context here—now—he couldn't ensure the outcome. So easily could he slip between her thighs and take what had been denied him. His blood heated, his pulse sped. The need to possess her, brand her, bordered on obsession.

Chastity's head snapped up. "No!"

The sudden dissent was a knife to Seth's gut. He flinched from the blow as if she delivered it with an undercut to his stomach.

Monty smiled. "I believe your slave has earned her first punishment." The servant boy handed Seth the whip.

Confusion glistened in her eyes. "Punishment? *Seth*?" It was a definite plea. As she scrambled to her feet Seth caught a glimpse of the swollen flesh between her thighs that he ached to caress.

"Face the curtains. On your hands and knees," Seth demanded in a tone of indifference.

Chastity hesitated, then obeyed, arranging herself as he'd commanded.

But when he got a good look at her perfectly sculpted ass facing the masses, he wanted to retract his command. Not only was her ass on display, but everyone could see her pussy lips, too.

Seth wanted to spread her cheeks and drive his cock deep between them. He held his breath, the mental image of his erection thrusting into her tight ass sent a wave of ecstasy through his body. He'd never taken her that way, but the position had great promise.

Speechless, he stood and stared at the two heavenly globes, so smooth, so firm. They had fit perfectly in his hands two years ago. His palms itched to touch. He barely stopped himself from reaching out and stroking their softness.

Here he was about to flog her, when all he wanted to do was fuck her. Delve into her hot, wet pussy. Feel her breasts slide against his skin, the weight of her ass in his hands.

Instead, he snapped the whip, striking the object of his attention.

Chastity startled at the sharp crack of the whip. Her body jerked forward as the shiny thongs met tender skin. She released a gasp somewhere between surprise and pain. Recovery was swift. Before the second whiplash hit she was prepared for the discomfort and took it without a sound. She remained rigid as pink splotched her alabaster skin.

He hadn't meant to hit her that hard. Regret surfaced. What he wouldn't give to kiss the hurt away.

He leaned into her, his bare chest feeling the warmth of her back. "Chastity, I'm sor—"

Over her shoulder she flashed him a look that would kill most men. The coldness in her eyes made him take a step back.

Through clenched teeth she hissed, "The clamps…have someone…from the audience…" She turned her head away from him unable to complete her sentence.

She didn't have to finish her request. She didn't want him to touch her.

He backed away from her and turned to the crowd. "A prize for a lucky man in the audience." It was a physical strain to force a smile. Like always, he performed for the cameras. "Who wishes to apply my slave's nipple clamps?" From the corner of his eye, he watched Chastity's shoulders fall with relief, an action that set his blood boiling. The leash glittered, swaying from her collar with her rapid breathing. A wild vision of the strap wrapped around his fist forcing her head up as he fucked her mouth filled his mind.

Right there he made a vow. Over the next week she would learn to enjoy his touch. In fact, she'd be begging for it.

Chapter Two

Be careful what you wish for. How many times had Chastity heard that saying? And how many times during the last two years had she seen a good wish go bad? For example, her most recent desire to feel Seth's hands caressing her body, his cock buried deep inside her. By no means was a nipple clamping and whipping what she had in mind.

After her first strike against him failed she should have stopped there. But, *noooo.* She had to wish him to the devil. And right before her eyes he had taken on Satan's form. Chastity's ass burned and her nipple ached, as well as her pride. Being flogged with a cat-o'-nine-tails on intergalactic cinema was not her idea of a good time. Now she was to endure yet another humiliation and more pain, but at least it wouldn't be directly from Seth's hands.

Chastity got up from her hands and knees as best she could with her hands cuffed. She slowly faced the crowd, her chin high.

After a moment of total chaos, a security guard ushered a man up the stairs and onto the stage. Chastity should've known that it would be a LA Annihilator in full combat attire. The audience was saturated with current and past players and more than a few wannabes.

Seth Allen worshippers.

Like little boys, they wore their khaki-green and tan uniforms and paraded around like warriors of the twentieth century. Only they weren't in the Skyforce, they chased an astro-ball around the interior of a dome, for heaven's sake.

With a flattop haircut, the young man couldn't be more than a year or so out of training guards. At least five years younger than her own twenty-six. Maturity lacking, the randy man high-fived Seth, then raised his arms, jumping up and down and roaring like a lion, a childish act of raging hormones. When he turned his intense brown eyes on her with a hunger that could only match that of a vulture, her skin crawled across her arms.

This decision had been her call. She had no one to blame but herself. But in reality she'd had no choice. Her hands were bound physically, as well as metaphorically. At this moment two things were raging out of control…her temper and her lust. If Seth touched her now, she didn't know which one would explode first.

Steeling her jaw, she drew Seth's attention, forcing him to look at her. *See what you're doing to me? Enjoy it, because after this week you'll never see me again.* Okay, so anger was in the lead. This was good. If she could keep this attitude up throughout the week she'd be home free.

Yet for now she had to prove to Seth that she wasn't frightened. That his fiercely dark looks didn't move her, affect her in any way. He was just a man. Feet parted, she slowly lifted her arms high above her head, the movement pushing her breasts up and out, presenting herself on a silver platter to the man from the audience.

With a sexy purr she murmured, "I'm ready, big boy." But she was far from ready when the young man took her nipple into his hot, wet mouth. His hands ravished her body, stroking her ass, attempting to work his fingers between her legs.

Sucking like a newborn babe, he slurped, and then bit down—hard. Chastity barely held back a scream of resentment and pain. Instead, she groaned. A sound that the idiot took as passion.

Seth shifted from one foot to the other, his discomfort apparent. A discomfort that Chastity knew couldn't possibly match her own. She was the one half-naked, whip marks on her buttocks, and an imbecile nursing at her breast while his fingers played hide and seek.

But she was game.

Chastity closed her eyes and threw back her head, crying, "Yes, *yes*." Yes, she would suffer at this man's hands, but so would Seth. Was there anything left between them that would force Seth's hand?

Her little act was enough to set Seth into a fury of motion. He jerked the young man off his feet, tearing him from Chastity. She grimaced, sucked in a breath as teeth scraped against her sensitized nipple. With ease, Seth slung the man across the polished floor. She took pleasure in watching the twit gather his scattered senses, push from the ground and stand like a tough guy, as if he thought to confront the raging man before him.

Smoldering silence, then a fierce growl rumbled low from Seth's throat. A glance at his savage expression—teeth bared, eyes black with dark emotion—and Chastity understood why the young man cautiously backed away.

Not a word. Not a threat of retribution was uttered.

The audience held their breath. The young man never turned his back on Seth as he backed his way off the stage and down the stairs, putting distance between them. The game show host took several steps toward safety as the servant boy fled the stage. Which left Chastity bound and alone to bear the brunt of Seth's anger.

Their eyes met and the air between them shimmered. Electricity crackled. And she swore the lights dimmed. No, it was just lightheadedness, she had forgotten to breathe.

"I've changed my mind," he murmured beneath his breath. He jerked the leash, dragging her reluctantly toward him.

Had she pushed him too far? Fear made her take the last few steps on her own. So close to the fire, she felt the heat of his anger rising from his body like steam. Felt the warmth of his breath fan her cheeks. The scent of his cologne took on a deep, dark redolence. Ten strong fingers wrapped around her neck.

She tensed. Her pulse leapt wildly, beating a staccato rhythm through each fingertip.

Would he kill her in front of a billion eyes? He nudged her closer, his thumbs slowly stroking her throat in the vicinity of her jugular. He leaned forward. For a second she thought he would kiss her while he crushed her windpipe.

Time stood still. Then he withdrew, the spell broken.

Roughly, he clenched her breast in his hand, pinching the clamp tight around her erect areola. Her chest arched forward, a moan escaping her lips. Whether from the pleasure-pain the ring induced, or the feel of Seth's hands on her body, she wasn't sure.

Breathless, she awaited the warmth of his mouth, desired his tongue teasing her other nipple. Instead, he rolled the nub between his fingers until it peaked, and slipped the clamp over it. Instant pain shot through her breast. This time there was no pleasure. Without hesitation, he pulled on the chain connecting the clamps to encourage her to follow him.

She held back a cry, but barely. When the air finally flowed back into her lungs, she gasped, drawing his attention. The infernal regions of hell basked in his eyes.

What an utter fool she was. He didn't care about her. Revenge was his goal, his only goal. This was a game she had started two years ago. Now Seth was one-upping her. Emotions and hearts were involved. There could be no winner.

Resigned, she surrendered. This was her trial to bear. The man she had loved was more interested in issuing pain than pleasure. And maybe she deserved it for leaving him without giving a reason. Would he ever believe she had no choice? That she had left to save his reputation and avoid gossip? Would he ever believe that she never stopped loving him?

If this was the way it was going to be, so be it. She would give him the pound of flesh he demanded and then disappear from his life.

"...and to ensure that each of you know the parts you're playing." Did the man have no scruples at all? The game show host continued as if nothing had just occurred, "Voyeur II is supplying you with your own training coaches. Tor Thorenson will assist Mr. Allen."

A golden god entered the stage. His attire was a toga made of white Egyptian linen and a gold medallion and chain around his waist. Brown sandals with black straps wound around each powerful leg to mid-calf, where the strings of leather were tied. Additionally, he carried something that unraveled like a snake before Chastity's feet. The six-foot whip he held slithered through the air and then snapped.

The evil sound made her flinch. She grasped Seth's arm and then released it just as fast.

Chastity Ambrose, what have you gotten yourself into? As if an ex-fiancé's rage wasn't enough, Voyeur II had hired King Dong and his minions. Two men followed, each a replica of the first. Shoulder-length blond hair and artificially enhanced muscles, bulging in every possible place a man could bulge. The taller of the two men, the one with green eyes, Mr. Dong introduced simply as Master Shawn. The hazel-eyed devil with a scowl was Master Terrance.

Seth's physique was natural, from his sinewy biceps and his artfully carved chest, to his tight, firm ass.

From the thunderous roar of the ladies in the audience, Chastity knew she was the only female not appreciating the new intricacies of the game.

When the three mammoths surrounded her, she stood her ground. Their daunting scowls were meant to intimidate. Each slow, calculated step closed the distance between them, a quiet takeover of her personal space and her confidence. But she would not yield to the menacing bullies waiting for her to cower.

"Cast down your eyes, wench," the one called Tor demanded. "You're not worthy to look upon us."

She winced, still refusing to divert her gaze. *Fuck you* was on her tongue, but before she could speak he grabbed her breast. He twisted the clamp and she dropped to her knees. White-hot pain imploded at her nipple and ripped through her body. She fought for air. Her stomach pitched. The sensation of rolling waves crashing against her insides made her drop further onto her cuffed hands.

Fuck, but her nipples hurt. At the pace she was going, she'd be listed in the Feats Book of Records for the most titty-twisters in one day.

Jaws clenched, she pondered what she might do to the man when she caught him asleep. Maybe a phazer-gun to the backside of his balls would put him in a more cooperative mood. The thought was interrupted when he grabbed a handful of hair and jerked her to her feet.

"Low-planet *son of a bitch*!" Dangling in the air, Chastity attempted to regain her footing, while remaining as still as possible to avoid ripping out any more of her hair. If he didn't release his hold soon she'd have a bald spot as big as an orange.

When she was placed firmly on her feet, punishment came swiftly. Two stinging slaps to each bare ass cheek. She could feel the outlines of his large palms marking her skin. When he smoothed his hand across her burning ass she wanted to strike out. Mouth agape, preparing to issue a string of expletives, she paused. This was intergalactic cinema. If she fought back she would simply feed the frenzy that had already taken hold of the crowd.

One man's happiness was another man's pain.

Only it was *her* pain, and the crowd loved every aspect of the exchange. From the audience she heard someone scream, "Pinch her tit again." Another yelled, "Fuck her doggy style."

The man beside her was bigger, stronger, and he had backup. From the corner of her eyes she saw his powerful cronies poised—ready to restrain her if she decided to retaliate or bolt. She couldn't win this battle. At least not here, not now.

Breathe. Inhale. Exhale. Chastity calmed herself. When she was young and scared, she'd learned to disassociate, to move inside herself. To form a shell to block the ugliness of the world and withstand the anguish it held. Slowly, she drifted to her knees resting on her haunches. Head bowed.

Inhale. Exhale. She felt a soothing blanket of calm cover her as she went into that safe place in her mind where nothing and no one could touch her.

"Nice." Like an arrogant man, Tor took her acquiescence as submission. Only she knew the truth. Well, Seth did as well. In fact, it might be the only weapon she had to fight him.

"Now, as you're aware—" The host of the Voyeur II series' voice was muffled—hollow—as though it was being forced through a funnel. Chastity lingered on the edges of consciousness, floating in a realm of peace and tranquility. If only she could linger here for the next seven days.

"The cameras of Voyeur II will check in several times during your stay at Ecstasy Island, located on the planet Zygoman. Chastity will meet her coach, the lovely Passion Flower, upon their arrival. She will learn the art of submissiveness and how to pleasure her Master. If she's successful she'll win *one...hundred...million...dollars.*" He paused for effect. "Now enjoy yourselves and don't do anything I wouldn't do."

Zygoman! It sounded like the vacation of a lifetime. But by the smirk on Monty's face and Seth's menacing expression, it was going to be anything but, for Chastity Ambrose.

Seth paced impatiently outside Chastity's dressing room. He didn't know relieving oneself could take so long—or was it his anxiety and need to get on with this charade that made him uneasy?

When Chastity finally exited the room, his pulsed jumped. He gathered up the leash and gave it a jerk, earning a frown from her.

The crowd separated as Seth led Chastity backstage. Hearty slaps on the back came his way as he moved passed. Men were envious—as they should be. The woman tethered to him was a virtual sex goddess. And for the next week she was his. Anticipation swelled his testicles. His cock hardened, lengthening with alarming speed. What would she do if he bared himself here and now, and demand she take him in her hot, wet mouth? Would her lips willingly embrace him, her tongue caress his erection?

When the leash was almost jerked from Seth's hand, he glanced over his shoulder expecting another confrontation. Instead, he was surprised at the wild look in her eyes. Fear? Panic?

Were the realities of the next week and what was in store for her finally setting in?

Would she renege? Steal his chance for revenge?

"*Wait*! I can't leave this minute. I must…uh…I need to…" The handcuffs had been removed earlier so that she could attend to personal matters. Desperately, she held onto the strap connected to her collar like it was a lifeline. Whatever urgent matter had her upset was important enough to expose her to additional punishment.

Or was it a stalling tactic?

Anxiously, she pulled against her restraints. Blue eyes looked up pleadingly. "Please, I can't leave now."

What was she up to? "Why?" he asked. Then he chided himself for even asking.

"A trans-planet call…just let me make one trans-planet call and then we can leave."

Anger flamed inside him. "What, Chastity, need to call your lover, Josh?" Savagely, he bit out, "If it's a cock you require, I will more than fulfill your needs every minute of the next seven days, six nights."

She flinched at his sarcasm. Resentment flashed in her narrowed eyes. She stood, arms akimbo, fists buried in her round hips.

Her rigid stance shoved her breasts forward. His mouth watered, wanted to taste them, feel them pressed against his chest, her naked body sliding over his. God have mercy on his soul. He ran a shaky hand through his hair.

Once again, she stood before him, proud, defiant, heat glowing like embers in her eyes. A breathtaking sight. And a reminder of what he had been deprived of. He would crush her before the week was over. A week was sufficient time to drive the thoughts of her lover from her mind and her body.

"No. If you must know, I need to trans-call my mother."

"Mother? But your parents are d—" Vexed, he shook his head. She was doing it again. "*Lies*. Damn you, Chastity, if it's the last thing I do, I'll teach you to never lie to me again."

Regret flickered in her eyes. Hands floating to her side, her stance softened along with her voice. "You don't even want to listen to my explana—"

"*Stop*! Not another word." He extracted the handcuffs from a strap connected to his pants. "Your wrists," he grounded out. Reluctantly, she shoved her hands out and allowed him to cuff her. He focused on the clicking of the locking mechanism as he snapped shut each wristband.

Control. He had to gain control of the situation, not allow her to manipulate herself back into his heart. Two years he had waited for this moment. She would not take it from him.

"This has nothing to do with the past." Now it was his turn to lie.

"Seth, it has *everything* to do with the past." He jerked away from the hand she laid upon his arm. He didn't want her pity. He had gone beyond the suffering. He had no more sleepless nights. Well, almost. His appetite was back. In fact, he'd gained ten pounds. On the field he was a brutal animal. And women? He had a different one every night to warm his bed. Yeah, he was doing just fine, thank you very much!

"There are rules to this game. And, that's what this is, Chastity. A game." With a dismissive action he brushed his hand through the air. "Unfortunately for you and me, the fates have thrown us together at different ends of the spectrum." Another lie—he was getting good at this.

A harrumph of disbelief pushed from taut lips. So. If she knew, all the better!

"You will walk behind me with your head bowed and your hands behind your back."

She responded with a "Yes, Master". But it came out more like "Fuck you, bastard". She raised a brow and then the wrists he had cuffed in front of her. He held back a chuckle. She was feistier than he remembered.

Seth met her glare. He sprung the lock on each of her handcuffs so that she would be able to follow his mandate. He fastened the manacles to the strap on his pants.

"Remember...the rule is to pleasure me. If I demand that you drop to your knees and take my cock in your mouth—" her eyes widened, "—you will do it without hesitation."

"But—"

"You will not speak unless I permit it. When you do speak, you will refer to me as Master. This is my last warning...before the punishments begin." Even he heard the menacing edge in his voice. She backed away and pivoted, presenting him with her back.

Damn, but her obstinate attitude was infuriating. Fingers closing tight around her biceps, he jerked her around, eliciting a squeal of surprise. "And, you will never turn your back to me. Now, a transport is awaiting us."

"Master, may I speak?" Her teeth were clenched so tightly he wondered how she got the words out.

A "no" was on his lips. "Yes."

"I need clothes, toiletries."

"I will decide what you need, and if I choose to provide them."

"Yesss, Master." Then, like a coiled snake, she sprung to life. "I can't do this." She frantically pulled at her collar, attempting to separate herself from it. "If you think that I will stand by and let you strip me of all dignity, you're crazy. There were…*are* valid reasons for what happened two years ago."

Frantically she searched for the neckband's clasp. "*Fuck it.*" She gave up trying to rid herself of the collar and focused on the leash that Seth refused to part with. A scowl skewed her features. She jerked harder on the leather strap. "Let go," she growled vehemently. If she were a dog, she'd be foaming at the mouth, ready to attack.

What a turn-on. He'd give anything to throw her on the floor and bury his cock deep within all that heated fury, a place that had once welcomed him. The backstage area was filled with people, their eyes riveted on the pair. But all Seth could think of was getting between her legs, feeling the wetness of her excitement as her pussy sucked him in.

"Is there a problem?" Monty asked, approaching. The gleam in his mischievous eyes revealed his enjoyment. "Miss Ambrose?"

Her body shook with rage. She clawed again at the neckband and jerked against the leash. For a moment she couldn't speak.

Concern flashed across Monty's usually jovial face. "Miss Ambrose? Are you all right?"

She swallowed hard, forcing words from her mouth. "Release…m-me. I-I c-can't do this," she admitted weakly, shame evident in her tone and posture. Blue eyes pooled with emotion. Red welts rose on her neck where her fingernails continued to dig.

"Quit?" Monty looked toward Seth for direction.

No! Seth mouthed firmly.

For a moment his friend floundered. Then he said, "It's your decision, Miss Ambrose. Just transfer the funds on your way out."

Flustered, she stopped struggling. Face flushed, chest rising and falling with each agitated breath. Confused and wild-eyed she glared at the man. "Funds?"

"Surely you read the fine print?"

"Fine print?" Her voice was barely audible. The trembling had subsided some. But her usually bright coloring had been replaced by a pasty-white hue.

Leave it up to Monty to ensure there were no escape clauses in the contract, unless of course, they were to his benefit. "Yes, you agreed to fulfill the contract or pay us five hundred thousand dollars. Recompense for the station's losses, finding a new contestant, rescheduling the reservations at Zygoman, et cetera, et cetera…"

"What?" A strangled cry of disbelief shot from her mouth. She went boneless, swaying, and her knees buckled.

Seth grabbed her arm, steadying her. She was cold to the touch, her skin clammy. Cradling her against his chest, he worried about shock.

Placing a finger beneath her chin, he guided her head up. When their gazes met, defeat was written on her face. Dark, haunted eyes stared back at him. She blinked back unshed tears, but one renegade drop rolled down her cheek. Hands shaking, she released the grasp she had on the leash and dropped her chin back upon her chest.

Seth had won.

But instead of his victory laying sweet upon his tongue, it tasted sour.

Even Monty seemed affected by her sudden acceptance. The coat of indifference he always wore wavered as he again looked toward Seth for direction.

"Is the transport ready?" Seth *had* to go through with this. If he let her walk out now he would regret it for the rest of his life.

"Yes." Monty's earlier hit-her-below-the-belt attitude had vanished. Chastity had a way of drawing people in. She was easy to like, easy to love. She could be tender and loving.

Then rip your heart out with the next breath, he reminded himself. His friend was just another man taken in by her lies.

Seth released his hold and stepped away from Chastity. He tugged on the leash, half expecting her to resist. Instead, she took an unsteady step behind him. Quietly, she followed him through the studio hallway leading outside.

A gust of warm air hit him square in the face. Catching his breath, he listened as the metallic conveyor revved its ion engine and a stream of radiant energy released into the atmosphere. Chastity hated this mode of transportation. You'd think in all the centuries of medical advancements that the cure for motion sickness would've been discovered.

From the corner of his eye, he watched the appreciative glances she received from men and women alike. She was a rose among thorns, but just as prickly. Her stance said that she had regained some of her defiance. The woman was resilient, he knew she wouldn't be down for long.

Still, she refused to look at him.

Motioning to a teleporter he held his hand out, palm side up and allowed the boy to scan his fingertips. Then he said, "Load my bags and possessions." He shoved Chastity's leash into the boy's hand. Her head twisted to meet the teleporter's gaze, an expression of pure disdain distorting her features.

The teleporter flinched. "Miss." He stepped back, obviously eager to place as much distance between him and the angry woman as the leash would allow. "I'll show you to your compartment." He waited for her to take a step and never exerted pressure on the leash to lead her.

"A wise choice." Seth chuckled under his breath.

As Chastity pivoted to follow, Seth could've sworn he heard her breathe, "Bastard." Punishment was in order—or he could pretend he didn't hear her. The latter was the course he took. All he wanted was a drink and a moment to gather his thoughts. But Tor and his assistants marched toward him with determination, robbing him of the opportunity.

"Master Seth." The leader bowed. "Your training begins now."

Around a table in the dining room of the transport, Seth listened to Tor explain his role as a Dominant and what should be expect of Chastity as a submissive. While Tor openly enjoyed his dinner, Seth thought of Chastity and her desperate plea to make a trans-planet call.

Was she in love with Josh? Why had his cousin waited until the wedding ceremony began before whisking her away? And why had Chastity even showed up at the church? For two years he'd asked himself these questions, almost daily.

The painful memory flashed across his eyes.

He stood with the woman of his heart before the priest, pledging his love, a vow of eternity, when a commotion from the back of the chapel halted the ceremony. Agitated, Josh struggled against the attendant firmly ushering him back toward the open door. His voice rose, desperation in his tone, "Chastity!"

Seth's fists clenched. His heart pounded. How many times had he replayed the events in his mind? Both he and Chastity had turned around. He remembered Josh's pleas to speak with Chastity alone, and how she went to him.

From the altar, Seth had watched his cousin's animated movements and heard Chastity gasp. She'd spun on her heel, stood for a moment staring at Seth as tears streamed down her face. Then without a word she fled from the church, Josh hot on her heels.

Neither had offered an explanation that day, nor the ones that followed.

Why would Josh allow a woman like Chastity to participate in a game show that would expose her to other men's fantasies? If she were Seth's he would keep her naked and tucked away securely in his bed.

And what drove Chastity to continue with the game when it was obviously causing her mental anguish? There were too many unanswered questions making him uncomfortable with the entire situation.

"…a safe word," Tor finished saying.

Distracted, Seth tried to focus. "A safe word?"

A disapproving glance was shared between Tor's assistants.

"It's a 'key word' or a 'stop word' that you and your slave agree upon. Using a safe word allows the submissive to scream, beg for mercy, or threaten revenge, all in the spirit of the game. When she is truly frightened or the pain too intense, she has a way out. A good Dom also remembers that during intense sessions a submissive can forget the agreed upon safe word."

Is this what he wanted? Confusion and uncertainty were both messing with his mind. What had Monty got him into? He hadn't expected anything like this. He shifted nervously in his chair, as the second course of baked *Henna-henna* bird with glazed red potatoes and asparagus dipped in red wine was set in front of him. Seth picked up his fork and stabbed at the poultry, suddenly losing his appetite.

"Your slave has the ability to tune out, or as we call it 'endorphin-out', does she not?"

The man was amazingly observant—too observant. "Yes, she can."

Tor's scrutiny was unsettling, as if he could peer into Seth's mind, read his thoughts. There were things in his head even Seth didn't want to know, much less a stranger. Mixed emotions battled against one another. Self-doubt hung in dark corners, awaiting the right time to spring out and overtake him. The contest between he and Chastity was the first game in his life where he wondered whether he would emerge the victor.

"Her technique is smooth, she's quite skilled. Yet if she goes too deeply within herself, to what is known as 'subspace', she won't be able to object or to express her limits. You could hurt her, inadvertently."

Appalled at where this talk was leading, Seth pushed back his plate and stated emphatically, "I would never hurt her." Not physically. But emotionally? Wasn't that what this was all about? This was revenge, and if she didn't hurt, if she didn't feel loss, then all was for nothing.

Tor studied him a little longer then he laughed. "It's a thin and dangerous line you walk. Love. Hate."

"I don't love her," Seth responded a little too quickly.

The knowing look in Tor's eyes said he wasn't buying it. "Ecstasy Island doesn't condone cruelty or abuse. Whatever you do together must be consensual. If you are asked to stop, you must." He laughed again, only this time it was laced with skepticism. "But after talking to Monty, if Miss Ambrose were a man, I'd say you had her by the balls. The woman nearly signed away all her rights. An act of a desperate person...or a stupid one."

Stupid? No, that was one word that didn't describe Chastity Ambrose. Desperate? Before he could ponder further, Tor said, "As a submissive begins to reach her limits she will become intense. You need to be aware of her body, her breathing."

There was no problem with being aware of her body. Long, long legs, rounded hips, a small waist and succulent breasts, what more could a man ask for?

"Well, from Chastity's reaction at the station, she's already reached a nine out of ten on the tension scale." Seth picked up his glass and downed his beer. The antiquated drink was still a favorite even in the twenty-second century. The foamy, bitter ale endearingly called a "brewskie" quenched a thirst like no other drink could.

"...signs to look for—her breathing will become tighter, more labored, her muscles will grow rigid. Stop immediately. Remember that it may take time for her to 'swim back up' or return from where she's gone. Even more time if she has fine-tuned the art of escape."

A slit in the table opened and another beer appeared in front of Seth. He picked it up, smelling the mixture of malted barley, yeast and hops. "This doesn't sound safe."

"It can be either very dangerous or as innocent as playful experimentation. I want to invite you to attend some of the bondage demonstrations at the club. There's even a Master-slave dinner and a slave auction. Do you think your slave would be agreeable to be auctioned?" Tor's eyes shifted nervously. A finger began to trace the rim of his glass. He seemed restless, uneasy.

"Oh, Chastity would be agreeable. Anything to get away from me." The question was more if Seth could allow it. Could he watch another man take his woman? Sour acid gurgled in his stomach. Hell, it wouldn't be the first time.

"And you?" Tor was testing Seth, for what he didn't know. But it was a test. He was sure of it.

"She's just another piece of ass," he responded nonchalantly. But inwardly he thought, *over my dead body*.

Tor tilted his head to the side, a knowing look in his eyes. "That much between the two of you?"

As skilled as Seth was at masking his emotions, something had slipped to betray him. So he gave the only answer he could. "Yes."

"No chance that your need for retribution, while in the throes of inflamed hormones, would cause you to hurt her? Trust and safety is essential. BDSM is not about genuine anger." Tor looked at Seth as if he was once again attempting to read his mind. "I'd hate to have you misuse this experience, when it can be gratifying for both of you." He cleared his throat. Indecision was on his brow, as if he'd left something unsaid. Hesitating, he added, "You know, playing with humiliation is like lighting the fuse to an emotional bomb. Some things you say and do can't be taken back."

Seth thought about that one. His answer was, physically, no. He never wanted to hurt Chastity. But mentally… emotionally?

Damn it! He wanted her to suffer as he had these past two years.

Chapter Three

It had been a wretched evening. Locked in her compartment, Chastity's mind reeled with thoughts of what the week ahead would hold. She had arrived at Voyeur II knowing that she could face something distasteful or uncomfortable. Never had she anticipated it would test the very limits of her being.

Still, if retribution was what Seth wanted, she would accommodate him. Well, as much as her pride would allow. Since the moment she'd laid eyes on him today her emotions felt bound to a skycoaster. Up, down…fight, surrender…it wasn't in her character to just roll over and play dead. If anything, her mother's situation had taught her patience.

Mom! Hope rose as she scanned the chamber looking for a trans-communicator. Every compartment had one. Then, as quickly as her anticipation had risen, it plummeted. The room that had once been well-appointed elegance was now stripped. Two chairs and an end table positioned in front of a fireplace, a beautiful chaise lounge that she stopped briefly to admire, and a cinema-max. She frowned at the walled entertainment center thinking back on this evening's fiasco. The knowledge that the show would be transmitted across the universe later tonight made her ill. She shivered at the thought before continuing her search. Every nook and cranny had been rid of possessions, all comforts removed except for the chaise lounge.

Downcast, she tugged at the collar around her neck and the leash swayed, rubbing against an exposed nipple. Then she drifted toward the chaise covered in manmade snow leopard fur. *Ooooh, soft.* Her fingers caressed the thick, plush hair, pale gray dotted with brown spots, like snow littered with golden chestnuts. With each stroke the settee purred—low, soothing.

Her fingers stilled. The sound disappeared. Her hand moved again across the surface and the drone started anew.

Pleased, she slid the full length of her body against the pelt as she lay down. She had to get one of these things. It wouldn't need to be fed or watered or cleaned up after. Two for the price of one. She'd have a new piece of furniture *and* a cat. Not to mention it felt wonderful on naked skin. Her ass never had it so good. She almost felt like purring, too.

Then she heard the door slide open and her gaze cut toward it. Seth walked in and she thought vomiting would be more apropos. The subtle motion of the transporter was always rough on her stomach, but being in a room alone with Seth Allen was enough for a girl to lose her cookies.

Okay, what was she supposed to do now? Stand? Drop to her knees and praise the almighty Master? Were there appropriate words of greeting? She began to rise.

An outstretched palm stopped her. "No, stay where you are." He took the last couple of steps to close the distance between them. "Tor said that the nipple clamps need to be removed." He stood over her, his eyes riveted on her breasts. She wondered what the tensing in his jaw meant. Was he nervous or anxious about the Master and slave role?

Glancing down at her breasts, she reached for one of the clamps.

"No, let me do it. Lay flat. Relax." He sat down on the edge of the lounge. She scooted over to make room as she apprehensively stretched out. Eyes still on her breasts, his tongue made a slow path across his bottom lip.

A gasp stuck in her throat. She thought about his touch, his mouth hot and wet on her nipple. The last time he had played with—no, *worshipped*—her breasts was at Christmas, just before their doomed wedding.

Seth was a breast man. And he had always loved hers. He had spent hours caressing, kissing, sucking, and biting her taut nipples, then fulfilling her wildest expectations with his tongue, fingers and cock.

Her pussy hummed with need, the subtle vibration setting the chaise to purr. Would the lounge roar if they got down and dirty atop it? The vision of slick, naked bodies sliding against each other, gliding through the fur, was more than she could take.

He cleared his throat and the image evaporated. "Tor said that removing the clamps would be painful."

Seth's earlier anger had seemed to vanish. He almost appeared…uncertain.

"He recommended that I distract you while removing them."

Distract her? What the hell did that mean? She found out when his hand slipped between her legs and a finger delved into her heat. She squeaked her surprise as he slowly began to finger-fuck her.

No! she inwardly screamed, scrambling on her elbows and heels to move away. She wasn't strong enough to withstand his assault.

With his free hand on her shoulder he immobilized her. "Don't move." It was a firm command.

The *Master* had returned.

So it begins, she inwardly acknowledged, allowing her facial features, narrowed eyes and a disapproving scowl, to express her displeasure.

And what did her traitorous body do but let loose a downpour, a veritable flood of welcome. Talk about conflicting messages.

The hard angles of Seth's face softened. A mischievous grin spread across his face, one that she was all too familiar with. One that said *I know you're mine for the taking*. Haunting dark eyes came to life and glowed, victory in sight. His pleasure evident at the skillful way he made her pussy weep as his finger slid easily across her slick, wet folds.

Her thighs trembled, threatening to part, but she wouldn't make it easy for him and clenched them tightly.

"Spread your legs, Chastity." His tone was a deep, throaty command.

She refused. A defiant act that she had to reach deep into her soul to find.

But when he touched her clit, stroked, her damn legs popped open like a flower seeking the sun. A warm glow of humiliation spread across her cheeks.

He plunged deeper, withdrew and traced her vulva and then groaned, "You always had the wettest pussy."

Oh yeah, talk dirty and I'm a goner. Or better yet, say that with your tongue buried deep inside me. Let me hear your words vibrate through my aching pussy.

His beautiful blue eyes looked at her, the heat of desire burning in them. She wanted him to make love to her. Thrust his cock inside her until all the loneliness was gone and she could once again feel safe in his arms.

Back arching, her hips undulated to his rhythm, wanting his fingers to fuck her harder, faster. Her fists clenched in the fur, knuckles white with anticipation. She needed him to slide his hard erection into her warmth, fill her…complete her.

A shaky breath and a gasp was the beginning of a climax she hadn't experienced in years. Just as she reached for the apex, Seth plucked one nipple clamp off and then the other. Pain and pleasure imploded, intertwining into an overwhelming summit. A scream tore from the depths of her soul. She wanted to cry out from the numbing ache in her breasts and laugh at the overpowering emotion. Eyes closed, she savored the moment.

When her heavy lids finally opened, the nipple clamps were gone…and so was Seth.

Chastity went through a range of emotions. She hated him. She loved him. Yet one emotion was clear—she lusted after him with every beat of her heart. She wanted him in every way.

Wanted to taste his essence, feel him slide deep into her wet core. But most of all she wanted him to kiss her like he had two years ago. Just a single, intimate kiss, a sharing of one personal moment before this all ended.

And she wanted to slap the shit out of him. How dare he finger-fuck her and then leave without a word! The more she thought about it, the angrier she got. But anger wouldn't get her anywhere. Talking wouldn't get her anywhere. Seth wanted his revenge and he would continue until he got it. In other words, she was screwed.

Feeling sorry for herself, she didn't hear the transport door slide open. A young lady in a green and yellow uniform walked in. Her blonde hair was pulled back in a severe ponytail. She looked to be right out of high school. On her tray she carried a tall glass, its contents spilling over the sides, and a small jar.

"Miss Ambrose." The girl knew her name.

When Chastity tried to rise, white-lightning stung through her nipples and breasts. "*Eeoow!*"

"This drink should help the pain." The girl pressed the tray toward Chastity. "And the cream will cool the fire."

Now how did the girl know about the clamps? Embarrassment rolled across Chastity's face like a red carpet. "What is it?"

"Blue Illusion. It's an analgesic."

Chastity felt like a disobedient child. "I don't want it."

The girl, whose name chip read Starlight, was focused on Chastity's breasts. "Pardon me, but by the looks of your swollen nipples you may want to indulge. We're still ten hours from Zygoman."

"Ten hours?"

Starlight nodded. "Can I get you anything? Would you like to watch cinema-max? That new show, Voyeur II series, is on in fifteen minutes."

No, but hell *no.* "No thank you, I think I'll take your suggestion and drink... What did you call it?"

"Blue Illusion. The cream is a special mixture of an analgesic and a coolant. You should feel the relief immediately. Would you like me to apply it?" The young girl seemed overly excited. Her brown eyes darkened, her tongue swept across her bottom lips.

What the hell. "Yes, please. But no cinema-max, I want to sleep." The last thing she wanted to do was watch a replay of her earlier humiliation.

Why? Because she was sure that more humiliation awaited her on the exotic planet of Zygoman.

The drink felt icy-cold going down and then instantly began to warm her body as the flavor shifted from fruity to minty. Sitting the glass back on the tray she watched Starlight as she dipped a finger into the cream, then approached and sat lightly on the edge of the lounge. When the girl's finger touched Chastity's nipple, she gasped at the instant icy relief penetrating through her swollen nub—and the strange erotic feeling it elicited.

The girl released a tight giggle. "I told you so." She gently massaged the salve into Chastity's skin, slipping beyond the edge of the material to stroke the fullness of her breast. "Miss Ambrose, you have a lovely figure. Maybe we could..." The aroused look on the girl's face said that she had moved beyond helpful to hopeful.

In the twenty-second century the sex act had taken on a more medicinal viewpoint. Attitudes had shifted, recommending the therapeutic benefits of stimulation and release. Studied and approved by the DNMA (Development of Natural Medicine Association), sexual assuagement was encouraged. Migraines were almost a thing of the past. Sex was prescribed as a stress-reliever, instead of mind-altering drugs. Fear of disease or unwanted pregnancy had nearly been conquered.

Now, if only they could give every woman the opportunity to carry a child in her womb. Even in this day and age a small minority of women were deprived of that blessed gift. The dream of a life growing inside Chastity, Seth's child, was one that had shattered two years ago.

The thought was a downer, a depressant. "Starlight, thank you for the offer, but I just want to sleep." *Sleep and forget.*

"An orgasm on Blue Illusion can be very relaxing," Starlight insisted as she applied cream on Chastity's other nipple, her breathing becoming more pronounced. The firmness of her hand squeezing Chastity's breast became uncomfortable.

"Thank you, but *no*," Chastity said adamantly, pulling away.

The crestfallen girl rose, picked up her tray, and without another word slipped through the door before it slid shut.

Relieved to be alone, Chastity snuggled up on the chaise, her fingers moving through the soft fur. The soothing purr sung low in her ears. Disheartened, she wondered if she could live through another day like this one. A deep yawn forced her mouth open, the air filling her lungs released on a sigh. Heavy eyelids drifted closed…

On the cold, gray moon Chastity watched the eight snow leopards guarding the forbidding fortress. For miles and miles it was the same — huge mountains and flat plains of nothingness. A natural satellite of Earth, the moon lacked an atmosphere. It had no weather, no clouds, no rain, and no wind. Sound didn't carry. There was no air to breathe.

Nothing.

However, this small section was shielded by a dome erected during the mid-twenty-first century. Artificial light and air was provided. Food and water was transported. Its inhabitants were those that no one cared about. Earth had exiled them to a vacuum of emptiness and left them on this dismal place to die.

How Chastity had arrived on this barren satellite, she had no recollection. Still, something about the imposing structure looked familiar. Each time a flicker of memory flashed in her hazy mind it disappeared, elusive.

The sense of loss and pain swamped her. Someone she loved was inside. She was that person's only hope, only salvation…and she was failing.

A cry from inside set the cats to pacing. Agitated, they raised their heads and roared. Their powerful paws rose, swiping the air. Chastity thought if she could only get closer she'd pet them, make them purr like her chaise. They were beautiful animals, agile, graceful, and dangerous. She couldn't forget that fact.

Would they submit to her, as Seth wanted her to do for him?

Where did that thought come from? *Her thoughts and memories were scrambled, seeping out through dark crevices.*

Seth, hurt, angry. God, she'd made a mess of things.

A lunar wind created by the ventilators blew back her hair. A wisp of moon-dust stung her eyes. Rubbing them, she tried to remember why she was here. What was she supposed to do? Whatever the risk, she knew she had to get past the leopards and into the building.

As Chastity approached, the cats stooped low, bellies to the ground. They crawled toward her. Sharp canines glistened in the artificial light. No purring emerged, just sorrowful, heart-wrenching cries to match the weeping coming from within the fortress.

She wanted to take their pain away, wanted her pain to vanish.

Reaching out with her mind to calm the animals, the felines turned as a unit and lunged, powerful jaws snapping. Stumbling, she fell over a cluster of basalt moon rocks, hitting the ground hard. The gravelly minerals dug into her backside. Everything was a whirl of motion and sounds. When her vision cleared she stared into eight pairs of menacing eyes, felt the cats' hot breath on her face, and smelled the rancid stench of decay and rotting meat.

She screamed.

In a chair across the room, Seth watched Chastity sleep. Restless, she moaned and cried out in pain. Her body arched and he held back the desire to comfort her.

Damn those nipple clamps. Someone should've told him that they shouldn't stay on longer than thirty minutes. From his pocket he extracted the menacing contraptions. They looked innocent enough, but then so did Chastity.

Had she ever loved him? Or had she just been one of the other astral-ball bunnies that hounded the players for their fame and fortune? Stardom and money hadn't meant a lot to her back then, however, it sure seemed to now. Getting her face in front of a camera would help her modeling career…and the money? Hell, he had no idea what she had planned for the money, nor did he care.

Seth tossed the nipple clamps into the air and caught them in his palm.

Had she enjoyed the pain? She was aroused. He had seen it in her eyes when he placed the first clip on her nipple. The cloudy look of desire had made him rock-hard. If he had tasted her then, sucked her nipple into erection, there would've been no chance in hell that he'd survive attaching the second one without a total meltdown.

Another cry, her body squirmed. God, he wished she was squirming beneath *him*. Crying out in ecstasy.

Would she ask him to place the torturous things on her again? He smiled at the thought. How would she react to the things he would do to her over the course of the next couple of days? What about the things Voyeur II had planned? She certainly hadn't found the whippings pleasurable. In fact, they did more to enrage than inflame.

He watched her svelte body move—even in her tormented sleep she exuded a sensuality that drove him crazy. Monty had definitely thrown him into an absurd situation.

Yet the pinnacle of this crazy day was when he had finger-fucked her, removing the torturous devices from her nipples as she climaxed. He had stood just outside heaven's door. So friggin' hot for her, his cock almost exploded in his pants. He'd barely escaped the room without embarrassing himself.

It had taken him fifteen minutes to regain his composure and move away from her door, when what he really wanted to do was return and bury his throbbing dick between her thighs.

Next time...if there was a next time, he would fuck her with his cock. Feel her warmth, wetness, her inner muscles contracting around him, pulling him deeper. And he would hold her close, just like the quiet times they had shared in the past.

No! He shook his head adamantly, and then pinched the bridge of his nose. He had to stop thinking like that. He couldn't allow her to screw with his mind.

Pocketing the chain, he leaned forward, his forearms resting on his thighs. She was beautiful. But then again, so was the deadly celestial spirit flower, commonly called the Death's Angel on Baccarac, a nearby planet. Its scent, an intoxicating blend of sweet and tart, was a poisonous gas. Hidden beneath a soft layer of fleece were leaves as sharp as a razor and as lethal as rattlesnake venom.

Yeah, that was Chastity Ambrose. On the outside a delectable treat, on the inside destruction waiting to be released.

A sorrowful whimper surfaced from her full lips. She whispered his name between cries. He stood and then just as quickly sat back down. Confusion pulled at his mind. His first thought was to comfort her, but his conscience overrode the basic instinct to go to her. Chagrined, he acknowledged that even in her sleep this woman held power over him.

Her body sunk into the couch as though an invisible weight pushed her down. Immediately, she began to thrash against the constraint. A fist swung out as if she was fighting someone or something. Her face was twisted into a semblance of pain and fear as she clawed the air. Then her mouth parted and a strangled scream ripped from her throat.

Before he could lunge from the chair and reach out to her, she began to weep, big soul-wrenching tears. She cried as if her heart were breaking.

Without a second thought, Seth gathered her up in his arms, settling her on his lap. "Chastity, honey, are you okay? Wake up, baby." But the drug she had taken refused to release its hold. Pressed taut against his chest she seemed to take some comfort as she again whispered his name and snuggled closer. In time, her sobs died. Still, the irregular sniffling that accompanied a crying spell shook her body with every breath she inhaled. Gently, he wiped her remaining tears away, pressing his lips to her forehead.

Confused and dismayed, he wondered how he could feel so much compassion toward this woman, a woman who felt so right in his arms—yet in the same breath loathe her, want to destroy her.

For almost an hour he held her, caressed her. Felt her skin against his, smelled the clean, sweet scent that was uniquely hers. And, he tasted her. Gently kissed her minty-fresh lips, trailed the featherlight kisses he knew she liked along her jawline to the sensitive spot behind her ear, and onto the hollow of her neck. The soft mewing sounds she made as her back unconsciously arched into his touch was a kind of agony he had never anticipated. Even after all she'd done, he still wanted her.

Seth eased her off his lap and back onto the chaise, stood and stretched. Her body, so close to his, had brought back old memories, old desires—ones that were best forgotten. What had he gotten himself into? Willpower flew out the window when it came to Chastity.

Control. He had to get his shit together. See this week through. And then get on with his life. He just had to remind himself that she had already proven untrustworthy. In fact, she had decimated him.

"Seth?" Chastity's voice was drowsy and oh-so sexy. It flowed over him like sweet red wine, intoxicating and inviting.

One word had brought him to a dead halt, sent his pulse racing. He faced her. "Yes?"

Eyes closed, she stretched her long limbs, reaching, her chest pushed out invitingly. Rosy nipples peeking through leather called to him. The vision of sexuality thundered through his groin, promising an exquisite pleasure that heated his blood. Then her heavy eyelids opened, pulling him like a magnet into their depths.

Desperation crashed down upon him. He had to get away, break the trance she had over him. But the more determined he was to refuse his desire, the more fierce his need to possess her. He wanted her beyond reason. Past the realm of madness.

Chastity rose into a sitting position. Her ruffled hair had that just-been-deliciously-loved look. Her lips were shaded a delightful pink from his earlier kisses.

"We need to talk." Such a sweet, guiltless voice, more lies he couldn't stomach.

Seth's body stiffened. If he didn't leave now he might never get out whole.

"You had two years to talk to me. The time for talking has passed." Bitterness was his only hope. Hastily, he headed for the door, allowing the sound of metal sliding against metal to consume him as it automatically slid open at his approach.

"Seth!" Her cry of despair gave him pause. Slowly, he pivoted to face her.

She stood before him, her eyes swollen and sorrowful. "Can't you give me ten minutes?"

Anger knotted his stomach. His body trembled with emotion. "I gave you two *years*." He turned and walked through the exit, the door sliding closed behind him.

For what seemed a lifetime, Seth stared at the metallic barrier—just one more thing wedged between them.

Chapter Four

As Chastity stepped off the transporter, she saw her four male escorts had already exited and stood impatiently on the transport platform of Ecstasy Island. Arms crossed upon broad chests, identical frowns of displeasure plastered on their faces. Four angry glares pinned directly at her were not a good sign.

A bevy of activity bustled around them—teleporters transferring luggage, guests arriving and departing. It seemed like a madhouse to Chastity as Seth waved her to his side. She obeyed without comment, but regretted it when she saw the smirk of pleasure Tor and his minions gifted Seth with.

Their attention was quickly redirected toward the crowd. As if silently ordered, the crush parted and a young Asian woman emerged. An exotic beauty with long black hair, almond-shaped eyes and golden skin gracing a shapely body. A sting of jealousy assaulted Chastity as she witnessed the sexual appreciation in Seth's eyes.

Tor moved away from their party to meet the woman. Without a word, she fell to his feet. With a gentle hand beneath her chin, he commanded her to rise. Then he took her into his arms and kissed her with the passion of possession. The woman returned his ardor, her reaction as intense. Finally, they parted and the two approached Chastity and Seth, the woman several steps behind Tor. Without a word he motioned her to Chastity's side.

It was then Chastity noticed the sign that read "Master Registry" and at the further end of the platform another that simply read "slaves".

As Chastity expected, a barrage of Voyeur II cameras were poised and ready to film their arrival. Well, Seth's anyway, as they surrounded him, bombarding him with questions.

His hand went to his chin, and he rubbed his neatly groomed mustache and goatee, pondering each question asked.

The man had a wonderful profile. The camera loved him, the reporters loved him, and sadly, Chastity loved him, too.

Attention intently focused on Seth, Chastity started when the woman beside her spoke. "I am Passion Flower. Please follow me, slave Chastity."

Chastity's brows rose. *Slave Chastity*? Before yielding to the woman's request, she glanced over her shoulder in Seth's direction, but Tor had already ushered him through the Master's entrance, the crew of Voyeur II hot on his trail.

"Where are we going?"

"To prepare your body for your Master's pleasure."

Well, of course. That would've been my very first guess, if I wasn't wondering why the hell I'm here in the first place.

A woman, dressed...no, *dressed* wasn't the appropriate word—nearly naked would be more apropos, stood before the door, her body swathed in chains. Chains used to lift and accentuate particular body parts, but not covering anything of real importance. Passion Flower's own attire wasn't much more than a floral printed flap that covered her mons. Her breasts were covered with either body paint or tattoos of exquisite lotus blossoms. Her name was obviously derived from the fruit that induced a dreamy languorous ardor.

Chastity glanced back at the woman draped in chains. "What does this preparation consist of?"

Passion Flower pushed open the door and held it for her to pass through. "You must be washed, perfumed and dressed for your Master's pleasure."

Chastity tossed a nod back toward metal woman. "I hope he's chosen something less revealing than her Master has, or yours, for that matter."

As they entered a sterile, white room, a bustle of activity buzzed around her. Clearly the women and men of slave status were looking forward to their adventures as they laughed and spoke with each other. Two women and one man openly shared their newly acquired piercings, a gold band through each nipple. Chastity smiled at the thought of the incredible orgasm she had experienced when Seth had removed her own nipple clamps. Then she remembered his abrupt disappearance and her smile fled.

Several staff members in togas approached. Immediately they began to disrobe her, despite her initial protests. Off came her skimpy little red leather outfit, then her boots and finally the collar around her neck. Thankfully, she wasn't the only one receiving this treatment. Several other women and men were being stripped in front of all.

No one seemed to be affected by the nudity, except for her. Nervous energy made her shift her feet, taking a step forward that nearly sent her sprawling across a man kneeling at her feet.

Where the hell had he come from? The man dropped to his hands, on all fours before her.

Bewildered, she looked to Passion Flower for an explanation.

The woman smiled. "Slave Chastity, place a foot on slave Henry's back." Chastity did as requested and a woman standing to her left lifted her foot and slipped a thin transparent bracelet over Chastity's ankle. Immediately, it adjusted to fit.

The band looked harmless, so Chastity decided not to resist.

"Now, the other," Passion Flower said, and Chastity obeyed. Again a bracelet was slipped over her other ankle, adjusting on its own. Next, similar ones were placed on both wrists.

Chastity tugged at the band on her left wrist.

Passion Flower stilled Chastity's hand with one of her own. "They cannot be removed without your Master's permission."

"They look fragile, as if you could tear them off without much effort." She tugged again, finding them amazingly sturdy. "What are they for?"

"You will see." Passion Flower guided her to another entrance. When she pushed open the door, Chastity came to an abrupt halt, gasping.

A magnificent waterfall cascaded into a pool of crystal-clear water, so pure the bottom was visible. Large, flat, green leaves with flowers that looked like white Moth orchids floated upon its surface. Every few minutes the broad petals would close, and when they reopened a fountain of water sprung from their center. Sand that felt like foam, soft and light, squished between her toes as she entered the garden. The sensation of walking through whipped cream was highly sensual as she strolled to the water's edge.

"It's beautiful." Chastity tilted her head and listened to the sweet song of birds high in the trees. Clusters of tiny flowers that looked like pink balls of fur were sprinkled throughout. Any moment she expected the breeze to lift the flowers high into the air creating a heavenly cloud of velvet catkins.

"Slave Tatiana will bath you." Passion Flower waved toward the pond. "Enjoy." Then she disappeared behind a mountain of rock, covered in moss.

The petite woman with short dark hair and eyes to match guided Chastity into the water. "Welcome to Zygoman."

Wide-eyed, Chastity stopped short. "There's something in the water." Invisible hands skimmed lightly over her skin, as if she shared the water with a million living creatures. A shiver slithered up her back as her feet began to move toward the bank.

The woman giggled. "Synthetically enhanced amoebas."

Chastity jumped and yelped, "One-celled organisms? Parasites? Like the kind that live off a host?" Panic rose in her throat as she made a beeline to the shore. Sprays of mist went everywhere with her efforts.

She had to get out of the water.

A misstep brought her down face-first, water gushing over her head. She came up sucking in a breath as she choked and spat, gagging at the thought of swallowing the tiny parasites.

This time the woman threw back her head and a stream of laughter burst forth. "The key word is *synthetic*, manmade." She helped Chastity to her feet, pulling her resisting body deeper into the bug-infested water. "Everything on this planet is created to stimulate the senses. Here in Zygoman the amoebas have been modified to cleanse instead of feed. We use no soaps, no shampoos—the creatures in the water break down and dispose of impurities. And it's a great conditioner for the hair and skin."

Was the woman jerking her leg? "You're bullshitting me."

"No, I'm not '*bullshitting*' you," the woman mocked.

Chastity swallowed nervously. Then she quickly dipped down and began to wash her body. There was no way she'd stay any longer than necessary in the water. Her hands briskly brushed down her arms, but the tiny fingers touching and caressing her most intimate parts made her pause, relax. With a deep sigh, she drifted deeper in the water. The amoebas were casting a spell as they stroked and stimulated, allowing her to enjoy the erotic experience.

Beads of water slithered down Chastity's body as she exited the pond. Tatiana used a big fluffy towel to pat her body dry. Then she began to towel-dry Chastity's hair.

The woman's hands were as gentle as her voice. "My mother and father live on Earth with my younger sister and brother. We're a close family, but when this opportunity arose I just couldn't resist."

"Opportunity?" Chastity asked.

The woman's rapidly moving hands stilled. "Working on a pleasure planet." Her light, easy conversation helped to put Chastity at ease. Maybe this experience wouldn't be too bad.

Tatiana spoke so dearly of her family, Chastity wondered whether she could elicit her help. "Tatiana, do you know where I can find a trans-communicator?"

"Slaves are not allowed such luxuries. Our Masters take care of our needs."

"But Tatiana, I need to call my mother. I haven't spoken to her in several months." The woman paused, and a sense of hope filled Chastity.

Tatiana began to dispose of the used towels in a receptacle close to the door. "I am sorry, slave Chastity, but the rules cannot be broken."

"Surely it wouldn't hurt to break a rule for something as important as family?"

Still, the woman replied, "I cannot."

Disappointed, Chastity knew she had to find another way to make the call.

After her bath, Tatiana led her to another room. Here she lay upon a cushioned table, while the strong, large hands of a gorgeous male slave, dressed in the same toga attire as Tatiana, massaged her body with oils and creams. Even her breasts and mons received attention from the muscular hunk.

Tatiana explained that in order to achieve total balance, no part of the anatomy should be ignored. When Chastity moaned, coming as the man stroked her pussy, she knew complete balance had been achieved.

Next, she was perfumed with a fragrance she had never before smelled. In fact, the scent seemed to change every time she thought she recognized its contents.

Evidently her confusion was obvious. Tatiana laughed. "Unusual, isn't it?"

Chastity inhaled deeply. "What is it?"

"It's a mixture of ingredients guaranteed to heighten arousal. Let me show you." With two fingers the woman stroked a path from the hollow of Chastity's throat to her breasts. The distinctive odor of sex rose.

"Actually, it's a conductor. Heat and friction release the incense of your body." The same aroma arose when Tatiana teased the inside of Chastity's thighs. It wasn't a hot, sweaty musk, but a mere wisp, an invitation to touch, to taste. The soft perfume seductively whispered, *I'm ready, take me now.*

Heavy breasts, tingling nipples and a wet pussy confirmed Chastity *was* ready for the taking.

While the perfume was gentle, the black leather outfit Tatiana presented next spoke loudly. It screamed, "Tear my clothes off, please!"

Stiletto heels adorned buttery-soft, thigh-high, black leather boots. Their wild look set off the leather thong and scanty bustier lying beside them. The collar and handcuffs she'd previously worn completed the ensemble.

Chastity briefly closed her eyes in disbelief. "Did *he* choose this outfit?"

Tatiana grinned. "Your Master must be very proud of your figure." An appreciative gaze raked up and down Chastity's body. "You are very beautiful. Now, let me help you dress."

The boots and the thong riding high on Chastity's hips lengthened her already long legs. The bustier was tight, barely restraining her breasts. She feared that a single breath would release them, revealing her nipples. Still, when she admired herself in the mirror she had to admit that she looked good—damn good.

When Chastity finally exited the bathhouse she felt confident, ready to face anything. Well, almost anything, she amended as she saw Seth and Tor enter the gardens. Stepping behind a statue, she withdrew from sight. Deep in conversation, the two hadn't noticed her. She breathed a sigh of relief. For the first time today she actually felt relaxed. Now if she could just avoid Seth for the next six days, not to mention nights, she'd be okay.

Yeah, right.

Appreciatively, she gazed at her surroundings. The interior courtyard was a place of beauty. From her position she inhaled the profusion of flowers and vines—hibiscus, bougainvillea, gardenias and a variety of other plants she had never seen before, bloomed and sweetened the air.

Only when the men turned a corner and disappeared behind a building did Chastity step out from her hiding place, pivot, and run smack-dab into Passion Flower.

"*Jesus!*" she cried out in surprise. "Where did you come from?"

The calm, unruffled woman smiled and said, "Slave Chastity, it is time for your lessons to begin."

Shoulder to shoulder, Seth walked with Tor toward the main structure of the compound, an elaborate edifice formed by a series of rounded arches, a tall, vaulted roof and shingles that looked like slabs of gold. In the sunlight the roofing glistened, creating a halo effect of glowing amber. Several smaller replicas surrounded the huge building, emphasizing its grandeur.

As they stepped through an archway, Tor asked, "I trust that your experience in Zygoman has been pleasurable so far?" A knowing grin and a twinkle in the man's eyes revealed he already knew the answer.

Zygoman was every man's fantasy. Sex and more sex, as far as the eye could see. Couples and multiple partners engaging in various sexual acts actually littered the walkway. He counted four interludes in the garden alone. One in particular had caught his eye, two women at play. A voluminous blonde was diving into an equally luscious brunette's thighs. As the brunette's hips thrust, he watched with appreciation as the blonde's heavy breasts swayed in rhythm. The globes begged to be fondled and sucked.

The woman receiving the tonguing was in the throes of passion, twisting her own nipples, her back arched, screaming in ecstasy. As she moved faster, the blonde's breasts jerked back and forth. It took a great deal of willpower not to join them.

Yet he couldn't imagine any sexual pleasures here that didn't include Chastity.

"I'm enjoying myself very much," Seth said, remembering the beauty that had thoroughly massaged his body. Paying special attention to his cock, her oily hands had slid up and down his length, massaging the sensitive tip until he couldn't hold back, his seed spilling into her palms. Then the woman, slave Marcy, had slipped a finger into her mouth, closed her eyes and moaned, tasting his essence.

The only problem was that the whole time she had stroked him, all he could think about was Chastity's mouth on him instead.

"I'm especially good at mouth massages." Desire had flashed in slave Marcy's emerald eyes as she gazed up at him through feathered lashes. "If your slave does not satisfy you, Master Seth, I will be available for purchase at the slave auction."

Tempting. But Chastity had always satisfied him, body and soul. For her, he had been willing to give up his bachelorhood, retire from a job he loved and focus on family and home.

A sting of regret pricked him.

Dreams lost.

A woman's scream tore Seth out of his personal pity party. He tensed, scanning the multiple doors before him. Another scream. His adrenaline surged as he darted toward the third door on the left. A strong hand stopped him from bursting in.

"Master Seth, Terrance and Shawn are in lesson."

Seth couldn't believe the calm exterior of the man before him. He attempted to push pass the brawny Viking, but was held tight. "They're hurting her."

Tor smiled. "Yes, and she's loving every minute of it. If you'll remain calm, I'll show you what I mean."

Slowly, Tor pushed open the door. Seth held his breath and peered into the room. A naked woman stood before Shawn, her palms on the man's shoulders as Terrance struck her again with the leather side of a rounded paddle.

She whimpered, her ass red-hot.

Then he flipped the paddle over and gently rubbed the side covered in fur over the tender area. "Does it feel good, slave Lydia?" he asked.

"Yes." Her tone was breathless.

Terrance's stilled his hand. "Yes, what?" he asked, displeasure obvious in his gravelly tone.

"Yes, Master," she corrected.

Slowly his hand moved, making slow circles with the paddle on her buttocks. "You know you will be punished for your forgetfulness."

"Yes, Master." Her head was bowed, but Seth could see the smile that crept over her face. The woman was indeed enjoying herself.

"Kneel before Master Shawn."

Her hands dropped from Shawn's shoulders and she sunk to her knees, her face level with the man's bulging groin.

"Release Master Shawn's cock and take it into your mouth," Terrance ordered.

The woman quickly, eagerly, removed Shawn's toga. Her eyes widened in appreciation as his erection sprang free. Without hesitation, she leaned forward, closing her lips around him. Her eyelids shut in peaceful bliss as she began to suckle. Shawn's fingers threaded through her hair, holding her head still as he thrust his hips forward. He growled and plunged again.

The movement along her slender neck and her cheeks as she feasted upon Shawn's dick made Seth's harden. He wanted Chastity like this—down on her knees, at his mercy. His tongue traced a hungry path between his lips.

When the woman's hands grasped Shawn's buttocks, Terrance swung the paddle, striking her hard on the ass. She choked as Shawn's cock thrust deeper down her throat.

"You are not to touch Master Shawn. Place your hands behind you." She did as Terrance ordered. He stepped behind her and tied a silk cloth around her wrists, binding her.

Seth sucked in a tense breath through clenched teeth.

He watched as Terrance shed his toga and then approached the woman. The man's erection jutted out as he anointed himself with a white cream. Slowly Terrance drifted to his knees, his buttocks resting on his calves. Reaching from behind, his hands cupped her breasts and a moan of pleasure squeezed from her full mouth.

"I'm going to fuck your ass." Caressing her waist, he lifted her up and penetrated her tight rosebud. Her cry of surprise was muffled. But judging by the thrust of the woman's hips meeting his, she was having the time of her life.

"Do not come until I give you permission," Terrance grunted as he plunged faster, harder. Shawn matched his rhythm, pushing in and out of her mouth. Perspiration beaded the woman's forehead, her expression almost painful as she strained to obey.

How she did it, Seth would never understand. *Shit*! Even he was on the verge of release.

When the men roared in unison, their bodies spent, Seth thought the woman would pass out, she was quivering so badly. But she held steady, drinking from both men. Terrance and Shawn pulled out from her and stepped back. She shook violently with need.

"Do you wish to climax, slave Lydia?" asked Terrance.

"Yes, Master…please, Master."

"Touch yourself."

The woman slipped a finger into her pussy. Her hips frantically moved as her digit pushed in and out, her thumb pressed against her clit.

Seth watched, mesmerized, as she pleasured herself. Her heat, her excitement was enough to stir the blood of any man.

Then the woman screamed, her body convulsing as she reached completion.

Stunned, Seth just stood there until Tor grasped him by the arm.

"Amazing, isn't it? Servicing our customers is what I live for," Tor chuckled. "God, I love my job."

Seth was ushered through a hallway of exquisite art and marble flooring and into a room similar to a large den. A fire burned in the fireplace—an optical illusion, as he felt no heat and he knew the temperature was regulated on Zygoman.

Tor motioned for Seth to sit in one of two chairs before the hearth, sitting in the remaining chair. Silence lingered for a moment between them until a slave entered and handed each of them a glass of Bordeaux. Quietly, she backed out of the room, shutting the door behind her.

Tor gazed at the red liquid and then sat the drink down on an end table and shifted nervously in his chair. The anxious movement placed Seth on edge. *This can't be good.*

"Master Seth, I know that you came to Zygoman with an agenda. But Voyeur II has an agenda of its own, as well."

Seth's fingers tightened around the stem of his glass. Why hadn't he had the foresight to ask Monty details? Seth loathed surprises and he felt a doozy was coming.

"Their goal is for slave Chastity to fail."

Of course, Seth should have realized that when money was involved there would be a catch. Even for a friend, Monty, not to mention the network, would not willingly allow Chastity to walk off with one hundred million dollars.

"To ensure this is accomplished, Voyeur II has paid for the Ultima-Erotic Experience, including add-ons."

Why did it feel like Seth was waiting for the other shoe to drop? But he asked the question anyway. "Add-ons?"

"Just a few small…uh…interesting things." Tor added quickly, "Nothing that will actually harm her. There's the slave auction. Of course, you have the right to purchase her, if you so choose." The man's Adam's apple dipped nervously. "And, then there's the four-way."

"Four-way?"

"The four-way will require others to touch your slave similar to what you just saw."

Aha, that little exhibition had been staged for his benefit. What was he supposed to say, yeah have a go at Chastity?

Seth stood and began to pace the room. "The contract states that she will not be physically harmed." Heat rose in the room, kicking on the temperature regulators.

"Yes, that's true. However, creatively, there is a lot that can be done to a person without physical harm."

Chastity wouldn't be cooperative. Hell would freeze over before she would surrender. Seth jerked to a halt. *Had* hell frozen over? It didn't take a brain surgeon to see she didn't want to be here.

"I'll need your agreement that you will not interfere with the mandates of Voyeur II."

"Monty's a dead man," Seth growled. He sat his wineglass down so hard the stem snapped in two. Wine splashed on the end table and the glass tumbled off and shattered across the floor.

Tor stood, picked up an identity screen, and held it out to him. When Seth made no attempt to give his consent, Tor added, "If you have concern for the woman, remember that if you don't go through with this, Voyeur II will get someone else to. Slave Chastity seems determined to win the money, or clearly she wouldn't be here."

Okay, the inevitable twist the arm trick. Seth couldn't leave Chastity with the unknown. It seemed ironic that he should be taking the position of her champion when what he wanted was revenge.

He placed a shaky hand on the screen. A florescent green line scrolled down the monitor. Then a multitude of information flashed across the screen in a blur. His head made several quick, jerky movements side-to-side as he attempted to read what he had signed.

"A copy of the agreement will be awaiting you in your room. Additionally, you are free to choose anything off our Register of Pleasures. You can view the list on the cinema-monitor. Any wish, any desire, can and will be fulfilled."

Seth quietly turned and stared into the blazing fire. "Where is Chastity?"

"She's in training."

"Training!" Seth snapped his head in Tor's direction. "Who's conducting the training?" He tensed, not ready to hear the answer.

"Terrance and Shawn."

Seth sunk down into a chair. "Fuck." His thumb and forefinger pinched the bridge of his nose.

Tor chuckled. "Not like what you just observed. At least not tonight."

That last part tied Seth's stomach into a knot.

"There are basic instructions she needs to know, to understand, in order to serve you better." Tor leaned against the hearth. "In fact, your assistance is required tonight."

"How?"

"On the first night of bondage, she must remain blindfolded for the entire night."

"Why?"

"A blindfold will increase her vulnerability and the degree of surrender involved. Her auditory and sensory skills will become more acute. Listening to you move around the room, wondering what you're doing, will drive her crazy. Let her listen to the distinct sounds of you undressing, preparing for the night. Allow her to touch but not see the articles you plan to use for your enjoyment. Let her caress your body so that she knows you're naked."

The picture Tor painted was making Seth's balls ache with need. His cock lengthened, hardened. She'd go wild, but whether with anger or lust he didn't know. Either way, she would be his to do with as he pleased. And it would please him to thrust deep inside her hot, wet pussy. To sample the nectar of her lips, ravish her breasts with his tongue. And when he was through he'd fuck her again. Enter her from behind so he could watch his erection slide in and out of her swollen heat and—

"I see that this interests you. Bind her and the stakes go higher. She will have to depend on you to see to her every need."

"Chastity will never go for this."

"Then she will fail and you can go back to Earth tomorrow. But I say you're wrong. Something is driving her," Tor paused. "And I don't think she is here for excitement. She certainly isn't weak."

"Not weak, but damn hardheaded."

Again, the man went quiet. His hand stroked a candlestick on the mantel.

Unease slithered across Seth's skin as he stood. "What? There's more, isn't there?"

"Tomorrow night she will again need to be blindfolded." Tor paused.

"And?"

"Well…we…Terrance, Shawn and I will—"

"Wait just one damn minute."

Palms outstretched, Tor took a step backwards. "Okay, okay, we need to at least give her the illusion that we are participating in the night's activities. We'll work with you, for now."

Some of the tension drained from Seth's body. Then it returned, when Tor added, "Allen, you need to loosen up. There are things out of your control. We can't be fighting you every inch of the way. We didn't sign up for that. This is a place of pleasure. Relax. Enjoy yourself. If you can dream it, it can be experienced. Now, would you like to see your slave-in-training?"

Seth nodded and they exited the room.

As they walked down the cobblestone sidewalk, Tor offered more of the rules on Zygoman. "Part of training is to strip a slave of all comforts. A slave is more receptive to a Master when they rely on them for the littlest of needs. Therefore, your slave's request to use the trans-communicator was denied."

Seth almost tripped over his own feet.

Son of a bitch! She was still attempting to contact her lover. Consideration and sympathy for Chastity disappeared in a cloud of smoke. Rage was alive and moving through his veins at top speed. It was time to teach her a lesson.

Chapter Five

A narrow brook of sparkling blue water weaved its way from one end of the garden to the other. From where Chastity sat in the grass she could hear a waterfall pounding in the distance. All along the banks of the creek, yellow trumpet-like flowers on long green stems arched as if seeking a drink. Giant birds of paradise with large banana-shaped leaves and orange and blue flowers added to the Eden-esque atmosphere. It was peaceful here.

Passion Flower stroked Chastity's hair, the caress having a calming effect. Her voice was low, soothing. "To submit is to yield control."

"But I don't want to submit or lose control." Chastity picked a daisy and began plucking its petals. To lose control was a weakness she couldn't afford.

"There is joy in serving another. A spiritual rebirth when you subjugate yourself to a Master."

Disbelief was on Chastity's lips. Surely she wasn't hearing this from another woman. "Joy? You're joking? Happiness is to be paraded around like a sex toy and to be humiliated and disrespected by a domineering man? Joy?" she repeated. "Passion Flower, how can you stand to be subservient to that— that barbaric Tor Thorenson?" Chastity crushed the remainder of the flower in her palm and then tossed its crumpled remains.

Passion Flower hesitated, her hand stilling. "He is my husband. I love him." She spoke soft, firm words that left no room for skepticism.

If there had been a breeze in the air it would have blown Chastity over. The sex king of Ecstasy Island was married? And this gentle creature was his wife? Okay, so the world had slightly tilted off balance. But then again, this whole day had been a scene from the *Twilight Zone*.

"Please accept my apology for my rude comment," Chastity said with sincere regret. Who was she to judge another? Hell, at least Passion Flower had the man she loved.

Through long, dark lashes the woman peered up at Chastity. "Tor told me of your first meeting."

Yeah, and Chastity's nipples and ass still ached from that meeting.

Slender fingers again began to comb through Chastity's hair. "He only wished to help you adjust to your role. He is a loving and gentle man."

Chastity's jaw dropped. The woman couldn't possible believe what she was saying.

Then Passion Flower smiled, a mischievous twinkle in her eyes. "But he can also be an ass. And if you tell him I said so I will deny it."

Both women broke into giggles. Their laughter was quickly squashed when they were jerked to their feet by two pairs of strong and angry hands. Shawn and Terrance both glared down at Passion Flower.

"Your Master will not be happy with you." Terrance spoke harshly to the Asian woman, while Shawn firmly held Chastity.

Passion Flower cast her eyes downward. "Please forgive me, Master Terrance. We were awaiting you and—and Master Shawn. It is our desire to know how you want to proceed…we seek only to please you."

The men glanced at each other, and then in unison they released the women.

Passion Flower had been quick with her response and the two muscle-headed men had bought it—hook, line and sinker. Chastity started to shake her head in disbelief. When she saw Passion Flower's warning expression, she refrained from further verbal or nonverbal comment.

Men were stupid. Just stroke their ego and they'd buy anything. Maybe this little bit of knowledge would be useful in this crazy world of testosterone and machismo.

"Have you taught this wench anything?" Terrance's demeaning glance from head to toe sparked a fire in Chastity.

Her fingers curled into fists. "No, she hasn't. But one thing I have figured out *on my own* is that this planet is overrun by a buttload of egotistical men high on themselves."

So much for stroking the male ego.

Instead, she found herself quickly subdued, facedown on the ground, Terrance atop her. Her body bucked, struggling to get free. But the more she fought, the tighter his grip. Forcibly, her arms were pulled behind her, ankles bent back resting on her buttocks, and then she felt something cool twining around her limbs. Chastity let loose a scream of fury as he released her and stood.

The damn man had hogtied her.

She squirmed, tugging against the ropes that held her ankles and wrists. "Bastard, let me go!" And then as if the humiliation wasn't enough, Seth and Tor arrived with the crew of Voyeur II in tow.

Okay, now what was she supposed to do? The air filled with tense silence. Seth just stood there like a statue, his eyes agape.

"*Seth*, make this cocksucker let me go!" She wiggled, trying to get loose, but only succeeded in baring her ass to the cameras focused on her.

Regaining his composure, Seth calmly faced Terrance. "My slave has offended you."

Wide-eyed Chastity glared at Seth. "Are you fucking *mad*? Look at me."

Deliberately, he ignored her. "What punishment would you feel appropriate for her disgraceful behavior?"

Ohmygod! Seth was putting her right into the man's hands. "Wait just a fucking minute. My contract is with Voyeur II and you not this—this *imbecile*." The soft cushiony grass was quickly turning into a hard bed of concrete. Her muscles were stretched tight and aching. And the cameras riveted to her ass put a new meaning to the words indecent exposure.

Seth looked toward the cameramen, shook his head, and sighed. "Again, she insults Master Terrance."

"Seth," her tone was a low, threatening growl.

Using his name as an admonishment was the wrong thing to do. Kneeling, he grasped a handful of her hair and jerked her head back so that their eyes met. "You are my *possession*. The sooner you accept it, the sooner we can experience pleasure. But for now, you will treat each of these men with respect. And, why?" he snarled. "Because it pleases me, and you are here to please me." Releasing her hair, he stood and faced Terrance. "Now, how would you like to punish my slave?"

This can't be happening. Chastity shifted against her bonds. She had to give it to Terrance. The man knew how to tie a knot. There was no play at all in the ropes.

"For slave Chastity I choose the chastity bell. She is to wear it during her lessons and orientation this evening."

Did he say bell or belt? wondered Chastity.

Whatever, it didn't sound too bad. Visions of the crude belt used in the Middle Ages for abstinence came to mind. The image quickly vanished when Passion Flower brought him a satin pillow holding something that looked strangely like an erect penis, but it wasn't any bigger than two inches.

"Master Seth." Seth took the miniature dildo Terrance offered and approached Chastity.

Chastity winced at his touch. "I'm *warning* you, Seth, don't do it." The caveat was issued through clenched teeth.

"Shut up, Chastity, or I'll cram it in your mouth. Now roll on your side and spread your knees." His languid tone made her stiffen.

"And how exactly do you expect me to manage rolling over?" Sarcasm lifted her voice. Her position left her helpless. A position she loathed. Too many times over the last two years she had found herself helpless.

Harshly, he pushed her over to her side. She groaned at the sudden movement, but was thankful when he placed himself in front of the cameras. Still, she knew the audience would feed off her humiliation like pond-sucking scavengers.

When Seth's hand slipped between her thighs, nudged past her thong, spreading the folds of her pussy, Chastity thought she'd die a slow death. Twice in one day. She'd dreamt of Seth's touch throughout the years. But never had she imagined this. His fingers probed and then slid between her nether lips. No way could she halt the shower of damp pleasure that flowed into his hand.

His breath faltered, betraying his desire.

Satisfaction tipped the corners of her mouth into a smile, a smirk that vanished when she felt the cool, metallic dildo slip inside her. Immediately, the small foreign object began to move, shaping to the walls of her sex. The solid mass was like liquid mercury, contorting, thrusting and filling her. Then it hardened and began to vibrate, plunging deeply. Her sheath gripped the invader, welcoming its presence.

Terrance's deep, menacing voice was the last thing she needed as she fought against the tantalizing effect the bell was having upon her. "The bell is devised to heighten sensation."

No *fuck*! Her pussy throbbed. Her body was aflame, reaching a level of stimulation she'd never before experienced so quickly. She desperately craved release, but not in front of the cameras, not in front of Seth. So she fought the inevitable.

Terrance's thumb and forefinger gripped her chin lifting her forward and slightly off the ground. Fiery eyes met an almost demonic grin, making a sliver of fear shiver through her. "But…" he hesitated.

Oh, no, not the dreaded *"but"*. She arched her back, straining against her bindings, the man's grip and her growing need to climax.

"It will keep you *from* fulfillment." He released her chin causing her to fall back. An unladylike grunt squeezed from her throat. "You'll beg for your Master's touch before the night is over," he said, amused. Then he reached down and untied her.

Seth, *hell*. She'd almost let *Terrance* screw her, if he could ease the devastating need between her thighs.

Sprawled on the ground, she wanted to stretch her sore limbs, but her body convulsed as shards of lightning shot through her sex. She held her breath, bracing herself for the climax of a lifetime. So close, so very close to the zenith.

Then...*ZAP!*

All sensation disappeared. She moved her hips, flexing her inner muscles, searching, reaching. Frustration rose like steam from a boiling pot of water. She repeated the movements, still nothing. She was an empty shell. No trace of the object lodged inside her remained. Only a cold numbness lingered, the sense of sexual pleasure unfinished. The devastating experience left her bereft and feeling a deep sense of loss, a miscarriage of desire. But at least it was over.

She climbed to her feet, refusing to acknowledge Seth's presence or the chuckles from onlookers. Gathering her aplomb, she brushed grass from her ass. Just one more humiliation to put behind her, she needed to focus on the training and get through this horrible nightmare one way or another.

At least, that's what she thought before Terrance said, "Master Seth, stimulate your slave."

Chastity's body went ramrod straight as Seth's sinewy chest pressed against her bare back. She arched away but not before his palms closed around her breasts. Immediately, her breasts grew heavy, her nipples tingled and warmth flooded her pussy. And that little dildo appeared once more, growing, thrusting and filling her.

Thrown back into the violent sea of passion, she arched into Seth's kneading hands, felt his arousal burn into her back. Hot, hot, hot… *God*, she needed to feel him plunging between her thighs.

As if he sensed her need, one hand abandoned a breast and caressed its way down her stomach, pausing atop the thong. When his fingers slipped beyond the leather, dipping into her heat, her knees buckled. He gripped her tight against him, saving her from falling, succeeding in driving her higher. A whimper made her cringe. She was pitiful as her pussy sucked on his finger begging for more.

Then…*ZAP*!

Nothing.

She couldn't feel his hand on her breast teasing her nipple. She couldn't sense his finger invading her sex.

Nothing…absolutely nothing.

Frustration hit a new level as she flung herself from Seth. Whoever had developed this little torture toy should be strung up by his balls. Surely, the inventor was a man hell-bent on tormenting a woman, an ex-wife, an ex-girlfriend or perhaps an ex-fiancée.

"Be forewarned—" Terrance's eyes sparkled with mischief, "—you cannot remove the chastity bell—any attempt will set it off. Only the hand that implanted it can dislodge it. Therefore, obedient behavior will be rewarded. Disobedience will be punished."

A colorful metaphor perched on the tip of her tongue preparing for flight when she caught the warning in Seth's eyes. She gritted her teeth, forcing back the words. She truly tried, but they slipped out anyway.

"You *son of a bitch*!"

Chastity was magnificent in her fury. Seth's cock tightened in appreciation. A bolt of energy, she glowed vivaciously as she stared up at her tormentor. Her five-foot-ten-inch frame looked small against the formidable man. Yet, if looks could kill, he knew Terrance would be dead. Hell, *he'd* be dead.

Still, Chastity needed to learn submission. Only then would she come to accept him as her Master. Only then would he be revenged.

She stood—proud, defiant—even when Seth grabbed her arm, dragging her about-face and bringing her nose-to-nose with him. He stared into her icy blue eyes.

"Apologize."

The men operating the Voyeur II cameras moved in for a closer shot of her bold resistance. Their smiles revealed their delight, the bulge in their pants their arousal.

Fire sparked in her eyes at his command.

Her chest rose, skimming across his, lighting the fuse to his desire. Heavy breathing kept her breasts in motion, her taut nipples poking against the thin material of her bustier. He couldn't stop himself. His head dipped and his mouth closed over a peak. Reactively, her back arched into him, pressing her closer, deeper, as he suckled. When he released her a warm, wet spot appeared where his mouth had been.

"Apologize," Seth repeated firmly.

Eyes narrowing, she met his glare with the same intensity. "No."

"You will be punished for your rebellion."

There was a moment of silence, except for their heavy breathing. Then her eyes clouded over. All expression disappeared from her face. A cloak of indifference covered her as her body relaxed. She was drifting, slipping into her safe zone.

"*No*." Seth hadn't meant to speak his objection aloud. Desperation clenched in his stomach. He couldn't lose her, couldn't let her escape him. So he did the only thing he knew to do. He kissed her.

At first there was no response as he gently brushed his lips across hers. Her eyelashes were dark crescents against rosy cheeks. Controlled breathing lifted her breasts in a slow, steady rhythm. She was stripping him of his revenge. Frantically, he crushed his mouth to hers.

Finally, he felt a break in her breathing. Then her lips parted and she whimpered in invitation. His tongue plunged deeply — the same way he wanted his cock to fill her pussy. He stroked and caressed and tasted. It was blessed torture to dwell in her warmth, to taste the memories of the past upon her tongue.

As she drifted back to him, her passion woke and a fierce battle of tongues ensued. She clung to him, her hips grinding against his. He met each thrust, one hand holding her close, the other cupping the weight of a breast. Seductively, she slid her body up his until she wedged his erection between her thighs.

Yes, she enjoyed his touch, no matter that she would deny it. She wanted him so badly that she was quivering, her arms clinging to him. Then he remembered the chastity bell. She wasn't reacting to his kiss but that damnable pleasure toy.

Savagely, he pushed her away. His ego had taken another blow. "Bring me a paddle."

Passion Flower waved to a slave across the garden.

Chastity stumbled. Confusion lit her bright eyes. Lips slightly apart, her skin was flushed with arousal. "Seth, I-I need…"

"What, Chastity? What do you need?" *Me*, he inwardly whispered. *Say you need me.*

"Nothing," she groaned, pressing her thighs together. "I need *nothing* from you." She released another guttural sound. Eyes closing, she moaned, her body moving slowly, sensually. A temptress' seduction — her body was an invitation that promised a man a slice of heaven and hell. And he had tasted both.

Damn her! Seth wanted her to crave *his* touch. He wanted her to need the feel of *his* cock plunging deep into her core, not some artificial fuck toy. And he wanted to hear his name screamed from her lips as she came.

Passion Flower took the paddle from the young male slave and handed it to Seth.

"Chastity, do you want to end this game?"

Chastity glared at him.

"Your safe word is 'red'. Use it when you've had enough. Understand?"

Her answer was to stubbornly lift her chin.

Angrily, he grabbed Chastity and whirled her around. Then his hand swung out.

Whack! Leather met skin.

Chastity's body arched. "*Aaaaah...*" She released a throaty cry.

Catlike she writhed, whimpering as another swat landed on her tender flesh. Incredibly, she acted as if the pain intensified the pleasure, as if each strike was a thrust into her pussy driving her closer to climax. Her body began to shake violently. Her breathing came in short pants. Then all of a sudden she collapsed to her knees.

"*Nooo!*" her voice strained. Fists pounded the ground in frustration. Her body shook uncontrollably. Once again fulfillment had been ripped from her grasp.

Seth felt no compassion, no sympathy. "Are you ready to apologize?"

Defeated, head bowed, her trembling voice whispered, "Master Terrance, please accept my apology."

The brawny man smiled triumphantly. Gently, Terrance placed his hands beneath her arms, assisting Chastity to her feet. "Are you ready to obey your Master without question?"

Eyes cast downward, shoulders drooping, she replied, "Yes, Master Terrance."

"Then we will begin your training. Master Seth, please take your slave in hand."

Chastity's face was drawn. All energy spent. No fight remained. Even when Seth attached his leash to the collar around her neck she made no effort to resist. In fact, her body swayed unsteadily and her eyelids appeared to be weighted as if she fought sleep. He wondered if she had again managed to wedge herself between her safe zone and reality. Terrance must have suspected the same as he asked her to repeat the words he had just spoken.

"I have but four basic duties—to serve my Master's needs, to obey his orders, to accept his domination and to please his desires."

To hear her acceptance of the subjugation sent a thrill through Seth. His body trembled with thoughts of how he would take her. His groin throbbed with anticipation. He'd order her to anoint his body with her love juices. Then he'd fuck her senseless.

"On your knees."

She knelt before Terrance at his command.

A shiver raced up Seth's spine. He gazed at her full lips, lips that would part on his command and take him deep within the tight warmth of her mouth. God, he wanted her. Seth wondered if he would ever look at Chastity and not see tumbled sheets, tangled limbs and their slick bodies in motion.

Terrance approach Chastity, hands on her shoulders he pushed her into a sitting position. "The appropriate position is buttocks resting on your heels."

Seth seethed as the man placed one hand on her back, the other on her abdomen. "Back straight and pelvis tilted slightly forward. Head held erect except for the very tip of the spine, which is bowed slightly forward. Gaze slightly downcast."

Surprisingly, Chastity followed Terrance's instructions without hesitation.

"The kneel-up command requires you to raise yourself onto your knees." When Terrance placed a hand beneath her buttocks and lifted her, a growl rose in Seth's throat.

"If you are requested to lie facedown, Master Seth has only to say the word 'prone'. *Prone*," Terrance commanded. Gracefully, Chastity slithered onto her stomach.

"Supine is the command for face up, lying on your back. *Supine*." Chastity rolled over onto her back. Her movements grew slow, unsteady. The tribulations of the day had finally taken their toll on her.

For such a passionate woman, this had to be hell. If she were to become conscious of the cameras still pinned on her, not to mention the audience that their display had accumulated, she would die.

Terrance stepped forward, inching her ankles apart with his feet, then he dropped to his knees between them. "Legs out means you must spread your thighs to a forty-five degree angle."

Seth's breath caught. He glared through a red haze as Terrance's hands started at her ankles and slowly caressed up her legs, grasping her inner thighs and wedging her limbs open, exposing her to him.

Chastity released a groan somewhere between desire and agony. Eyes heavy-lidded, her back arched off the ground. Then her hips rose in invitation. Once again, she had been thrown into the heat of passion and desire.

As her body writhed, the smile on Terrance's face revealed his actions were deliberate. Whether it was to torment Chastity further, or instigate a reaction from him, Seth didn't know.

In either case, it worked.

Fury swept through Seth burning like a brushfire. Fists clenched, his heavy footsteps beat a determined path toward the pair.

"*Enough*." Seth hooked his hands beneath Chastity's shoulders and jerked her to her feet, releasing her as if it burned him to touch her. Weakened knees buckled, every bone in her body melted. He lunged forward, gathering her into his arms.

Her head lolled back. Eyes smoky with arousal met his. She whimpered.

"Are you okay?" *What a stupid question to ask. Hell no, she wasn't okay.* Chastity was caught between the worlds of pleasure and pain.

"Master." Her voice was a fragile whisper.

He drew her closer, smelling the heat of desire damp upon her body, feeling the rapid beat of her heart against his chest. "Yes, Chastity?"

Through sensual lashes she gazed up at him, her tongue making a slow enticing path across her bottom lip, and then she purred, "Fuck me...please."

Seth felt his eyes widen in surprise. Those weren't exactly the three little words he had waited two years to hear. However, he couldn't say that her plea didn't please him. But not like this. Not with the use of artificial means. He wanted her ravishingly horny, wanton beyond all control for him. Yet, there was an important element missing—emotion. There would be no joy in taking her this way. Well, almost no joy.

"No, Chastity. Not now, not here." He heard an exasperated breath squeeze from her lips. She grasped his cock in a gentle hold. Magical fingers slid lightly over his sac. A tight breath caught in his throat. He had to hold tight to his convictions, else he'd be tearing his leather pants off in a heartbeat.

"P-p-please," she panted, before her knees collapsed and a grating, almost animalistic sound pushed from her lips.

Seth waved a free hand at the men holding the cameras, mere feet away. "Turn those damn things off."

He had to get away from her or surrender. Spread her thighs and cram his cock into her pussy. Although screwing her sounded promising, he couldn't let her take control. No pain, no gain. And she would learn to obey him.

Gently, he released her. She slithered down his body and crumpled onto the ground. Face hidden by her arms, her shoulders shook as she wept.

Seth looked at Terrance for guidance. He wasn't any good with tears, especially when he was partially to blame. *He had to stop thinking that way.* Chastity had got herself into this mess. She would be subjected to these trials whether it was him or some other unsuspecting man. She was receiving no less than what she deserved.

"Passion Flower, remove her from our sight." Terrance waved a dismissing hand through the air. "Clean her up and prepare her for orientation."

The woman hastened to Chastity's side. Seth heard her whisper, "You must get up. Please do not anger Master Terrance further." The desperation in the woman's voice prompted Chastity to push herself off the ground. She wobbled, and Passion Flower eased an arm around her waist to give support.

Her red-rimmed eyes burned into Seth. He wondered if Chastity would retaliate or if she had finally accepted her fate.

Chapter Six

The day wasn't over. Evening was creeping over the golden horizon as Chastity sank deep into the warm outdoor spa on the outskirts of the garden. She listened to the water bubbling, teasing her skin. It felt so good. The heated water bathed her aching joints, but did nothing to soothe her aching heart or the lack of sexual fulfillment that lay just below the surface.

Twice on her way to the mineral spring she had encountered couples in the garden in various states of copulation. Her unexpected arousal had her succumbing again to the tortuous dildo. But one man and woman's intimacy had been worth the agony. Their gentle coupling had been a display of love. Their bodies moved as one, creating music as ancient as time itself.

Once in her room, she had attempted to dislodge the hateful thing only to prove Terrance right. Her touch immediately set the thing to thrusting and vibrating, resulting in feelings worse than any of the earlier episodes. Right then she had sworn that if she was ever free of the chastity bell she was going to cram it right up Terrance's ass.

She giggled, the thought giving her some degree of pleasure.

God, it had been a hellish twelve hours, and undoubtedly there was more to come.

"Slave Chastity." It was Tatiana, the petite woman who had bathed her upon arrival. She was still dressed in a white toga that highlighted her olive skin. "I've been asked to assist you. If you will rise, I'll dry and oil your body."

Water beaded down Chastity's body as she rose. A warm bath towel was placed over her shoulders and Tatiana gently rubbed the moisture away. Then she secured the towel around Chastity.

The woman linked her arm through Chastity's and smiled. "When I'm tense and bothered I like to go to the glass atrium. Come."

They walked along the perimeter of the garden, passing by the observatory, and finally came to a glass structure hidden among a grove of trees. Long willowy branches hovered over the building as if to protect it from unforeseen attack, presenting an air of security, safety.

Chastity entered and breathed in its beauty. "I can see why you would seek out this sanctuary." It was a paradise, overflowing with greenery and exotic flowers, their fragrant scents used for aromatherapy, or so Tatiana told her.

The therapeutic effect on Chastity was amazingly effective as she inhaled. When she heard the door slide shut behind her it was like closing herself off from the world. She felt more centered, more relaxed and more herself. Although the universe seemed in harmony within this little glass house, she wasn't fool enough to believe it. She wouldn't allow this imaginary sense of equilibrium to confuse her. She wasn't an equal on this planet. She was a slave...Seth's slave. And with a snap of his fingers she could be any other man's property. The thought was chilling.

Tatiana removed Chastity's towel and then helped her upon a cushioned table, where she laid on her stomach. "It appears that you have had a trying day."

Chastity laughed. Surprised and thankful that she still could. "That's an understatement." From behind her she heard a squishing sound as Tatiana squirted oil into her palm. She was rubbing her hands together, warming the oil, when she stepped into view.

"There is more between the two of you than this game show, isn't there?" The woman began working the tight muscles in Chastity's neck and shoulders.

There was no reason to pretend she didn't know what the woman referred to. So Chastity simply responded, "Yes."

Gentle hands moved down to her tender shoulder blades working the knots out. Chastity hadn't realized just how stressful it was to climb the mountain of desire without tumbling off the other side.

"Do you want to talk about it?"

Moisture filled Chastity's eyes. "It doesn't matter." *Not anymore.*

"You know it does." The outside of Tatiana's hands began a steady chopping motion down Chastity's back. "How did you meet?"

It seemed like so many years ago. "I had just found out about my mother's death. I was told that she died in a solar accident. Her body lost in space. A couple of friends suggested I go to a party, try to forget for a night. I didn't want to go, but they insisted."

"He was there?"

Chastity almost moaned aloud as the woman massaged the soreness from her buttocks.

"No, not at first. The party was hosted by his cousin, Josh Allen." She sighed, remembering how Josh had fawned all over her. "Then Seth walked into the room. I don't know if it was love at first sight, but it certainly was lust at first sight. One thing led to another, and we found ourselves in bed, in love, and walking down the aisle in less than three months." Emotion hung tight in her throat. Memories assaulted her like the rapid fire of an Atmospheric gun.

Reliving what happened so many years ago was harder than Chastity realized. She opened her mouth, at first with no sound, and then strangled words emerged, "I-I didn't know it, but Josh was running a security check on me." She picked at one of the static wrist bands.

"Josh was Seth's manager. He ran checks on all of Seth's associates. The day of the wedding I received an urgent call from

Josh, fifteen minutes before I was to walk down the aisle. He asked me to stop the wedding. When I asked him why, he refused to say over the trans-communicator. He said it was important. He begged me to wait."

Tatiana's fingers pressed deeply into Chastity's thighs. One of the woman's fingers struck a spot that had Chastity flinching. "I'm so sorry." Tatiana smoothed her palm over the offended area.

"I guess I'm too out of shape to be kneeling on a full-time basis."

Tatiana laughed. "It does take time getting used to. So, what happened?"

"I didn't stop the wedding, but Josh did. He arrived just as we were exchanging vows. He asked to speak to me alone. He said that he had found my mother. She was alive." The memory brought a tear to her eye. "She'd been arrested for murder and wanted me to believe her dead."

A gasp of disbelief left Tatiana's lips.

Chastity heard the desperation in her own voice as she continued, "Josh begged me not to marry Seth. He said the negative publicity of a murderer in the family would tarnish the Allen name. Seth is a proud man. My mother was alive—locked up. She needed me. I was so confused."

Tatiana's hands stilled. "So you walked out on him without even an explanation?"

Chastity nodded, silent tears rolling down her cheeks. "In time, Seth would have come to hate me."

"But you never even gave him a choice."

Chastity's response was a single headshake.

Again, gentle hands began to massage. "No wonder the man is livid."

"It's even worse. Seth believes that Josh betrayed him, that I left him for his cousin."

"Turn over," Tatiana said, and Chastity rolled on to her back. "Where is your mother now?"

"Incarcerated on the moon."

A hand covered Tatiana's mouth in surprise. Moisture softened her eyes. "No."

Rising on her elbows, Chastity explained, "I've been working these last two years to gather the money for her release. If I win the one hundred million dollars this contest promises I'll be able to free her. Josh has been helping me keep in touch with the authorities. When I asked you earlier if you would help me use the trans-communicator, it was to call her. Josh received approval for the call." She shook her head. "I don't know what I would've done without Josh these past few years."

Tatiana placed a gentle hand on Chastity's knee. "I'll help. But we'll have to be careful. In this world it is our place to obey. There could be dire consequences if we're caught."

Excited, Chastity sprung from the table. "Now, can we do it now?"

"No, it's time you dress. You will barely make Orientation, as it is."

Powdered and perfumed, Chastity was dressed in a silky white toga that scooped low in the back, riding the swells of her ass, revealing a hint of the cleft. The front of the garment dipped to her navel, secured with three golden chains across her midriff, divulging enough to entice, but not exhibit. It was short. If she inhaled, her pussy and ass would be laid bare. Comfortable sandals were laced up her calves. As for underwear, there was none.

Tatiana ushered her through a grand hallway and pushed her toward two imposing oak doors that loomed at least fourteen feet high. Beyond the woodwork she could hear laughter and voices—a party she would have gladly missed was in progress.

The doors opened automatically on their approach. "Go now. I will see what can be done about the trans-communicator." Tatiana smiled and then disappeared, leaving Chastity to face the inevitable.

And what an outrageous spectacle it was. The room and occupants looked like a scene from an exotic skin flick. Leather and lace, chains and ropes, an innocent schoolgirl, a saucy French maid and a eunuch—*yeah, right*—not to mention total nudity were only a few of the costumes. It was shocking…disturbing…arousing.

Clearly these people were here to live out fantasies most people only dreamed about. Free of inhibitions, they could do anything, with anybody, and not be judged.

As much as Chastity hated to admit it, she was envious. And she was feeling the itch of excitement creep across her skin as the bell began to take shape. The tingle between her thighs warned her to think of something else fast, like sucking on a century-old egg. *Yuk!*

After a deep, cleansing breath, she relaxed, believing she'd succeeded, and then Seth walked into the room. Tight leather pants that molded strong calves, powerful thighs and a package that already looked semi-aroused made her pulse jump. No shirt—she watched the play of golden muscles ripple across his broad chest. Nipples erect as if a cold breeze had brushed through the room. What she wouldn't give to lave the tantalizing buds with her tongue. Feel his hot skin beneath her palms.

Across the distance someone called his name. He pivoted, sending a wave of ebony silk over his shoulders. He had great hair. Soft and sensual when sliding across naked thighs.

In profile, he was the epitome of sexuality.

Before she could halt the direction of her thoughts, the chastity bell began to have a field day with her body. The warning tingles in her pussy began to throb unmercifully. Electricity shot through her breasts, hardening her nipples. She bent at the waist, fighting the wave of desire that swamped her.

Chastity moved quickly across the floor toward a Victorian couch. She blanked out the elegance of the polished room, the lights and the people.

Where is a vibrator when you need it? But it, too, would be useless. Fully aroused, she'd climb the ladder of ecstasy and swan dive into nothingness and then begin again.

Heat scorched across her face, and then liquid fire blazed through her veins. A moan pushed from parted lips. Her control was slipping, her body's needs taking over. Briefly, she thought of retreating into her safe zone, and then decided against it. The last time Seth ripped her from her sanctuary, the result had been devastating. As she sank onto the divan she prayed this night would end quickly.

From across the room Seth observed Chastity. Something or someone had triggered the chastity bell buried deep inside her. Nervously, she attempted to sit. But when her ass touched the velveteen couch she rubbed her buttocks back and forth. Her back arched. When she realized her wanton behavior, surprise and embarrassment registered on her face as she literally flung herself from the sofa.

But it was nothing compared to the look of horror on her face when she discovered it was her own hand that caressed a breast, her other lodged between her thighs. And all in front of an audience, a group that was enjoying every minute of sensual play.

Seth couldn't resist a chuckle, watching her fight and then assuage her desire. She reminded him of a slinky cat in heat, the way her lissome body moved and stretched. Her soft mewling sounds made blood rush straight to his loins. The rosy nipple peeking out from her dress was mouthwatering.

Desire ripped through him—hot, strong, violent.

She was exquisite.

But when Chastity's expression went dreamy, and short, fast pants emerged, he knew it was time to rescue her. Rushing to her side, he caught her as her legs turned to rubber and an explicit remark squeezed from her taut lips. Sharp fingernails bit into his biceps as she held desperately to him as if he were a lifeline and she was going under for the last time.

Frustration, anger and a hint of pain lurked in her shadowed eyes. Like a magnet, her icy glare drew him in. Hypnotized, he didn't see nor hear another man's approach.

"Master Seth."

One arm circling Chastity's waist, Seth accepted the outstretched hand of a brawny man planted firmly before him. A mien of power, strength and elegance enveloped the man. Gold chains, diamonds and rubies adorned his richly draped sheik costume. Four colorfully veiled women stood behind him, their posture—legs slightly parted, hands clasped behind their backs and their heads bowed—told Seth that they were this man's possessions. A harem, concubines to service his needs, his pleasures.

"Master Dawson." The flamboyant man introduced himself. "Congratulations on your slave! She is lovely, a rather delectable morsel." His hungry gaze raked over Chastity.

Seth suppressed the urge to wrap his fingers around the impertinent man's neck.

Eyes focused on Chastity, Dawson's thumb rolled a massive gold band on his ring finger back and forth—a slow, calculating action. "Will she be available at auction?"

Chastity's grip tightened on Seth's arms. He glanced down and saw the apprehension in her fallen expression, felt her body tense. Evidently she had not heard of the exchange event offered by Ecstasy Island. Nor that she would have to participate.

Seth would rather die than let this man touch Chastity, add her to his stable.

Still, he responded dryly, "It depends on her obedience."

Chastity's gazed snapped to his, her eyes kindled at his thinly veiled threat.

Dawson saw the spark of fire in Chastity's eyes and grinned, his interest heightened. "Very good, verrry good. She promises to give joy, I'm sure. I look forward to bidding on her. But for now, I must tend to my own slaves. Until later."

A six-foot whip uncoiled from beneath the man's robes. It crackled through the air, sending all four women falling to his feet, buns in the air, chins resting on their hands. After winding up the black snake, he secured it to his sash. Cruel fingers threaded through two of the women's hair as he jerked them up, their feet scrabbling to find purchase. Dual cries arose. Pain etched across their faces. Releasing them, they fell hard, only to scramble back into formation.

"To the sedan," Dawson ordered. The women began to rise, when he added, "And crawl." His foot thrust out, landing hard against the ass of the woman dressed in different shades of yellow. Robbed of her footing, she fell, a throaty grunt leaving her breathless. Down upon their hands and knees, the remaining women joined her. The haste and the fear in their eyes said it all.

Seth flashed the man an expression of disapproval. Dawson's reply was to haughtily sweep a lecherous eye over Chastity. His deep laugh echoed through the room. He meant to have her.

Seething, Seth took a step toward the man. In a heartbeat Terrance and Shawn were at his side. "Don't do it," warned Terrance. "Orientation is about to begin. Take your slave in hand and have a seat."

Shawn stepped forward. "Dawson's behavior will not be condoned. I will speak with him."

Fists flexing and retracting, Seth grasped Chastity by the chin. "You are never to go near him."

Relief filtered across her face. She nodded in quick, short movements.

As far away from Dawson as possible, but within his line of sight, Seth sat in a wingback chair close to the stage. With a wave of his hand he motioned Chastity to settle at his feet.

Terrance and Shawn joined Tor on the dais. In unison they bowed low to the audience. Tor broke from the pack and stepped forward. "Masters, you are welcomed to Ecstasy Island, the pleasure palace of Zygoman. Tonight we will share with you some of the features available to you."

At a flick of his wrist, Passion Flower appeared at his side. Gently he raised her wrists for display. "Your slave is accessorized with static ankle and wristbands. These bands allow you to position your slave's body any way you desire. All you do is activate the force field and let the play begin."

Tor gave Passion Flower the command to strip. She shimmed out of her little skirt, revealing her shaved pussy. Pride flickered in his stern eyes. She was truly a beautiful woman. Still, Seth wondered how he could expose her to so many gawking eyes.

"*Prone*," Tor commanded. The woman sunk to her knees and gracefully slid facedown onto the floor.

"*Spread-eagle*." Her legs parted and her arms went above her head, assuming the position. Seth's cock rose to the occasion. He had a clear shot straight at the woman's swollen folds. Out of the corner of his eye he could see Chastity's cheeks flush red, a blush that was very becoming.

Tor held a small remote control in his hands. He pushed a button and the air shimmered around Passion Flower. "The force field will hold your slave in the position you desire. You can restrain singularly, or in total, her hands, her feet or any part of her body."

Another button raised the woman from the floor. Not a muscle moved, only a waterfall of ebony hair fell around her face. She stopped at Tor's waist-height. Then he pushed another button and Passion Flower was rotated so that she was gazing up at the ceiling.

"You can adjust the slave to any position or angle. No chains to interfere with your access." Beneath her, he ran his hand from her neck down her back, buttocks, and finally her legs. Then he stepped between her thighs.

"As you can see—" his finger delved in between her spread pussy, while his other hand fondled a breast, "—complete access."

Several other features were demonstrated while Passion Flower was in the spread-eagle stance, and then he moved on.

"One of my favorites…" Beneath lowered lashes Passion Flower smiled at Tor. Without need of instruction, she sat on the floor, spread her bent knees apart and crossed her feet at the ankles. Then she raised her hands above her head, crossing them at her wrists. Again the air shimmered.

Tor pressed a button and Passion Flower was raised to the height of his shoulders. "This position allows access to her genitals, great for cunnilingus." He stooped, then came up between her thighs. With his tongue he tasted her. "Ummm, beautiful."

Pushing another button, the woman moved down Tor's body until her pussy was the correct height for him to enter her with his cock. "Or, as you can see, great for missionary-style sex."

Another button was pressed and Passion Flower was again sitting on the floor. Tor stepped out from between her legs. "For those that wish to use the manual version of ropes and chains, I will need a volunteer to display the technique."

When Tor's gaze landed on Chastity, she died a little inside. Any movement sent that damn thing inside her vibrating like the finely plucked strings of a guitar. In fact, the dildo felt like the whole damn orchestra had just reached its crescendo. She had spent the biggest part of the evening with her eyes closed, humming loudly in her head to block out anything that might arouse her.

Then she relaxed, letting her air of confidence show with a half-smile toward the infuriating man. Seth wasn't an exhibitionist. And he knew that the outfit he had chosen for her had no undergarments.

"Master Seth, would you and your slave accommodate me?"

"It would be our pleasure," Seth responded, rising.

Figuratively speaking, Chastity swallowed her tongue. Speechless, she could only stare at Seth in disbelief. He had put one of his "for the audience" smiles on his face. His proffered hand hung in the air briefly as Chastity shivered, wary of the so-called punishment if she didn't cooperate. Slowly, her hand slipped into his.

God, she wanted to wipe the smirk off of Seth and Tor's faces with a big metal bat against the side of their heads.

Why was it that men got such a kick out of the humiliation of a woman?

Then it came to her. True submission was not about the body. Mind control was what a Dom, wanted — no *needed* and desired — because the mind was the hardest thing to submit. Mind games…

In this mental game of Domination and submission Chastity took center stage. Directed to sit on the dais, her feet dangling over the side, she wondered how — or if — she would make it through the week. Every eye was focused on her, a fact that made her self-conscious and uneasy. Seth took his position on the floor next to her. His large, imposing presence hovering over her made her feel insignificant in comparison.

Amazing how every word, every action, was planned to move each pawn into their slotted role. And, like the fool she was, Chastity felt herself slipping into character.

Tor's deep voice felt like acid burning her ears. "Master Seth, command your slave to raise her arms above her head." Without thinking, Chastity raised her hands, crossing them at the wrist like she had seen Passion Flower do only moments ago.

Her inability to await Seth's order received a frown of disapproval.

Leaning into her, he whispered, "Don't push me, Chastity. It's your choice whether you want to be punished in front of an audience."

Well, shit! She was damned if she did, damned if she didn't. And she was tired, physically and mentally. She just wanted him to get on and be done with it.

Terrance handed Seth a satiny rope which he used to bind her wrists. Her binding wasn't tight, or meant to cause pain. They were more for effect than anything.

"Master Seth will now have his slave bend her knees out flat, ankles crossed."

This time she awaited Seth's command, knowing full well that her spread legs would display her nether lips for all to see.

From the crowd she heard Dawson growl his appreciation. Heat flooded up Chastity's neck, growing across her cheeks.

Seth's body went ramrod straight. Fury turned his face to stone. Quickly he stepped in front of her, blocking the audience's view. She felt a moment of relief, until several disgruntled comments were expressed. Still, Seth stood firmly in front of her as he bound her ankles.

Their eyes met, held.

"Master Seth, please assist your slave to lie upon her back." Gently Seth guided her down, never once breaking the spell between them. "Now slip between her thighs. Your body weight pinning her down and holding her legs apart."

Spread wide, her pussy more than wet, her folds swollen, her clit throbbed to the tune of the chastity bell's hum. Chastity had never been in such a state of embarrassment and arousal and confusion all at once. Another gush of wetness seeped between her naked thighs. She squirmed against her bindings, her body aching so badly that she wanted to scream.

Damn, but she needed to climax.

Seth's nostrils flared with either anger or excitement — she didn't know, didn't care which. All she knew was that she had to feel him inside her.

As his head dipped, silky hair slid across her inner thighs bringing her back off the floor, white-hot desire flashing through her body. When his face was aligned with her sex, her hips rose in shameless offering. She was beyond the point of caring. In her mind's eye she could feel his stiff, prickly facial hair caressing her folds, his tongue driving deep inside and the exquisite suction of his mouth as he fed. Another wave of moisture flowed from her core.

Through sensual lashes, dark eyes burned into hers. He paused, inhaled deeply.

Chastity prayed the heady scent of her desire was enough to push him over the edge. Encourage him to take her, *now*.

All the while, Tor's deep voice continued, "As you can see, this can be a psychologically powerful position. It is nearly impossible for her to stand or bring her knees together."

Broad shoulders pressed against her thighs. She felt Seth tremble, felt the growl that surfaced from deep in his throat quake through her flesh.

He was weakening.

But just when she thought he would surrender, taste her, he moved further up her body. A hand placed on each side of her head suspended him above her. It was futile to attempt to separate their bodies when his engorged cock pressed tightly against her pussy. And there was nothing he could do about it.

This time Chastity refused to be denied. Wrists bound, her arms slipped over his head, drawing him closer, as her hips ground against his. Then she began a slow seductive rhythm, anointing him with her heat.

Elbows locked, he wrenched back against her attack, but she trapped him with her legs, drew him nearer with her arms. Like a cat enjoying a bowl of cream, she licked a path up his neck to the soft spot behind his ear. Gently she suckled his lobe, and then playfully nipped. Hissing lightly, she blew a warm stream of air into his canal, her tongue following it to caress.

The chastity bell vibrated, plunged, sending tremors in all directions. She squirmed helplessly against Seth.

Then his resistance faltered. Weak elbows gave as his body crushed hers, chest to chest, flesh to flesh. He joined her rhythm as they rocked together.

The dildo was driving her crazy. But her need for Seth was more, much more. She needed to feel his cock, hard and deep inside her, the heat of his mouth suckling her breasts, his hands caressing, their souls touching.

A calloused hand stroked the back of her thigh, moving up to cup her ass.

"Yes," she purred. *This* was what she had dreamt about for two years.

When his fingers entered her pussy, Chastity thought she'd died and gone to heaven. Like a bow, she arched into him, her mouth parting on a soft sigh.

And then his fingers stilled, withdrew.

Once again, disappointment crashed down upon her. Every muscle taut, nerves stretched to their limits, Chastity hated Seth Allen at that moment, at least until she saw the chastity bell in his hand. In one quick movement, he flung the menacing thing across the floor. Chastity's heart soared as the bell landed with a sharp clang and then rolled.

"Orientation is over." The finality in his voice was a warning to anyone thinking to stop him.

The room held a collective breath as he extracted himself from between her legs, untied her wrists and ankles, righting her toga before he assisted her to her feet. When his fingers touched the small of her back, guiding her from the room, she shivered at the responsive ache between her thighs.

He was hot and ready to take her.

Tonight she would experience paradise once again.

Chapter Seven

Dual full moons hung in the inky sky as Seth and Chastity silently walked toward their bungalow. The only sounds were that of the night, the light rush of water from the nearby waterfall, the cooing of a dove settling high in the trees for the evening, and the high-pitched serenade of crickets in the distance.

Neither spoke. Each vividly aware of the other's aroused state, their heavy breathing, the beat of their hearts.

Seth had exposed his hand, revealed his desire for her. A mistake he needed to remedy.

Hand still resting at the hollow of her back, he marveled at the warmth and smoothness of her skin, how right she felt beside him. Slowly, he dipped his middle finger down the cleft of her ass.

Her breath caught on an inhalation. Through heavy lashes she covertly glanced at him.

Without warning, he whirled her around to face him. With one hand he ground her hips to his, with the other he cruelly grabbed a handful of her hair and jerked her head backwards.

Lips parted, she stared wide-eyed at him. He could feel her heart pounding against his chest.

"You're mine," he grated through clenched teeth.

Short, quick nods of agreement were her response.

The warmth of her breath on his face heated his blood. "I can take you any time, any place."

Again, she acknowledged him with a series of rapid nods.

He would prove his point here, now. "Kneel," he ordered.

Without hesitation she drifted to her knees. Uncertainty glistened in the blue eyes staring up at him.

"Release me." He didn't need to say more. She reached for the waistband of his pants and peeled them away. His cock—engorged, erect—sprang into her hands.

"Touch me."

Soft, gentle hands cupped his sac, kneading, caressing. When her fingers curled around his member and stroked, he hissed a breath through clenched teeth. It felt good, damn good.

Still he needed more… Wanted more.

Fingers biting into her wrist, he eased out of her grasp. Confusion clouded her eyes until his hips thrust and his cock parted her lips, meeting teeth. He nudged forward. "Take me," he growled. "All of me."

She hesitated.

He tightened his grip on her hair and drove again between her lips. This time she opened to him.

Warm, wet heaven closed around him. Her movements were awkward at first. Seth half expected her to refuse. Then she took him deep, sucking and bobbing. Slender fingers magically danced across the underside of his balls before she cradled them in her palm and gently caressed. Gazing down, he watched his dick slide in and out of her luscious mouth.

Chastity was his tonight, and the next night, and the next…

Wild blue eyes focused on him as he fucked her mouth. Guttural sounds rolled out of her throat as he thrust between her lips. Her body trembled.

This is what he had imagined. Chastity on her knees before him, at his mercy. Lips wrapped around him, sucking, surrendering. It was a dream come true.

God, but he wanted to taste her passion, delve between her thighs until she cried his name. Just the thought made his body spin out of control.

His climax hit with a vengeance. It ripped through him like a runaway transport, tearing everything in its path to pieces. He arched his back, his mouth opened, and a roar of triumph lifted to the sky as he released his seed.

Holding her tightly against his hips, he growled, "Swallow." The concave of her cheeks, her throat pulsating as she milked him, made him harden further. He eased from between her swollen lips. She licked them as though savoring his taste. Her breathing was labored, her need apparent as she reached for him.

He stepped away. "What is it you want?" He toyed with her, needing to hear her ask.

Heavy-lidded, she gazed up at him through feathered lashes. "To make love." Her response was a mere whisper.

"Love?" His laugh was scratchy with sarcasm as he tucked in his cock and fastened his pants. "You mean fuck, don't you, Chastity?"

She flinched, eyes narrowing. Slowly she stood, her shoulders squaring. "Forgive me, Master," she said with a degree of dryness that bordered on the acerbic. "If you don't mind, I'll just retire for the evening." She spun on her toes.

His hand shot out, staying her. "Oh, but I do mind."

He wasn't through with her quite yet. The night was young and he had two long years to make up for. "And I believe you have earned a punishment," he added.

"What? Why?"

"Forgetfulness. You will retire when I wish you to. Trust me, Chastity. If you learn to trust and obey me without question, then you will want for nothing."

Jaws clenched, she replied, "Yes, Master." Her tone clearly communicated her unspoken rage. Her anger was so palpable it filled the air like a cloud of dense smoke.

Aaah, but the night looked promising.

As they entered their bungalow, Seth left Chastity standing at the door. He smothered a chuckle as she nervously scanned her surroundings.

One corner of the room was a den of iniquity. It was a playground for sensual exploration. Tools of the trade—whips, paddles, floggers, chains and a variety of other erotic toys—hung from the wall, as well as shackles and a swing with stirrups.

In the other corner a flagstone fireplace burned low, a polished wooden floor held a sunken tub brimming with bubbles, and a majestic bed waited silently for his pleasure.

Remembering Tor's instructions, Seth picked up a black sleep mask from a nearby table and approached. Cautiously, she backed away. A single raised brow stopped her in place.

He knew Chastity hated the dark. Still, she didn't falter as he slipped the blindfold over her head, drawing it down so that no light filtered through. She would have to rely on her other senses to experience the evening's entertainment.

"We're going to have a little fun." His promise held a slight tinge of menace even to his ears. She shivered beneath his palms resting on her shoulders. Loss of sight would add to her vulnerability and increases the degree of surrender involved, Tor had said.

And Seth wanted her total surrender tonight.

Standing where he left her, she cocked her head, listening as he moved around the room. She spun, shifted nervously, and then swayed as if she might lose her balance and fall.

Approaching undetected, she startled when his hand caressed her breastbone. With a quick snap he plucked the first chain of her toga loose. "Let's make you a little more comfortable." The second dislodged and finally the third. With a flick of his hand the silky garment fell to the floor, pooling around her ankles. Seth's eyes followed the path of the material, breathing in her lovely skin.

He gloried in her full breasts, their rosy peaks enticing him to taste. His head dipped, taking a nipple and the dark areola surrounding it in one mouthful. With his hands, he cupped her, kneading and stroking their fullness.

She was gorgeous. And she was his.

A soft moan broke his concentration. "Chastity, during our play you are not allowed to come until I say. Do you understand?"

"Yes," she muttered.

"Yes?"

"Yes, Master," she corrected.

"Undress me," he commanded, stepping away.

Palms out, she blindly felt toward the sound of his voice.

"Here," he said, moving as he spoke. As she followed, he watched the sway of her rounded hips, the curve of her small waist, her breasts rising with each breath. "Here," he repeated, allowing her to finally catch him.

Long, slender fingers moved across his chest stroking the hardness of his abdomen. When her fingers tucked into his waistband, he sucked in a tight stream of air. Slowly, he stepped out of his pants, allowing her full access to his body. When she touched him and stroked his erection between her hands, he shuddered and breathed an oath against her cheek as the pleasure grew too much to hold silent.

Gently, he eased from her grasp. Taking her by the hand, he led her through the room, her free hand moving side to side, attempting to gauge her surroundings. When she heard the creak of the bed, he saw her smile.

"Now for your punishment." Her grin disappeared as her body stiffened beneath his hold.

He sat on the downy comforter, and then drew her rigid body across his lap so that his cock was wedged between her thighs. Her pussy was warm, wet, inviting, as the head of his dick nudged her swollen folds.

Silence beat down upon them as he dragged out the anticipation. Beneath his circling palm her ass was tight and tense, waiting.

Oh, yeah, he had every intention of spanking her, but not now. A finger delved inside to feel her heat. He had to chuckle. She tried so hard to be unaffected by his touch, but always her body deceived her—even now a gush of hot liquid welcomed him.

When he pinched her clit she groaned, her hips rising to meet his thrust. After that her body seemed to relax, settling into a slow rhythm.

He'd never known a woman so responsive to his touch. Nothing had changed between them physically. They were prisoners to each other's needs and desires.

The thought sent a wave of anger coursing through Seth's veins. His hand lashed out and landed hard against her ass.

She yelped, struggling to rise.

"Be still," he ground out between taut lips. Then he struck the other cheek, watching the tender skin brighten and flush with his handprint.

Once again, Chastity grew rigid beneath Seth's touch. He began her seduction anew, moving his finger in and out of her pussy until she drenched him with her arousal. This time, when his digit was slick with her juices he slipped it into her anus and began to finger-fuck her ass.

Chastity flinched at the unexpected intrusion. Fire lanced up her. She whimpered, squirming to be released. Never before had he done this to her.

With one hand he held her down, while the other slid in and out—slowly at first, then increasing the pace. There was a wickedness to his actions, going where no man had gone before.

Not to mention the sensation of being filled in that sensitive area was new...and exciting. Blindfolded, there was nothing to do but feel. Her anal muscles tightened around him. Her sex itched to be scratched. Pressure built in her abdomen, so intense that her breathing hitched, coming in small pants. She strained, arching and holding back the inevitable, waiting for something more.

Her body drew inwardly upon itself and then stretched tight, becoming something foreign to her, seeking things that she had never before sought—adventure, variety…and yes, even pain.

Chastity raised her ass, needing more, wanting something larger, thicker in her ass, in her pussy, both at the same time. Like a firestorm, heat spiraled through her veins. She was moments away from climaxing, but she held out.

He withdrew his finger. She tensed. When his palm landed hard against her ass, she threw back her head and a scream of ecstasy tore from her throat, her body shattering.

Deep-seated tremors went on and on, stripping her soul naked as she writhed, squirming against his cock. Hot, wet tears dampened the sleep mask. Her heart beat so wildly against her chest, she half expected to die of a heart attack. Yet, it wasn't to be.

When the last of her tremors subsided, Chastity finally released a breath of relief.

"You have earned another punishment." Seth's disapproving voice echoed in the room. Once again she had fucked up. A sigh of despair shook her. "Do you know why?"

Her chin trembled, a show of weakness that pissed her off. "I came without your permission."

He nudged her off his lap. She lost her balance, landing on the floor with a thud. A burning ache throbbed through her hip. She lay quietly, wondering how he would punish her, fear and excitement warring in her.

"Stand," he ordered, his voice deep, rough against her ears.

Stumbling, she rose to her feet, grasping at the air, struggling to orient herself in her darkened world.

"Spread your legs and raise your arms." Chastity gave up seeking her bearings and surrendered to his request. She wedged her thighs apart as she lifted her arms above her head.

He must have activated the controller, as her static bands locked in place.

Nervously, she wet her lips, swallowing hard. Her head made sharp movements following the path of sounds he made throughout the room.

When Chastity sensed Seth's approach, she tensed, wrenching back as he brushed something cool across her breasts. Her sensitive nipples beaded into tight buds, a layer of goose bumps rising on her skin.

She shivered as Seth dragged the cool object across her shoulder, down her back, then through her legs. When he struck her thigh with the *thing* she strained against her bonds. The mask never allowed a hint as to where or when the next sting would fall, which only served to raise her frustration and anticipation. Even before the thought left her mind, she felt the whip bite into her leg. A whimper slipped from her lips.

This was wrong, so wrong. The man she loved, dreamed of sharing her life with, was flogging her. And what was worse…she liked it. Never had she known that pain and vulnerability could be so erotic, so exciting.

Sometime during the chaos, her inner struggle had manifested into central elements of exotic pleasure.

Was that sick, or what?

Was she so different from other women? Did every confident woman want a man who was stronger, one that could control, dominate her? No decisions to be made, no distractions, no responsibilities. Erotic control and sensual surrender, a world filled with mystery and illusion, of fantasy and delight.

After all, it was the fight that was the spice of life and kept a relationship riveting, exciting.

Chastity inwardly smiled. This was Zygoman, a pleasure planet that was advertised to make all fantasies come true.

It was clear that Seth wasn't focused on her pleasure. In fact, the opposite was true.

But if she could push past their history, Seth's mastery would allow her to explore the darker side of her sexuality. Heart pounding, endorphins pumping, her pussy tingled and her breasts grew heavy. Slowly but surely, she felt the walls of her resistance being torn down, replaced with a feeling of power, of freedom.

Under the illusion of force she could permit herself to be subjugated as Seth's slave. Take whatever he had to offer before their time came to an end. Afterwards, well, she'd deal with it then.

Roughly, he pinched her chin, drawing her head up to his gaze. "Now, I'm going to fuck you." His hand slid down her throat, fingers closing around her neck. His pulse beat rapidly in his fingertips. The firmness of his grip was both frightening and exciting.

Yes, *yes*. Finally, she would have his cock driving into her pussy, feel his mouth suckling her nipples, his hands caressing. She hid her excitement behind a mask of indifference, not allowing any emotions to show in her body and what little expression showed beneath her blindfold.

The pressure in his fingers tightened disapprovingly.

Good! She wanted him angry, forceful. This was a game two could play.

Chastity jerked her chin from his fingers, receiving a growl of displeasure from him. She heard the flogger hit the floor and slide. Then the sounds of Seth fumbling with something, his curse of frustration followed.

"Damn this thing! Which button is it?"

When he finally succeeded in locating the button to release her wrists and ankles, his hand clutched her arm, dragging her toward the bed, she hoped.

Struggling, she put up a display of opposition even her acting coach from high school would have been proud of.

Without warning, she was heaved off her feet and thrown into the mass of down. A high-pitched squeal squeezed from her taut lips. Before she could scramble off the bed, she sunk deeper into the covers as he landed on top of her. She fought, resisted and inwardly glowed with anticipation.

With one hand he grasped her wrists, pinning them high above her head. A warm gush of air told her that his mouth was mere inches away from her nipple. The peak tingled, aching to feel him.

Seth's other hand delved between her legs, none too gently. She twisted, turned, laboring to escape, only to have his caresses grow bolder, harsher.

Chastity was so friggin' hot she thought she'd explode when he jammed three fingers deep inside her. Hissing in a breath, she attempted to buck him off, forcing him to use the strength of one knee to pry open her thighs. He was rock-hard as his cock parted her swollen folds. He teased her unmercifully, rubbing his erection against her clit, nudging her entrance with the tip of his swollen head.

He played.

She suffered. And just when she thought she'd die, he entered her with one powerful thrust that had her head banging into the headboard.

Pain, ecstasy — what a turn-on.

Every bone in her body melted. She stopped her struggle to bask in the length, the firmness of the man invading her body. It was total perfection. Two bodies uniting as one.

Being blindfolded brought a whole new dimension to sex. There was nothing to do but feel, smell and taste the nuances of hot sweaty bodies sliding against one another. She didn't need to have his cock in her mouth to taste the saltiness of his pre-come. She didn't need to be between his thighs to smell the sweet aroma of their juices blending. And she didn't need to see to know that Seth felt she was under his power.

Like everything in the universe, power was illusive. Seth thought to dominate, but she was the one that had won.

In the struggle her blindfold dislodged. The intense look of hunger in his eyes sent a gush of liquid seeping down her leg.

Seth released her arms. His attention was pinned on her rising and falling chest. Tender hands cupped her breasts, weighed them, kneading softly.

She leaned into his caress, relishing the feel of his calloused hands upon her skin.

When his touch became too gentle, she rose, her teeth piercing his neck as her fingernails clawed a path down his back.

He closed his eyes and arched his back, a guttural sound emerging as he drove harder into her pussy.

It was heaven, the sound of flesh pounding against flesh, the scent of raw sex filling the air. She screamed at the exquisite pain when his mouth covered a nipple, biting hard and then suckling. Fingers lacing through his hair, she jerked his head back, scraping his teeth across her tender bud.

Seth muttered a curse, his mouth coming down hard on the other breast, lavishing it with the same heated attention. A storm was building inside him and Chastity wanted to drown in his downpour.

Strong biceps flexed as he looped his arms beneath her legs, cradling her knees in the crook of his elbows, spreading her wider for his assault. The muscles of her thighs protested against the blissful torture of being pulled in different directions.

A gravelly sound emerged from deep within his throat as he pushed to his knees and gazed down at their bodies coming together. A fierce expression distorted his features as he watched his cock sliding in and out of her wet pussy.

The intensity in his dark eyes nearly plunged Chastity over the edge.

Breathlessly, she asked, "May I come now, Master?"

"*No!*" he hissed, driving harder, deeper.

Damn if it didn't feel like he was beating a path through her entire body. "Please," she begged, as tremors filtered through her like tentacles seeking something to grasp onto and devour.

Then, just when she thought all was lost, he cried out, "Jesus Christ! Chastity, come with me, *now*."

It was as if someone had lit a series of fireworks off inside her. Sparks and fire rained through her body until she lay, a trembling mass in Seth's arms.

Seth, too, was dealing with the aftermath. The last pulse of his cock echoed inside her. His hips slowed, and then stopped, his body heavy upon hers. For a brief moment she thought he had fallen asleep. Then she heard a sigh of contentment and he rolled over, taking her with him, holding her after lovemaking just like he had so many years ago.

Chastity snuggled closer into his embrace. He brushed a kiss on her head, hugged her and murmured something inaudible.

Then he froze.

His body tensed. An invisible wall slipped between them. She smoothed a hand across his back and down his ass, trying to entice him to relax, to forget what had forced them apart.

As if her touch burned, he released her and plunged from the bed. Silent accusation etched his stern face, and he glared at her as if she had just committed the foulest of sins.

Seth would lay a bet that the confusion on Chastity's face matched his own.

"Seth?" Cautiously, she pushed back the covers and began to rise.

Seth took a hasty step backwards.

Had he really whispered, "I love you"? Had she heard his declaration of love?

A trembling hand brushed through his hair. Everything was getting too complex, too messy for his liking. He tried to convince himself that it was just a reaction, something a man said to a woman during sex. But try as he might, his brain just wasn't falling for it.

Once again, she had bewitched him. Worked her wiles on him and — for a brief moment — made him forget.

Man, he couldn't believe it. The great Seth Allen had just fucked the enemy and reveled in the act. Then lay in heavenly bliss with her afterwards. The damnedest thing was that, given half the chance, he'd do it again and again.

"Get up." He barked the command before realizing that she was already standing. He needed to pull himself together and get things back on course. "You will be punished for removing the blindfold."

Her blue eyes widened as her jaw dropped. "You're kidding, right?" Then her body seemed to relax. She smiled and began to move toward him.

His outstretched hand stopped her cold.

Confusion seeped back onto her face. "What have I done?"

He motioned to the black mask lying among the tangled sheets.

Her gaze followed the path of his finger. Slowly she turned toward him. Fists planted on her hips, she glared, and then she leaned slightly forward.

"You fucked me hard enough to blow the roof off this building." Her hand angrily swung a path from her side to the ceiling. "Not to mention causing a sleep mask to move. And you want to punish *me*?" She waved her hand dismissively and turned her back on him.

A defiant action he couldn't allow.

"You're fucking nuts," she grumbled, looking over her shoulder.

Outraged, he lunged for her. She dodged, barely evading him as he stumbled and rolled on the floor. With a growl, his hand swept out and caught her by the ankle. She fell, grunting on impact. Stunned, she lay motionless as he crawled to her side. Her eyes were closed.

Had he hurt her?

"Chastity?" Seth brushed the brunette curls from her face, only to catch the bend of her knee in his balls as her eyes popped open.

"*Aagghh!*" Pain lashed through his groin as he folded at the waist. Breathlessly, he held onto her. With all the fortitude left in him, he raised up, pulling her beneath him and pinning her with his weight as he collapsed.

"Stop struggling, Chastity." Every move sent pain coursing through his genitals. She would pay dearly when he could function again.

"Fuck you," she retorted sharply.

He would accommodate that request before the night was over. But for the moment he needed to lie quietly and gain back his strength.

Then he'd wring her pretty neck.

For the next few minutes she lay quietly beneath him. All the while, he was forced to endure the rage burning in her fiery eyes glaring up at him.

"Let me up," she ordered.

With his potency revived, he carefully moved from atop her. In a blink of an eye she tried to crawl away from him, but he held her firmly by the arm. Then he shook her hard enough to hear her teeth rattle.

"I'll give you this warning once and only once." His words were slowly drawn out. He rose and loomed over her before jerking her to her feet. A grunt pushed through her pinched lips. Cruelly, his fingers bit into her arms as he pressed her to his chest.

"If you ever do that again…you'll not live to regret it." With a quick shove he released her. "Now put your hands behind your back."

Seth didn't know if it was what he said or how he said it, but Chastity complied without comment. Using the static controller he locked her wrists and ankles together.

Hands fused together, she was helpless. The snap of her feet dragging together made her body sway like a tree caught in the wind. He pivoted, prepared to walk away, when he heard a thump, a sharp intake of air and then a very agitated growl that made him glance over his shoulder. Chastity lay sprawled upon the floor.

"You son of a bitch!" Snakelike, she squirmed around until she could see him through a web of mussed curls. Her agile body arched and she tossed her head, slinging the mass of hair over a shoulder and out of her eyes.

"You fucking son of a bitch!" She sucked in a long breath, gaining strength. "You cruel, ruthless, fucking son of a bitch! Let me go, *now!*" Her voice dropped an octave as her temper soared.

There was nothing like a hot woman, not to mention a knee to the gonads, to get a man back on track. He wasn't here to make *love* to Chastity Ambrose. He was here for revenge.

"*Silence!*"

Seth was mad. His anger smoldered around him like heat vapors off pavement.

What had happen? What had changed the beauty of what they shared only moments ago?

He stomped over to the bed, whisked the sleep mask into his hands, and headed toward her.

Chastity cringed, worming her way into a sitting position in the corner. At least the walls gave her the illusion of support. She didn't like the dark, or the unexpected. But this whole arrangement was a blind dive into the unknown. Surprises hid around every corner.

When Seth stood before her, it took everything she had to remain still as he slipped the blindfold over her eyes, plunging her back into darkness. Motionless, she waited for him to say something, anything. He didn't speak nor did he walk away. Through the blackness she sensed his glare burning into her.

Relief filtered through her when she finally heard him turn, his angry footsteps sounding as he put distance between them.

Seconds seemed like minute, minutes hours, as she listened to him move about. Every quiet moment made her that much more uneasy with her situation. She had never imagined how vulnerable it was to be left without vision.

Water splashed. Her head turned in the direction of the tub, or at least the direction she believed it to be. He was enjoying a bubble bath while she lay crumpled in a corner. The smell of sex hung on her skin, her thighs were sticky, her body ached, and she felt like crying.

Nothing made sense. Not Seth's reaction and most definitely not how her body still hungered for his touch.

Heavy feet padded across the room, coming closer and closer. She tensed, sensing that he stood near.

"Rise."

Great. It appeared their conversations were now to consist of single words. But so as not to further agitate him, she placed her back against the wall, drew her feet beneath her and used the wall to awkwardly inch herself up into a standing position.

When fingers folded around her biceps she flinched, an action that resulted in increased pressure. As he began to pull her forward she noticed that he had released her ankles from bondage. Her wrists were still fused tightly together in front of her.

Disoriented, she didn't know exactly where in the room she was when he stopped.

"There's a table in front of you. Raise your hands and lean forward." A hand pushed her down until her chest was resting on the cool wood, her arms lying above her head. "Spread your legs."

Her pulse leaped. "Seth?"

"No talking." His voice lacked emotion. In the dark it felt dull, empty to her ears. With trepidation, she wedged her feet apart.

Silence reigned, except for her thudding heart and a ceiling fan that made whirling sounds as it spun air currents that teased her nether lips—exposed for Seth's eyes.

Fingertips stroked the outside of her ankles before moving around to the inside and traveling upwards, sending goose bumps across her heated skin. The gentleness of his touch made her relax. He caressed her calves, moving up her legs, brushing the inside of her thighs, kneading her buttocks.

Her pussy wept for him. She felt her inner muscles contract and tighten, readying to receive him, take him deep.

With every inch of skin he grazed, Chastity's nipples tingled, her breasts grew heavy with need. Then his body covered hers, his cock wedged between her thighs. She sighed with the exquisite feel of him moving against her nether lips.

The fine hairs on his chest tickled her back. She could smell the faint scent of bubble bath and the masculine scent that was unique to Seth. As he moved, thrusting against her swollen folds, she noticed something different about his erection. It was slick, as if he had covered it in lubricant.

Without warning he stood and plunged his cock into her ass.

Chastity screamed. Her breath caught as fire lanced through her body.

He stilled. His breathing labored. His weight was heavy as he pressed their bodies together.

Breathe—in—out.

After what seemed like forever, the burning sensation dissipated, leaving an incredible fullness. But it was nothing compared to the feeling when he rose and slowly began to thrust in and out of her ass.

Her muscles pulsated around his cock.

Seth sucked in a tight breath. A hiss she knew was inhaled through clenched teeth. His fingers buried in her hips trembled. His arousal sent her into a frenzy of desire.

"You're so tight." His throaty growl was breathless.

Perched on her toes, she arched her back and leaned into him, wanting him deeper, reveling in his excitement. She was unbelievably wet between her thighs. Her breaths came in short pants as her heartbeat threatened to burst through her chest.

A hand left her hip and she felt it settle upon her clit. As he pumped he stroked her pussy. Heat radiated off his hand, setting a tidal wave building inside her. Her nipples stung as she pushed against his hips.

"Oh, baby," he groaned, his body stiffening. Just the deep resonating sound of his strained voice threw her over the edge, plunging her into space.

Something snapped inside her. Chastity felt consumed by his climax as if their souls were intertwined, something bigger than the universe itself. No words could describe the incredible feeling. It was nothing short of a cosmic orgasm.

Tremors easing, Chastity sighed, only then noticing the table she was draped across was biting into her legs. Seth's weight pressed into her ass and back increased the discomfort. But she didn't complain, content to listen to his breathing, his heartbeats radiating into her body.

He pushed from the table, their flesh parting.

She smiled, the ceiling fans cooling her heated skin.

Without a word Seth helped her from the table. Her body ached as he led her through the room and, once again, she found herself in a corner.

"Wait," he said, leaving her for a moment but returning quickly. "Sit." He assisted her down upon a fluffy pillow and then released her. His footsteps grew faint as he moved away.

Snap! Chastity felt her ankles drawn together. He had activated the static bands, a fact that bent her slightly out of shape, both figuratively and literally. She shifted, anxiously wondering when he would release her. She was tired, and the thought of a bath and a snuggle with Seth was tantalizing.

Blindness amplified the sounds in the room as Seth moved about. She heard the splash of water, the sound of him dressing, and then silence filled the empty space.

Her brows rose beneath the sleep mask. "Seth?" No answer.

"Seth, come on, this isn't funny." Still no response.

Chastity let out a scream of fury. He'd done it again. Fucked her and disappeared.

Their night together had meant nothing to him but vengeance, an exercise in carnal desire. He wanted to use her body, torment her mind.

Well, then she would just play the game according to her own rules from now on.

Chapter Eight

Chastity woke to silence and what was obviously an empty room. She sat on the floor exactly where Seth had left her. Her body ached, not to mention her heart and soul. Last night something beautiful had gone terribly wrong. They had made love and Seth had held her as if there might still be something salvageable between them.

She was a fool to have ever believed that anything had changed between them.

Chastity shifted her weight and began to fall. Her numb hands were of no help as she tumbled off the pillow and onto the cold wooden floor.

"*Aghhh.*" A burning sensation tore through her limbs.

How long would Seth punish her? She hoped he would release her soon. She didn't know how much longer she could take the darkness, the loneliness, and she had to pee so bad her eyes felt like they were swimming.

A light knock drew her head in the direction of the sound. She heard a familiar swish as the door opened.

"Chastity?"

It was Tatiana.

"Oh, my!" Anxious steps approached quickly.

As the woman neared, Chastity's bindings released, wrists and ankles parting.

The first thing she did was tear the sleep mask from her head. The sudden light burned her eyes. She shut them as moisture pricked her lids. Were they tears of sorrow or discomfort? Both, she reasoned, choking them back before they could fall.

"Chastity, are you okay?"

Chastity squinted, seeing the woman through a veil of emotion. She raised her wrists. How had Tatiana released her without the controller?

The woman understood her question without it being voiced. "Your Master must have set them on a timer. I was told to be here at exactly 9:00 a.m. to assist you with your needs." As she helped Chastity to rubbery feet, she added, "You must've made him awfully angry."

Chastity's mouth was parched, filled with cotton. "Bathroom?" she squeaked.

Tatiana pointed to a silky white partition. "Behind the screen. Do you need my help?"

Chastity responded with a shake of her head. Cautiously she tried her legs. It took a moment to gather her strength, to move on her own. At first she took baby steps, one and then another until she disappeared beyond the three-part hinged screen and through the bathroom entrance, shutting the door.

"You'll feel better after a bath." Chastity heard the woman's muffled voice through the door. "I bet you haven't eaten." There was a sharp rap on the metal barrier. "I'll see to breakfast while you bathe."

Then the outer door slid closed, leaving Chastity alone again with her thoughts.

Toiletries taken care of, she drifted back into the main room. A crashing sense of dismay hit her as she looked at the rumpled sheets. Memories bombarded her. She blinked her eyes, fighting back tears as she willed herself to forget about Seth, forget about restoring what they once had.

Chastity inhaled a ragged breath. A bath awaited.

Cautiously, she dipped a toe into the water. It was perfect, not too hot, not too cold, as if it had just been prepared. Rubbing her sore wrists, she slipped into the bubbly water that percolated like a boiling teapot. Warmth encompassed her, pulling her deeper, magically working to loosen tight muscles. She relaxed and allowed the movement of the water to cleanse her of the night's trials.

When Chastity was sure her skin was pruning she stepped from the tub. Dripping on the wood floor, she ignored the door as it slid open. "Tatiana, can you please hand me a towel?" A fluffy towel was draped over her shoulders. She snuggled into the warmth. "Thank you."

Briskly she dried herself. "What has the Master designated I wear today?" She bent at the waist, winding the towel around her wet hair, and threw her head back, rejuvenated from the bath.

A dark voice rose from the silence, "Nothing... You look lovely as you are."

Startled, Chastity spun on her heels, meeting the devouring stare of Dawson, the contemptible man from orientation. Hungry eyes devoured the sight of her naked breasts, sending a shiver up her spine. Briefly she faltered, then threw one arm across her chest, the other futilely attempted to cover her mons.

A sardonic laugh slipped from his thin lips. He took a step forward. "You mustn't hide your treasures from me. After the auction you will be mine to do with as I wish, at least for a night."

There was something about this man that made every hair on her body scream with warning. The man was dangerous, it oozed from his pores.

Frantically, she searched for something to cover her nakedness, the wrap atop her head forgotten in her turmoil. As if he read her thoughts, he moved to the stack of towels next to the sink. With slow, drawn-out strokes his large hand caressed them, teased her.

Her mouth went dry. There was nothing close to grab, not a robe or even a blanket, not without putting herself into the man's reach.

Where was Tatiana? Where was Seth?

Bottomless dark eyes gleamed with laughter, feeding off her fear. The more panicked she became, the more aroused he appeared. Chest rising and falling rapidly, his long, pointy tongue licked his lips, while his cock pushed against its restraints. He reached down to adjust himself. When her eyes inadvertently followed his hand he growled his delight, giving his erection a caress.

Somehow Chastity had to take control of the situation. A deep, calming breath filled her lungs. She squared her shoulders pulling an indifferent mask across her face. "What do you want?"

Uncertainty flashed across his face, distorted his features, and then as quickly as it appeared, it vanished.

A heavy brow rose. His sardonic smile deepened. "Mmmm." Another step drew him closer. "Your Master has not broken you."

It took all the fortitude Chastity had to remain still, to not run. She didn't want this man near her, much less touching her. But she couldn't show him fear, couldn't give him what he wanted.

Her defiance fueled him to take another step, and then another, until he stood before her. His expression hardened.

"I look forward to snuffing out your fire—" he licked his index finger then pinched it to his thumb, releasing it quickly, "—like the flame of a candle. Sssssss," he hissed.

A tremor shook her body. He began to chuckle, stopping abruptly when she hid her trembling through laughter. She tossed back her head and the wrap securing her hair released, sending wet curls tumbling down her shoulders. She caught the towel in midair, bringing it against her as she casually stepped back, putting distance between them.

"Oh my, Mr. Dawson, you have such a delightful sense of humor." The stunned look on his face gave her encouragement. "I can assure you that my participation in the auction is doubtful. You see—"

Dawson lunged.

It happened so quickly, Chastity didn't have the opportunity to defend herself. Cruel hands burned into her skin as he yanked her to his chest. Arms pinned beneath his, she struggled, but it was useless.

She was trapped.

One beefy arm secured her, while the other hand grabbed a fistful of hair, jerking her head back. Malice spewed from his eyes. "Bitch, don't think to *ever* laugh at me."

The hot breath fanning her face made her nauseated. Her stomach churned, pitched.

"I'll have you." Dawson licked a path up her cheek. "In fact, there is nothing to stop me from tasting you now." His mouth crushed hers in a cruel assault. Her jaw clenched, refusing his tongue entrance. He countered by wrapping his fingers around her throat and squeezing.

Chastity's mouth opened on a gasp. The invasion was swift as his tongue plunged deeply, choking her. She gagged at the continued pressure around her neck.

Lights dimmed. The roar in her head grew quiet as she began to slip into her safe zone, into death. If not for her mother, it wouldn't matter.

The swish of the door sliding open and heavy footsteps approaching didn't faze Chastity's journey to safety, but Tatiana's scream did.

Dawson released her. She stumbled and fell to her hands and knees, gasping. Out of the slowly clearing haze she saw the shadow of a man. Seth? No, it was the imposing Viking. Shawn.

The man pinned Dawson with a glare. His furrowed brows and penetrating green eyes spoke louder than his words. "Poaching, Master Dawson, is not acceptable. You will leave now and never return to this bungalow."

An airy laugh met Shawn's scorn. Unaffected, Dawson turned and with a swipe of his foot, pulled Chastity's hands from beneath her. With a surprised grunt she crumpled in a heap on the floor.

Shawn moved so quickly it was as if he flew across the room. This time it was Dawson who found himself in a stranglehold. Nose to nose, Shawn's whisper was almost inaudible, "Touch her again and I'll kill you." If his controlled, confident demeanor had not convinced Dawson, then the man's steely tone should have.

Chastity had no doubt that the large man meant every word.

Released, Dawson sucked in a hungry breath. Red-faced and seething, he flashed Chastity a look that said, "This isn't over," before he pivoted and stomped out the door.

The thought that Dawson would concede defeat had never entered her mind. Dawson was a man who got what he wanted. For some unknown reason he had fixed his desire on her.

Maybe desire was the wrong word. Perhaps it wasn't even her he was after. It wouldn't be the first time that a man tried to thwart Seth through her. Seth's notoriety was a magnet, provoking envy wherever he went.

Anger welled inside Chastity. It seemed that Seth was at the root of almost all her trials.

Tatiana ran to her side. Thankfully, the woman reached for the towel on the floor and draped it over Chastity before helping her to her feet.

A series of tremors assaulted her. Tears burned her eyes, at remembering how close she had come to being violated. Tatiana's supportive arms folded around her.

In a small voice, Chastity murmured, "Thank you." Then she acknowledged her rescuer, repeating the same words of appreciation. "Thank you."

A silent nod was the big man's response. Without comment, Shawn turned and disappeared before she could say more.

Chastity's laugh was scratchy. "I believe that was the first time I've ever heard the Viking speak."

Tatiana guided Chastity to a chair. "Master Shawn is a man of little words. It's amazing isn't it? Those brothers are as different as day and night."

Chastity sat, tucking her feet beneath her as her hands stroked rapidly up and down her arms, trying to warm the chills that refused to go away. "Brothers?"

Retrieving a blanket from the bed, Tatiana wrapped it around Chastity. "You didn't know? Master Tor, Terrance and Shawn are brothers. Tor is the well-spoken one and the leader, Terrance is a man of action and Shawn is the still waters."

Well, Chastity didn't know if she would've described them in such a way, but the revelation was indeed astonishing. It frustrated her that she hadn't noticed the similarities before now. She prided herself on being observant.

But how was a woman supposed to pay attention to others with a man like Seth constantly around?

As though her thoughts had conjured him forth, Seth walked into the room.

Unbelievable. It was eleven in the morning. He had given orders that she be dressed and ready when he returned from his business meeting. But here she sat draped in a blanket as if she had just risen.

The bondage demonstration they were scheduled to attend started at eleven-thirty. Because of her disobedience they would be late. Frustrated, he tugged at his tie, and the scrap of silk disengaged.

Lack of sleep, hours of roaming the grounds last night, and the fact that his business meeting hadn't gone well, had turned his mood sour. The last thing he wanted was to argue with Chastity.

To make it worse, the detective he had hired to investigate Chastity had been useless. Something just didn't smell right.

Chastity and this game show just didn't quite match up. Clearly she didn't want to be here. And if it wasn't for adventure, then it had to be the money.

But why? He knew she didn't need the money. Josh had become affluent working as his manager.

It was true that one could squander a lot of money in two years, but so much that Chastity had to degrade herself? Seth had thought more of his cousin, of Chastity.

And where were Josh's records regarding Chastity's security profile? There hadn't been time for Josh to steal anything. In fact, that betrayer had never stepped foot into his building again. Seth had personally made sure of that.

In a temper he removed his jacket, throwing it and the tie across the bed, and then he paused, looking at the rumpled linens where he had lain with her. The memories of the night assailed him.

He had fucked her mouth. Then they had made love, shared their bodies. He had held her and inadvertently confessed his love, an unbearable weakness that had disgusted him. To console himself he had misused her body. Used her like a whore.

Suddenly his inward anger burst free. He turned on Tatiana. "She was to be dressed and ready upon my return." He plucked at the neck of his dress shirt and the adhesive released, baring his chest.

Tatiana's head bowed. "Please forgive me, Master Seth, but—"

He held a palm out. "I want no excuses."

Seth had received enough excuses from the detective this morning. It seemed for the past two years Chastity had vanished off the face of the earth. There were no traces of her working. No paper path to where she had resided. Even her financials had been wiped clean. Nothing. As if she had ceased to exist.

Josh, it appeared, had gone on with his life. Still, there were holes in his whereabouts that made Seth uncomfortable. The one thing Seth knew for sure was that Chastity had not stayed with his cousin. Josh, the little fool, had even made several attempts throughout the two years to get back into Seth's good graces.

Josh's denial of anything intimate going on between him and Chastity had fallen on deaf ears.

Chastity and Josh had betrayed him. He could not forget their deception.

The dark-haired woman interrupted his tattered thoughts. "But—"

Before she could give some flimsy excuse he pointed to the door. "Get out."

As the door closed behind the insubordinate slave, he turned his attention to Chastity. "Why aren't you dressed?" *Better yet, why aren't you in my bed, legs spread wide, awaiting me?*

God, how he wanted to once again take his emotions out on her body. Make her submit to him. Prove that he was stronger, that the feelings he felt for her last night were fleeting. A huge mistake, simply due to being caught up in the moment.

With a swipe of his hand he tore the blanket off her. Chastity cringed, drawing her legs up and hugging her knees close to her chest. She looked so small, so threatened.

Speechless at her vulnerability, he stood like a damn statue, blanket swaying in his hand.

Then he saw the red, angry marks that marred her slender neck. When he reached for her she flinched. Cold to the touch, she trembled beneath his palm.

Had he hurt her last night? Was she frightened of him?

Damn that blindfold. Chastity's eyes were the windows to her soul. Her eyes laughed, they cried. You knew where you stood with her by the emotions she openly displayed. Or was it all a lie? He certainly hadn't known she would run out on him that day two years ago.

Fuck. His plan was to draw her to him, not push her further away. The contempt he felt for himself was immense. The rage he felt toward her was inconceivable. Still, he hadn't wanted to hurt or frighten her.

Chastity's stomach growled and he wondered when she had eaten last. He knew she hadn't on the transport. And he hadn't seen her eat since they'd arrived on Zygoman. "Are you hungry?"

Swollen eyes brimming with emotion stared at him.

Had she been crying?

Seth released her and ran a hand through his hair. "Dammit, Chastity. Are you hungry?"

Her stomach rumbled again. "No." Her voice sounded small, distant.

Clearly, she was lying. But what could he do if she refused to confide in him?

"Fine, then get dressed." His eyes raked her body.

Indifferently, he dropped the blanket. It slithered down her shoulders, pooling in her lap. "Or would you prefer going out naked?"

Fire sparked in her eyes, clearing away the clouds and shadows. Tossing back the blanket and pushing it to the floor, she rose. "What does the Master desire I wear?"

The room began to get warmer. The fire in her was back.

"Very little," he bit out before disappearing into the bathroom.

Man, was Seth in a snit of a mood. Here Chastity was licking her wounds after being attacked, and he came in like a tiger with a thorn in his paw.

Chastity ran a brush through her still-damp hair. Looking back at her from the mirror was a tired, worn-out woman. Quickly, she pressed her face to the Curative Resurrection Spa, a contraption that looked a lot like a huge suction cup, hanging on the wall next to the sink.

Warm air cleansed and soothed her skin. She felt the drawing agent pulling, caressing around her eyes and mouth, taking away the puffiness and lines. Her breath caught as a brisk rush of cold air closed the pores and sealed the EnchantMist into her face. The revitalizing vapor was the best invention, replacing plastic surgery.

When she looked into the mirror it was as if the morning's events had never happened.

Wasn't modern science wonderful? But what was there to heal the wear and tear on the heart? Absolutely nothing.

This place was like a skycoaster dipping in and out of heaven and hell, keeping Chastity in a constant state of confusion. She looked around the room. Lying on a chair before the fireplace sat something that could hardly be referred to as clothing. Underwear yes, clothing no.

She picked up the scanty lace thong and matching bra between her thumb and index finger. Black, silky thigh-high stockings and four-inch stilettos finished the ensemble.

"Well, it won't do any good to argue," she murmured. "If this is what the Lord and Master wants, then so be it."

She donned the skimpy underwear, rolled the nylons up her long legs, slipped her feet into the heels and braced herself for whatever would come next.

When Seth exited the bathroom he stopped abruptly as if his feet had anchored to the floor. His jaw dropped.

Chastity beamed at his reaction. She knew that her long, untamed hair and the delicate lingerie showed off her body's features well. The stockings and stilettos made her legs appear long and shapely. And the heated look in Seth's eyes made her want to peel each piece of clothing off slowly, one at a time, until the man couldn't resist touching her, spreading her wide and thrusting his cock deep inside.

A sensual toss of her hair and the seductive dip of her eyelids had him at her side. His palm grasped the nape of her neck, yanking her to him as his mouth met hers. The kiss was hungry, filled with possession and fire. Their tongues dueled. Then Seth quickly released her and moved away.

"Ready?" His voice was deep and throaty.

Chastity watched the rise and fall of his broad chest and the confusion warring in his eyes. He wanted her. She could feel it in the way he touched and looked at her. But there was too much between them that he couldn't—or wouldn't—let go.

If only she could end this game, just leave. Because the agony of the ups and downs was wearing thin. One of them was going to break, and which direction the pieces would fall was anyone's guess.

As they exited their room, Seth glanced at his watch. "Damn, we're too late to attend the bondage demonstration." He frowned at her, letting her know it was her fault.

Relief flooded Chastity. The last thing she wanted was to be roped into performing before a crowd. And she just knew that the sex king of Zygoman would insist on it, or his brother, Terrance, would have something distasteful for her to do.

Silently, they strolled down the path leading to the garden, Seth in the lead, Chastity several steps behind. Rounding a corner, the crew of Voyeur II spied them and hastened into position. Two men, cameras propped on their shoulders, stood in front of them blocking their exit, while a young anchorwoman sidled up to Seth. From the looks of her short, tight skirt and shirt, she'd dressed to entice the audience and to attract Seth, thought Chastity.

The woman held a transmitter-phone that she wedged between her and Seth. "Tell us, Mr. Allen, how things have been progressing throughout the last two days, especially *last night*." The woman's voice took on a dreamy quality. Her tongue made a sensuous path along her full bottom lip, eyes darkening with desire.

Anger scorched through Chastity as the blonde batted her long lashes. If the flirtatious woman didn't back away from Seth, and soon, Chastity would pluck every bleached-blonde hair from her head. But before she could ponder more acts of violence, Seth's reply had Chastity redirecting her fury.

"I'm pleased. My slave's walls of resistance are cracking, if not crumbling. Acceptance of domination is not always easy, but for a woman like Miss Ambrose, well—" he paused, " —she can benefit from exploring her sexual desires. I'm just here to help her in that discovery."

Oh, puleeeze! Chastity felt her brows rise and her jaw drop in disbelief. His words deserved a response, even if he couldn't see it. Standing behind him, but in full view of the cameras, her right palm landed hard in the bend of her left elbow forcing her fist to snap upwards in the age-old "fuck you" symbol of the Italians.

In unison, the cameras directed at Seth focused on her. The men's chuckles made the cameras vibrate against their bodies.

Seth glanced over his shoulder, but Chastity had regained her pose, feet parted, hands behind her back, head bowed.

He frowned. "Kneel." It was a show of his authority. One that Chastity didn't like one bit. Still, she drifted to her knees, casting her gaze to the ground until Seth again faced the cameras.

The anchorwoman smiled. "So, Mr. Allen, would you say Miss Ambrose is coming along as you expected?"

Chastity saw the devilish twinkle in the woman's eyes. Then she nodded toward Chastity in a sign of appreciation.

Hey, Chastity could get to like this newslady. She had spunk.

As Seth spoke, Chastity could envision his camera-ready smile flashing for his audience.

"Yes, in fact, she's right where she should be." He paused for effect and then added, "Beneath me." The crowd joined him, laughing at his witticism.

However, their heads dipped back and they released a roar as Chastity's middle finger raised, saluting Seth's back.

Seth whirled, only to find Chastity docilely kneeling, her head bowed in reverence.

Then Chastity's favorite nemesis appeared to wreck the day.

"Master Seth." Terrance moved to his side. "I believe that your slave has earned another punishment."

Shit, shit, and double shit! The barbaric Viking was going to be the death of her. Through feathered lashes she watched him as he explained to Seth what was occurring behind his back.

In a nanosecond the man's facial features went from bewildered to embarrassed to outraged. But like the professional Seth was, his expression softened. He threw back his head and burst into laughter, a sound that to Chastity had a little too much humor for comfort.

The camera saw a confident man taking the incident with grace. From her perspective, Seth was pissed.

"Perhaps a reminder of the rules and what is at stake is required." Then his eyes pinned Chastity, nailing her to the ground.

Yep. Pissed!

"It appears a firmer hand is necessary."

Chastity heard his words, but the unspoken meaning was the one that frightened her the most. Seth was a proud man and she had humiliated him on universal cinema.

But *dammit*, he had done much worse to her.

"If you will excuse us, it's time to get to work." With diplomacy, Seth dismissed the camera crew and reporter. His heavy footsteps beat a path toward Chastity. She cringed, wondering what was in store for her.

"Rise." There was no animosity in his tone, but of course the cameras were still rolling in the distance.

How could a simple word from this man send butterflies whirling in her stomach? She remained on her knees in reflection. Trepidation and excitement blended to raise the hairs across her skin. Even now, as his imposing frame loomed over her, all she could see was a man of sensual pleasure. A man that made her pulse speed, her nipples burn and ache against her soft clothing. Not to mention, a man that started a flood of desire, wet and warm, between her thighs.

Fiery eyes glared down upon Chastity. Then Seth's lips drew back into a snarl. "Master Terrance, would you accompany us? I believe you can assist in my slave's further training."

Like a fragile flower being crushed by strong hands, her ardor was squashed with Terrance's reply. "It would be my pleasure, Master Seth."

"I said, *rise*."

Chastity stood at Seth's command, wishing the cameramen hadn't disappeared.

Terrance produced a length of satin rope from somewhere on his person. Dangling it in front of Chastity's face, he grinned. "Might I suggest that you bind her knees? She will be able to follow behind, but it will be a lesson that you are in control, and can take away and give freedom as you see fit." The rope slithered through his fingers like a menacing snake, before falling into Seth's waiting palm.

Seth knelt. As the cool cord wrapped around and around her knees, Chastity silently cursed Terrance. If it was the last thing she did before leaving this planet, she would pay the man back for his interference.

The man in question pinched her chin, raising her gaze to his. Rich hazel eyes flashed a warning. "Don't even *think* about it." His tone was a deep, menacing rumble.

Speechless, Chastity jerked away from his hold. How the devil did he know what she was thinking? Was the man clairvoyant? Or just really, really aggravating?

Seth slapped his thigh as he began to walk. "Heel."

Heel? Like I'm some friggin' dog? Warmth heated her cheeks as she stood her ground. When Terrance glanced over his shoulder and smirked, fire raced through her veins.

Seth snapped his fingers. "*Now!*"

His blatant contempt startled her, but succeeded in putting her feet into motion. The first hesitant step, not to mention the four-inch stilettos, nearly had her tumbling head over heels. Quickly, she gathered her aplomb, concentrating on each footfall. Head down, she watched one foot move in front of the other.

Damn, but it was hard to look dignified when shuffling along like a geisha girl. So intense was she on staying upright, she didn't notice that the terrain had changed. As if the earth itself thought to torment her, a gnarled tree root curving across the ground snatched away her footing. She screamed and pitched forward.

"*Fuck!*" She grasped her skinned knees, the abrasion burning and throbbing.

Seth was immediately at her side. "Are you hurt?"

Chastity's brows lifted in an expression that said, *Duh*.

Only then did she look past Seth and at her surroundings. They had entered a forest, but it was unlike any she had ever seen on Earth. Bright, colorful flowers dotted the panorama and seemed to wink at her in the shadowed sunlight. A pond lay still, as if holding its breath. Tall trees, as large as the redwoods in California, sprung up to the sky. But their trunks, instead of the usual rough brown bark, were like polished marble. Red veins traversed their pearly columns. In fact, she could see their life force pumping, moving and breaking into new channels, creating a labyrinth of arteries. Golden vines embraced the magnificent trees like lovers.

Mesmerized, Chastity was still looking around when two strong hands tucked under her armpits and raised her to her feet. She crow-hopped, and then grasped Seth's arm to steady herself.

"It's beautiful." Her hand floated to her side. "Almost as if you can see and hear the heartbeat of life." The grandeur made her feel small, insignificant.

The last thing Chastity wanted to hear among all this splendor was Terrance's haughty voice. "The Forest of Immortality is indeed enchanting, but it also teaches a lesson."

"Of course, a lesson," she sighed. Did the man ever take a break from being an asshole? Exasperated, she turned to face him.

Terrance drifted to his knees. With a powerful thrust he buried a silver stake into the ground. Then he rose and moved several feet away and planted another.

"Mortality teaches us to cherish life, to live it to the fullest. Here you will be able to set your soul free. Find peace and surrender."

Terrance and the word surrender didn't give Chastity warm fuzzies, and neither did the four stakes looming before her.

Then it dawned on her what they planned to do. She took a cautious step backwards. "No way." But her bound knees took control forcing her down to ground and she landed on her ass. As Terrance slowly approached her, she desperately cried, "Seth!"

Seth gazed down at her. "Did you think you would go unpunished for your little act of defiance, Chastity?"

Fear and fury blazed in her eyes like flames trapped under glass. *Man*, how he had missed her spirit over the past few years.

The woman was a fighter.

Seth's cock stiffened in appreciation. Even Terrance's eyes showed a hint of admiration for her mettle.

No, Chastity Ambrose would not go quietly into the night – or any other time of day.

Half-crazed, she fought her bindings. When that didn't work she used her arms and feet to crawl. It was a losing battle, but she showed no signs of quitting. Each time they approached, her arms flailed wildly.

Then a lucky punch caught Terrance in the left eye. "Yeow!" One hand covered his battered eye as the other hand snaked out and caught her by the ankle. Seth leaped forward, using his weight to pin her to the ground.

With one hand Seth raised her wrists above her head. A guttural sound of rage arose from her. Her chest heaved, heartbeat throbbing fiercely against his chest. The wild scent of her fury caressed him. Savagely, his mouth crushed hers.

Defenses firmly in place, she bit his lower lip. He jerked back, spearing her with a warning glare as his tongue slid across his offended lip. The taste of his blood was a heady aphrodisiac. He had to have more of the hellion beneath him.

Terrance moved around them, but Seth was oblivious to him, even when the man drew one of Chastity's hands away and secured it to a stake. For the moment, no one else existed but the two of them locked in a battle of wills. When her other hand drifted from his grasp he turned his attention to depriving Chastity of her clothes.

Within seconds Terrance had removed the rope around Chastity's knees, bound her ankles to the remaining stakes, and then quietly disappeared into the shadows.

Chastity's eyes dilated, knowing what was coming. The snap of her bra and the feel of her breasts springing into Seth's hands was unbelievably erotic. The glorious mounds rose and fell rapidly, her taut nipples betraying her arousal.

Seth eased off of her and kneeled beside her. The sight of her arms high over her head and bound to stakes, legs splayed wide for him, was an amazing stimulant. Seeing her clad in nothing but a scanty thong, silk stockings and stilettos made him even hornier.

His cock pulsed against his leather pants, the ache growing as his gaze lingered on the delicate blue veins visible beneath her alabaster skin. With a quick movement he released his dick. He hardened, lengthening beneath her hungry stare.

She wanted him. The knowledge drove him crazy.

Pushing between her legs he nuzzled her mons, scenting her, and reveling in the perfume that was uniquely her own. Skin soft as silk met his hands as they caressed up the inside of her thighs, stopping when they came in contact with her thong.

He smiled.

Fantasies truly did come true on the pleasure planet of Zygoman. Now it was time to make one of his a reality. Seth grasped the loose cloth of her panties in his teeth and tugged. The small clasps holding the material together on each side snapped, slipping away, leaving her in nothing but stockings and stilettos. He grinned at her from between her thighs, ignoring the defiant glare she returned.

Chastity could fight him all she wanted, but the juices glistening on the lips of her pussy were a blatant invitation to take her.

But he wouldn't. Not until she begged for his cock. It had to be her choice to give herself to him, only then would he bury his erection deep inside her body.

"You're beautiful," he murmured, sliding flesh against flesh as he took her breasts in hand. "So succulent." He bent over her, taking a taut peak into his mouth. Chastity gasped and then tensed, as if to hold back her reaction. Fury was moving in the shadows of her eyes, but then again, so was desire.

As he suckled he slid his cock along her slick folds. He teased her, nudging her swollen flesh with the knob of his erection. Her hips rose, her thighs parting as far as possible with the minimal play of the ropes around her ankles. Still he held back, gently taunting, then withdrawing before entering her.

Cradling her rib cage, he thrust along her heated center, feeling her full globes bouncing against the back of his hands. Cupping their weight, he pinched her nipples, wrenching another gasp from her lips. He licked, lavished attention on the rosy buds, and then blew a light path of air across them.

She sucked in a tight breath and a hot wave of her excitement anointed his cock.

In a playful mood, he moved down her body again until his head was between her thighs. Elbows on the ground, chin resting in the palms of his hands, his eyes devoured her pussy. A single finger reached out, tracing her swollen sex, exploring and pushing on her clit, sending her hips off the grass. Then he leaned forward and tasted her essence.

A whimper escaped her lips. Triumphant, he moved again atop her and thrust his throbbing cock along the heat between her thighs.

Chastity tried to hide just how much her body wanted Seth. But it was the little signs that betrayed her. Erect nipples, a pussy wet and emitting the scent of her arousal. Even the ripple of muscles in his body, the power visible in his sensuous movements, made her body tighten with uncontrollable need.

When his breath fanned warm across her lips, she gave a shiver of pleasure. The anticipation of his caress, the feel of his goatee and mustache against her skin, was maddening. She wanted him inside her mouth and pussy now.

A featherlight touch, a wisp of skin brushing skin, teased.

"Please," her plea was breathless.

He grinned behind sensual lashes. And then their lips met and time ceased.

His kiss was a slow intimate knowing of her mouth. It was everything she expected and more. Passion. Tenderness. She tasted herself upon his tongue and sighed.

A soft whisper caressed her ear. "Do you want me to make your skin burn?" His voice was smooth as velvet, dark as night. The sound, low, seductive, caused her body to shudder.

She yearned, ached, to touch him. Her fingers twitched, her bonds holding her tight. It was a torment unlike anything she had ever experienced. And it was exciting.

"Yes." *Oh, God, yes.* Her body arched, asking for what he offered.

She watched as he licked a slow, sensual path down the valley of her breasts, stopping at her belly button. A carnal gaze met hers. His tongue dipped.

"Yes, *what*?"

Chastity couldn't take much more of this. Blissfully, she closed her eyes. "Yes, Master."

A strong hand found her clit and pinched. She moaned as electricity shot through her body. In slow, seductive movements he brushed his body against hers, teasing her and making her realize how much she needed him driving his cock into her heat, his mouth suckling her breasts. She needed to climax so bad she could taste the salty flavor in her mouth.

A wave of longing swamped her. She felt like weeping, her desire for him was so raw.

"Tell me what you want." His voice vibrated around her.

Chastity hesitated, not wanting to admit her depth of hunger. Then he flicked her nipple with a finger, sending fire radiating through her breast.

Like a river racing freely she blurted, "I want you buried deep inside me. I want to burn beneath your touch. I-I want you to make l-lo... Fuck me. Fuck me, Seth, please."

Still, he held back. He rubbed his cock along her swollen folds. Her body tightened, every nerve stretched to breaking. It would only take him entering her and she would shatter into a million pieces.

"I'll only give you what you want if you promise not to come until I tell you to." He parted her nether lips with the head of his erection, and then stopped.

"Yes, yes, I promise." Her hips ground against his, she had to have him now. "Please, Master, pleasure me."

"And you will obey me in all matters?" A finger pressed against her clit, sending a shot of white-hot lightning up her channel.

"*Ohhh*, yes, God, yes. *Now*, Master, take me now." Chastity was going to scream if she didn't come soon. She had agreed to all his demands—why wasn't he thrusting his cock inside her hot pussy? And it *was* hot, fiery hot and burning.

A cool gust of air chilled her body as Seth moved away. She opened her eyes to find him standing between her splayed legs, studying her. The sight of him, his huge member jutting out from the folds of his pants, made her even hotter.

Maybe he planned to untie her, take her back to their bungalow. Hell, she wanted him here—now—on the hard ground among the wilderness of the forest. Even in front of Terrance, who had made himself scarce, but was still visible just among the trees.

"I'm pleased with you, Chastity."

Bewildered, she looked at the man standing above her. "What?"

"I'm pleased that you trust me and have agreed to subjugate yourself to me." Rolling his hips he pushed his cock back into his pants. The strain on his face said it wasn't an easy task. Pressing the folds together he sealed his erection away from her view. "When I return, if you still deserve it, we will consummate our agreement."

In disbelief, Chastity's jaw dropped. The *son of a bitch* planned to leave her staked out in the middle of a forest where any wild animal could maul her, or even kill her. He had teased her, played her like a fiddle.

Her arousal cooled faster than water in subzero temperatures.

Seth knelt beside her, his shoulder-length, ebony hair falling in silken disarray as he inserted a finger into her pussy and began to thrust. Instinctively, her hips rose to meet his assault.

Okay, so she only *thought* her ardor had shut down.

She still walked a tightrope of desire—beyond help and lost to sensation as she faced the enemy.

Shrewdly, the bastard was wielding sex like a weapon. And what was worse, she had no willpower to resist him.

"From this moment on, you will not speak without permission. You will no longer fight my dominance." He retracted his finger and stood before he issued the final caveat. "If you do, I'll contact Voyeur II and end this charade."

Stung by his threat, she found a new courage as she squared her shoulders. His infuriating air of supremacy roused her anger and made her determined to thwart him. He had thrown down the challenge. All she had to do was accept.

"Forgive me, Master," she said with a degree of dryness that bordered on the acerbic. "I will not forget that I am only here to serve your needs, to obey your orders, to accept your domination and *to please your desires.*"

Then she closed her eyes to block out his handsome face. The final knife had been twisted. He had won her body and submission, but she would leave here with one hundred million dollars, save her mother, and then never set eyes on Seth Allen again.

Chapter Nine

From behind the cover of the trees, Seth watched Chastity. It was six o'clock in the evening, and for five hours she hadn't moved, hadn't cried out in a fit of rage. There were no tears. In fact, there was no emotion whatsoever. Her eyes remained closed, her breathing shallow and steady as if she slept.

Had she escaped into her safe zone?

Leaving her so aroused had almost killed him. He'd been so friggin' hot that it took only two pumps of his own hand to release his seed. The act had left him unfulfilled, empty. The desire to feel his cock buried between the folds of her pussy was overpowering. But he had no other choice. He needed to know what her motives were.

The fear in her eyes when he threatened to contact Voyeur II and end their game had confirmed her need of the money.

Now he had to discover for what purpose. But how?

"Are you ready for tonight?" asked Terrance. His gaze was intently focused on Chastity.

"Yes." Seth studied the man beside him. He'd be livid once he got a good look at his eye. Chastity had given him a hell of a shiner. Puffy, it already was darkening into shades of black and blue.

Something lay between Terrance and Chastity. Even if it was just animosity, Seth couldn't stop the tinge of jealousy that seeped into his bones.

Terrance turned and faced Seth. "You understand that Voyeur II wants your woman to fail."

"I do, but everything done to her must be within reason."

Seth didn't like the arrogant lift of the man's mouth as it slid into a grin. "Define reasonable."

Between Terrance and Tor, Seth worried about the outcome of the night. "Don't fuck with me. You know she isn't to be harmed. I'll call this thing off if you get any ideas to hurt or debase her."

The man's response was to deepen his grin, then he turned and disappeared into the forest.

Seth stood glaring at the place where Terrance had vanished, before he pivoted back toward Chastity. Quietly, he exited the trees. Standing before her, he gazed upon her perfect body splayed wide for his pleasure. A slight pink color tinged her skin. He had forgotten that she might burn in the light of the day.

Her blue eyes opened, but she made no attempt to speak. He smiled, pleased that she had remembered his first edict.

"Are you ready to consummate our agreement?"

"If it pleases you, Master." She closed her eyes and said no more, giving him the feeling that he was about to slay a sacrificial lamb, instead of fucking the woman of his dreams.

Even though she lay placid before him, he knew where to touch, to caress, to make her body react. In minutes he would have her where he wanted, hot and wild and begging him to take her.

A finger slid over her nipple and he watched with pleasure as it tightened into a needy bud. Gently, he kneaded her breasts, waiting for the sharp intake of breath that told him she craved his hands moving across her body.

But it didn't come. Neither did it appear when he sucked a nipple deep into his moist mouth and bit down hard.

Defiance would get her nothing but a fast trip back to Earth. Frustrated, he thrust a finger into her pussy. Wet and warm, a flow of heat released in his hand. Yet the expression on her face remained statue-like.

Anger pulsed through his veins. His little plaything had slipped into her safe zone, daring to deceive him.

"Chastity!" he barked, then gave her a rough shake.

Leaden lids lifted. "Yes, Master?"

She responded too quickly to be submerged into herself. He sat up, baffled at the situation. How was she able to physically react, but mentally tune out, deny his seduction? Whatever the answer, fucking a corpse left little appeal, and his hard-on died a quick death.

There was nothing left to do but untie her and figure out his next move.

Once released, she made no attempt to rise. He stood dumbfounded, wondering what her game was. Then it dawned on him. She awaited his command.

As soon as he said, "Rise," she stood, swaying weakly on her feet in nothing but her stockings and stilettos. When he turned to walk away she didn't follow. When he handed her the black silk robe that Terrance had supplied she didn't put it on until he told her to.

So they were to play the game of explicitness. No reaction would be offered—only that which was decreed.

Be careful what you wish for, his mother had always said, *because sometimes your desires blow up right in your face.* There was more truth than not in those words. He didn't want Chastity like this. He wanted her fight, her fire.

Maybe the Thorensons' plans for tonight would awaken the passion within her. Or maybe they would push her further into compliancy.

Sunset was bathing the mountaintops. As Seth led Chastity back to their bungalow she practiced slipping in and out of a conscious state. On the fringes, she wasn't sure she could fool him into believing that she was a participant in their Master-slave game. Already, she had failed, or at least left him wondering.

The episode had not left her totally unaffected. At first, when his dark eyes gazed upon her she had almost lost it. As she slipped into the haze of her mind, she'd successfully erased the hunger on his face by visualizing the cold shell of her body empty of emotions and feeling.

That was fine, until she resurfaced and found her nipples tingling, her pussy pulsating, and Seth's cock as limp as a noodle.

The walk through the breathtaking forest was over too soon as they entered the garden. Birds chattered noisily high in the branches of the trees. Laughter filled the air as a man chased a woman into the pond. With a growl he caught her and they fell with a splash. There was a moment of silence and then their heads broke the surface and the laughter continued until he kissed her with the passion and possession of a man in love.

Envy wasn't pretty, nor was it comforting. Chastity looked at Seth, noting the intensity of his features. Glare fixed forward, brows furrowed, his footsteps heavy with determination.

Something was up.

When they passed their bungalow, the fine hairs on her arms rose, as well as her anxiety.

Where is he taking me? More importantly, what's in store for me?

Arriving at the main complex, Seth ushered her through the large gaping doors. Midway down the hall, he stopped in front of an archway. "Do you need to use the restroom?"

Chastity nodded.

Seth pointed down the small passage, through the entrance. "Down this hall, first door on your right." Chastity pivoted, only to be jerked to a halt by Seth's fingers curled around her wrist. "Don't take all day. We're having guests tonight."

Guests? Now why didn't she like the sound of that?

After taking care of necessities, Chastity bent over the sink and splashed cool water on her face. She rested her eyes, and then opened them with a sigh. A wary woman stared back at her from the mirror. A sharp knock on the door made her jump.

Damn the man. Chastity nearly tripped in her stilettos as she raced for the door.

Seth's frown greeted her as she opened the door. His hand settled at the small of her back, and even through her silky robe his touch sent a frisson through her spine that exploded in her brain and between her thighs. Pulling on the strings of her safety zone, she fought to block the sensation.

Her concentration shattered as they began to walk down a set of stairs. The further down they went, the bleaker their surroundings. Lighting went from electricity to lit torches in cast-iron sconces mounted on the walls. The marble flooring and white plaster walls shifted to cold, gray stone. Before her very eyes the building was morphing from a beautiful palace to a dungeon.

The stench of danger filled her nostrils.

The door before them opened, screaming as if in pain against the rusty hinges. Before she could retreat, the palm that rested in the hollow of her back gave a push and she stumbled into the room.

Chastity couldn't stop the gasp that escaped her. She chastised herself and dug deep within to find the courage to raise her chin and square her shoulders.

But it was all an act.

Because as she looked around, Chastity knew that she had fallen into the past, as she stood in what looked like a medieval torture chamber.

Whips, crops, canes and paddles hung among chains and leather constraints. Nipple clamps and other, longer clamps, adorned with beads and precious stones, made her shiver. Fear crept into the room on cat's feet, slow and stealthy.

Seth moved around the room as if he had forgotten her. She watched him gathering items from the wall—handcuffs, rope, a feather, a whip, a paddle, a wicked-looking knife and her nipple clamps from the show.

Slowly, he slipped on a pair of gloves. The snap of the latex made her jump. Whatever he had planned for the evening, it didn't look good.

"Disrobe." His command was given with his back facing her.

Apprehensive, she paused, but only briefly as he picked up a whip with coarse thongs, almost like a horse's tail, and hit it across his palm.

Startled, she fumbled with the sash, fingers tearing at the robe. When she was naked except for stockings and stilettos, he turned and approached.

A ripple of muscles flexed across his chest. In his hands he held a sleep mask.

No, *not again*.

A knot formed in her throat as he placed the blindfold over her eyes. Blackness folded around her. She sensed his closeness, listened to his breathing, then she felt him move away and heard the squeal of hinges as the door opened.

Good, he was leaving.

Then she heard voices, male voices. Her heart crashed against the walls of her chest. Because there wasn't one, or even two, men in the room with her, but several. How many, she struggled to discern, the task a tormenting endeavor.

One was Tor, his deep, commanding voice was unmistakable. When Terrance spoke, apprehension slithered up her back. Then she heard the soft voice of the third part of the trio, Shawn. Her rescuer was now one of her tormenters.

"Are you ready?" she heard Tor ask.

Seth replied, "Yes. You'll find additional gloves on the table."

Chastity twisted her head, following the footsteps padding across the floor in all directions. Chaos exploded in her head as latex snapped once, and then again, and again…

She flinched. The taste of fear beaded on her tongue. She was going to be tortured by all the men, including Seth.

At least she knew his scent. Would know when he touched her.

Her head jerked back and she stumbled as a pungent scent was placed under her nose, robbing her of smell. She fought to hold still, not to struggle and give them the reaction they sought.

Two sets of strong, unyielding hands grasped her wrists. She bit down hard on her bottom lip to keep from crying out. The taste of blood was in her mouth.

A yank on both arms forced her backwards. Then she felt cold metal clasped around each wrist. The squeal that left her lips as her legs were jerked apart could not be held back.

Two forceful palms encased her face between them. Then something was slipped into both of her ears and she was released.

The silence was deafening.

The bastards had taken her ability to see, hear and smell. The only senses she had left were touch and taste.

Panic welled inside her, blocking out her ability to concentrate, to slip into her safe zone.

A scream rose in her throat. Instead, she heard her own muffled plea, "Please, don't do this."

Great. She had once again been reduced to begging.

The dull roar in her ears began to lessen. Suddenly the night came alive with sensation.

Hair lifting off her shoulders as it was fastened atop her head. Multiple streams of warm air brushing the back of her neck. Something cold and wet sliding down her spine, forcing her back to arch. Instantly, the chill vanished, appearing again at the very tip of her left nipple. The sting was brief, gone so fast that she wondered if she had imagined it.

Trapped in darkness, she anticipated the next place the ice would grace. Instead she felt the burn of fire, one drip at a time, on her breast. Her jaws clenched under the agony that was quickly appeased by a frosty touch.

Somewhere along the way, her fear dissipated. In its place was excitement as her mind played along with the game. Each time another place on her body was teased with fire or ice she felt the pull to relax and enjoy the exquisite sensation of the unknown.

But the decadent act that made her breath catch was when an icicle slipped between her swollen lips and disappeared into her pussy. Her channel relished the cold, the feeling so unique, so different. Even the water seeping down her legs, as her body heat melted the foreign object, was arousing. In her mind's eye she saw the ice growing smaller and smaller, consumed within.

Smack!

She screamed, unprepared for the sting of a paddle against her ass. Then she felt the caress of a hand, and wondered if it was Seth's soft touch.

Smack!

This time her anger surfaced. Surely it was Terrance wielding the instrument of pain. But before she let loose with a string of curses, the gentle hand returned. Easing and smoothing out the pain, applying ice to take away the burn.

Mind focused on the circular motions of the palm across her skin, she gasped when her nipples were sucked into warm wet mouths.

Mouths?

She froze.

Oh. My. God! Being comforted on one end while suckled on the other by not just one man, but several, threw her mind in chaos.

Who was doing what?

Did it really matter? her mind questioned.

No sight, no smell, no hearing—she was lost to the unknown and the desires of her body.

Then came the pleasure-pain she remembered when the nipple clamps bit into her. She arched into the palms of…well…who knew. She simply enjoyed the white-hot lightning shooting through her breasts, knowing that more was to come.

Chastity's breath was stolen by the sudden sting of pulsating needles, one right after another, on her thigh. Like a mass of bees attacking or a charge of electricity. She cried out, fighting her bindings. Then a wisp of something wet and silky magically dulled the pain before another series was released on her other thigh.

"Fuck! That hurts," she bellowed. The pain instantly vanished with another application of the wet silk.

All at once she felt slick bodies pressed against hers. Hard, rigid erections pressed into each of her sides, one to her back, the final one to her belly. In unison they moved, sliding up and down her own body, sending her into meltdown.

Chastity wanted to touch, feel, but her restraints held her tight. She rolled her head, moaning in ecstasy. She wanted Seth's cock inside her while the other men rubbed against her.

Was that sick, or what?

Never had she imagined that something so sinful could be so arousing. As if a floodgate had opened, fantasies of what she could do with four men poured into her head. But always it was Seth at the forefront.

The plug in one ear was removed. She listened to the heavy breathing surrounding her.

In a low, deep voice Seth asked, "What do you want, Chastity?"

No, no, no. It was happening again. Her body tensed. Her mind grappled to take control.

"What do you want, Chastity?" he repeated.

Remembering the agreement made in the forest, the one hundred million dollars, and her mother's situation, she whispered, "Whatever will please you, Master."

"You won't endorphin-out?"

The minuscule confidence she had managed to gather dissolved in the air around her.

He knew of her barrier. The last of her defenses had been stripped from her, leaving her helpless. She was his to do as he pleased and there was nothing, absolutely nothing, she could do to prevent it.

Resigned to her fate, she hung her head. "No, Master." For once she relished the darkness, the unknown, and prayed it would swallow her up.

As if by magic, her bindings fell away from her body. Strong arms lifted her, cradling her close to a large muscular chest. With one ear she heard the muffled scrape of a chair moving across the floor. Then a set of hands grasped her ankles, spreading her legs wide as she was lowered in a straddle position. It wasn't until a stiff cock pierced her pussy that she realized someone sat upon the chair. That *someone* was now buried deep inside her body.

Her ass nestled in his lap. Bare hands, free of gloves, cupped her breasts, then began to tease the nipple clamps, sending flames through their tortured peaks.

"Place your palms on my shoulders." Relief filtered through her body as Seth spoke. Even blindfolded, she felt his eyes burning into her flesh. He whispered her name and a warm, wet rush of desire flowed between her thighs.

"That's my girl." His hips began to thrust. "Ride me," he growled, his hand moving from her chest to her hips, forcing her to take every inch of him deep into her pussy.

Flesh slapped into flesh as he raised her and then stabbed into her with his dick. Not knowing whether she performed for an audience increased the sensuality.

Once again, Chastity found herself climbing the crest of ecstasy. But this time as she hit the summit, Seth jerked the nipple clamps off. The pain-pleasure hit with a vengeance. She threw back her head and released a scream, climaxing just as

Seth ejaculated. Together they soared, before landing in each others arms, sated and blissful.

Seth listened to the pounding of her heart against his. She snuggled up to him as she always did after they made love. Her kitten-like movements made him chuckle.

The electronic clip in her hair jabbed his chest. Grabbing the release, he pushed and a mass of brunette curls tumbled between them. His fingers threaded through the silk as he bent and kissed her forehead.

He reached for the sleep mask covering her eyes and gave it a jerk. She squinted, blinking watery eyes as she grew accustomed to the light. They were alone in the chamber.

When she gazed up at him he smiled. "Are you hungry?"

Her response was perfunctory, just what she thought he wanted to hear. "If it pleases you, Master."

Grasping her shoulders he squared her in front of him. "No, Chastity. What would please me is to know whether you're hungry or not."

She bowed her head refusing to break character. "Yes, Master."

He raised her from his lap, his cock sliding out of her pussy. "Come on, then. Let's see what we can round up."

As she slipped on her robe he noted that her ass and thighs were still pink from their play.

Had she enjoyed the erotic torture? Had she been turned on having four men touch her at once?

When their eyes met, a blush spread across her cheeks. A weak smile lifted the corners of her mouth.

No, he wouldn't let his jealousy spoil the remainder of the evening. For one night he wanted to enjoy Chastity's company. He would feed her and then enjoy his dessert between her sweet thighs.

Chapter Ten

In disbelief, Chastity stared at the midnight picnic gracing the banks of the pond she had bathed in upon arrival. Seth had left her in the chamber alone while he had spoken to someone outside the door. She had tried to hear the jumbled voices on the other side, but with no success. Clearly this was what Seth had been up to.

Stars twinkled in the ebony sky. The water gleamed with an inner light, as if it had captured rays of moonbeams and held them beneath its glassy surface. The Moth orchids floating on the surface of the pond were iridescent, glowing.

Seduction was the scene.

The tactics of the game had changed…again.

The day had begun with an attack, been iced with humiliation, decorated with bondage and temptation, sprinkled with a threat and then topped with erotic torture. Talk about keeping a girl on her toes. Chastity felt like she'd been beaten into submission, and now Seth was going to kill her with kindness.

As tantalizing smells rose from the basket, her stomach growled. She clutched her abdomen, remembering that it had been nearly a day and half since she'd eaten.

Seth laughed and extended his hand toward her. "Come on, baby, let's get you fed."

Shocked at the intimacy in his voice, she stared at him, unsure what to do. When she finally reached out, his fingers weaved through hers, pulling her toward the blanket.

A perfect gentleman, he helped her sit and then took a place next to her.

"Those heels must be uncomfortable. Here, let me take them off." Seth grasped the back of one stiletto and pulled it off. When his hand circled her thigh, fingers dipping into the top of her silk stocking, Chastity felt her heart leap.

Their eyes met. A roguish grin, one she had seen so many times, graced his lips. Without a word, he began to slowly slide the stocking down her leg, leaving a path of fire in its wake. As Chastity fought to control her emotions, he repeated the same on her other foot. And he wasn't through with her.

A breath caught in her throat as he pulled at the sash of her robe. He parted the material and paused, staring at her breasts as if he had never seen them, before sliding the garment off her shoulders.

"There." Eyes riveted on her nipples, she heard him suck in a tight breath. "Now you're comfortable."

No, Chastity was anything but comfortable. Averting her gaze, she stared into the silvery depths of the water and concentrated on breathing slowly and steadily.

"Hungry?" She heard Seth open the basket. "Let's see what we have."

Inhale…exhale.

Hell, she'd made it through two days and a night of bondage, she could survive this evening. For one hundred million dollars and her mother's release she could make it through anything.

"Here." She felt a cool glass pushed into her hands. Looking down into the amber liquid, she wondered whether Tatiana would truly help her.

"It's not poisonous," Seth laughed.

She stared at the goblet, her index finger and thumb holding the stem as if it were contaminated.

"It's only wine," he assured her.

Chastity clutched the glass in her other hand, bringing it up to her lips and downing it in several gulps.

"Relax, Chastity. Let's just have one night of enjoyment unfettered by the game...or the past." Seth poured more wine into her glass.

Skeptical, she glanced sideways at him. His tone sounded genuine. But even if they stole two or three hours, it wouldn't be long before they were forced back into character, Seth the Master, she his slave.

Could they, for a moment, forgive and forget?

You fool, Chastity rebuked herself. Seth tossed the hook, she bit, and now he was reeling her in.

She wasn't going to fall for it again. Let him wine and dine her—seduce her. This tactic was just another approach to the cruel game he played.

Beneath her breath she whispered, "Hit me with your best shot."

He did.

Seth reached for her glass, setting it aside. "Lay down," he said, his voice deep and sensuous, eyes twinkling with mischief.

She did as he bid, turning her head to block out his handsome face.

"Are you comfortable?" His voice caressed her ears and heated her blood.

"Yes." *Yeah, about as comfortable as a long-tailed cat in a room full of neo-gliders.*

No, no, no, it was the wine making her lightheaded, bending her resistance. The wetness between her thighs was a result of alcohol and no food. Not a need to feel his cock deep inside her, his lips on her breasts, his hands stroking.

When Chastity felt a moist coolness slide across a nipple she allowed herself a peek at what Seth was doing. He had rid himself of his robe, naked as she. His length lay in front of hers, his hand slowly anointing her taut peak with a juicy strawberry.

Their eyes met. He smiled, pressing the berry to her lips. It was sweet sliding down her throat. Extracting another plump piece of fruit from the basket, he bit the tip, the flow of red nectar drawing her gaze to his tantalizing lips. She watched a drip swell, felt the pull to taste. Before she made a complete idiot of herself his tongue skimmed across his mouth and the juice disappeared.

Okay, she was dying here. Her heart crashed against her chest, sending a reverberation tingling through her nipples. Liquid gathered between her thighs, forcing them slightly apart in invitation. Like a puppet, she waited with bated breath for him to yank the next string.

When his mouth inhaled her nipple, every bone in her body melted. She reached for her wineglass, lifted her head and pressed it to her lips.

He nipped.

She gulped.

The glass tipped and a stream of wine dribbled on her other breast.

Warm, rich laughter radiated around her nipple before his tongue made a path across her chest, seeking the golden liquid. His lips closed around the peak and suckled.

Damn Seth for playing the game of seduction so well. And damn her lack of willpower.

Protect your heart, her brain pleaded, as if down on bended knee. *Mind your own business and let him in,* her heart snapped, bringing to the forefront all the memories of the past, her hopes for the future. Yet it was her stomach that made the final decision, growling at the most untimely moment as his fingers slipped between her thighs, stroking her pussy.

Cool air brushed over her nipple as he jerked back. Staring into his dark eyes, she cursed her belly for its interference.

He rolled over and began to rummage through the basket. "Chicken, cheese, what would you like?"

Your cock thrusting between my thighs was her first thought. His tongue dancing between them was her second choice.

"Either one." Chastity rested her cheek on the palm of her bent arm. The slide of muscles beneath his broad back and the tightening of his ass when he moved made her hand reach out to touch, caress. He turned, and instead of tight buns, her hand brushed across his balls.

He raised a brow, a haughty grin on his face. "I've got an idea." He sat up, crossed his legs Indian-style. In a swift movement that forced a squeal from her lips, he lifted her above him, and settled her on his cock.

She felt his hardness slide deep inside. Felt the heat of him, his fullness, and she sighed, closing her eyes.

Something nudged against her mouth, forcing her heavy lids to rise. A piece of cheese glided between her lips.

"You eat." His hips thrust upwards, plunging further into her channel. "I'll fuck."

Shocked, Chastity nearly choked on the sharp cheese. Quickly, she chewed and then swallowed. He placed her arms around his neck their chests touching skin to skin. "You don't need to do anything but enjoy." The man was true to his word, offering her bites of chicken he held between his teeth, only to tenderly kiss her when their lips met.

And oh, what his body was doing to hers. White-hot spears of desire shot up her pussy. She held him tight. Like dry timber going up in flames, she burned with the need to climax.

"Master, may I come?"

Brows furrowed, he frowned.

Shit, shit, shit, she had made him angry. Then his face softened.

"Tonight I'm Seth, you're Chastity. And yes, baby, I want to feel you explode around me. Feel your body on fire for me."

Chastity needed no more encouragement. She threw back her head and screamed as shards of lightning rippled through her. When Seth's teeth bit down on a nipple, sparks splintered behind her lids, igniting a volley of tremors that shook her to the core.

Emotion welled in her eyes. She loved Seth Allen, would always love him. Beneath her embrace she felt him tense, heard him groan, his cock thrusting into her pussy as he filled her with his seed.

In the aftermath, Chastity held on tight. Tonight she didn't want him to pull away from her, to deny her the warmth of his arms, the comfort of his body. She didn't want the man she had turned him into. Bitter. Vengeful. She wanted the man he had been two years ago.

As his hands peeled her from him, her heart did a nosedive. Crushed, she watched him rise, pivot and walk away. In the shadows he waded into the water, disappearing an inch at a time until he was gone from her sight.

Chastity held her breath, staring helplessly into the depths where he had vanished.

Then Seth's head broke the surface of the water.

She could breathe again.

He shook out his long mane. "Join me, Chastity. The water's great."

Chastity? He'd used Chastity, not *slave*, to beckon her. He'd asked, not demanded. Could it be that their night of passion would continue for a little longer?

She leapt to her feet. Foamy, soft sand slid between her toes as she strolled to the water's edge. She hesitated, unsure of what was expected of her.

He opened his arms, and as if she had wings on her feet she flew into them, splashing all the way. Laughter filled her ears as he embraced her. Then he held her away from him, staring deeply into her eyes.

Hands on her waist, he lifted her. She spread her legs wide. Then with a single thrust his hard, slick cock impaled her pussy. He didn't move, only held her eyes and body locked to his. When he finally spoke, her heart stopped.

"Kiss me, Chastity—" he paused before continuing, "—like you used to." Emotion crept into his voice, need, desire, and a hint of sorrow.

Tears pricked at her lids. The happiness bubbling inside her was bittersweet. Tonight she'd take what he offered, even if tomorrow it vanished, like she had two years ago.

* * * * *

A warm mouth brushed over Seth's. He knew the shape of Chastity's lips. Knew her taste, as her tongue parted his lips and darted inside. Her body was warm atop his, moving seductively. When his arms reached to embrace her, they stopped short.

He tugged in vain, held helplessly immobile.

Had it been a dream? The decadent night spent with Chastity—making love by the waterfall, returning to the privacy of their bungalow to take her twice more before falling asleep in her arms.

From the haze of sleepiness he yanked his hands again, coming fully awake when he realized his wrists and ankles were bound to a bed. He jerked his ankles again. The straps didn't budge.

His breathing and his heart rate were surprisingly calm as he considered his circumstances. Hands tied to the headboard of a bed, his legs were spread wide. The woman he had tormented for two days and nights had moved from atop him and now sat at the foot of the bed watching his reaction.

Surprisingly, his cock seemed to enjoy the bondage as it arched, almost touching his belly button. In fact, he was incredibly turned on. He felt the corners of his lips rise in a faint smile of anticipation.

A twinkle brightened Chastity's eyes, as a playful growl rose from within her. Slowly, she began to move between his thighs like a lissome tigress, on all fours. Through heavy lids, she gazed up at him.

He felt his anger and the wounds of the past dissolve like mist on a windy day. What remained was one man, one woman, and the promise of a glorious morning.

His erection twitched, drawing her attention.

Sitting back on her haunches, she ran her fingernails along the inside of his thighs, goose bumps following in their path. When her head dipped, licking a path up his leg to his scrotum, his balls tightened. She hesitated, staring up at him. The arousal in her eyes pulled him deeper into their depths.

Itchy fingers clenched into fists, unable to weave through the long brunette curls teasing his skin as she moved up and down his body. He sucked in a tight breath, wanting to draw her warm, wet mouth down upon his throbbing cock.

God, how he wanted to watch her head bob as she took him deeper and deeper, filling her, as the head of his shaft touched the back of her throat.

"Chastity," he moaned, his hips rising off the bed.

Light, airy laughter met his frustration.

He looked at her and growled playfully, "You hateful vixen. If I don't feel your lips on my dick this minute I'm going to tear this bed apart."

"Are you?" She leaned closer. He shuddered when she blew a stream of warm air over his sex. Then her tongue caressed the undersides of his balls, making his breath catch.

She pinned him with a glare. "I believe that you are *my* prisoner."

The gleam in her eyes had him wondering for a moment whether his confidence was unjust. This woman had all the reasons in the world to retaliate. But would she?

Long, slender fingers closed around his cock and began to pump up and down his hard erection. In slow, tantalizing movements she brought him to the edge of madness, only to release him, allowing his body to cool before she began the torment again.

It was then that he realized retaliation was just what she had in mind. When her mouth closed around his erection, Seth knew right then and there that Chastity Ambrose was going to kill him with mind-blowing sex.

"Oh, baby, you're killing me." His back arched as he fought back his release. His jaws clenched tight. "I need to taste your wet pussy." His hips squirmed to break the hold her mouth had on him. "Let me go, so y-*youuu…aaagh*, can fuck my face."

Lips parting, she released him, her laughter floating on the air.

She was everything he remembered and more. He knew if he didn't taste her now he'd die a thousand deaths. "Come up here, baby."

Crawling atop him, she slid her nether lips over his erection. In slow, seductive movements she anointed his cock with her juices, using the tilt of her hips to lift and take the head of his crown into her warmth. He thrust, needing to go deeper. She countered by pulling back, so that he delved no further than the entrance of her pussy.

His fingers twisted around his silk bindings, giving him something to hold on to as she did with him what she wished.

Bondage was one of the most erotic things he had ever experienced. Not being able to touch her was driving him friggin' nuts. Not controlling the pace or the path their loving was taking was pushing him closer to the edge of madness.

His body tensed, needing to feel her heat. "Fuck me, baby. I need you now."

Still, Chastity dragged her body against his, across his abdomen, over his chest, until he could smell her arousal, almost taste her essence on his tongue. Her hips suspended above his face, he marveled at her pink lips glistening with heat. She eased down, hovering just out of reach. Just when he thought he'd go crazy, she sat, lightly burying his face in her pussy.

A wave of moisture released as his tongue entered her swollen lips. Hungrily, he sucked the sweet nectar, starving to take all of her into his mouth.

From his position he could see her hands clutching the headboard. It creaked to the gentle sway of her body. Her eyes, closed in an expression of pure ecstasy, filled him with such joy he thought he would burst.

Beneath a smile, he nipped and played with her clit, sending her body into spasms above him. He heard her gasp, felt the weight of her sex pressing into him. Unrelenting, he continued to suck and lick his way through a climax that took him to the brink. Still, he resisted the urges of his body, wanting to feel his cock thrusting in and out of her wet, warm pussy.

Sated, she rose.

He inhaled her scent. It lingered on his moustache and goatee. Carefully, she backed away. And to his surprise, she eased off the bed leaving him fully aroused…and unfulfilled.

In disbelief, he watched her stroll over to the wall where all the erotic torture toys hung. She reached for an eight-thonged whip, the nipple clamps that he had placed on her twice, a blindfold and a wicked-looking knife.

A shiver of apprehension slid up his spine.

She wouldn't dare.

A haughty expression brightened her face as she approached. The whip swayed with the rhythm of her hips, the blade glistening in the light.

"Chastity," he growled in warning, uncertain how far to push a woman with an attitude and a knife.

Despite his uncertainty, he found the experience of the tables being turned, the slave becoming the Master, heady and arousing.

Fingertips grazed along his jawline. Her head dipped to taste his lips in a gentle attack.

His pulse raced as she glided the sleep mask over his eyes, plunging him into darkness.

"Chastity?" Her name was all he could manage when he felt the leather thongs sweep lightly across his chest, his abdomen. When it brushed his cock he held his breath.

Fuck, the woman wouldn't dare. He fought his bindings, fear and excitement warring against one another.

Then the mattress creaked beneath her weight as she climbed onto it. He felt the warmth of her legs straddling his hips, his erection nestled between her thighs.

He startled when cold steel touched his wrist. His fingers curled in a fist awaiting her next move, wondering if she would draw blood.

Darkness intensified every sense…hearing, the sense of touch, the taste of her on his tongue. A multitude of sensations rushed him, bombarding him all at once.

When he heard the ripping of silk, his bindings being cut away, relief, trust and pride swamped him.

A warm breath caressed his neck. Her voice hummed low in his ear. "I want you to touch me when I take your cock into my pussy." Her words left him reeling.

Seth felt his other wrist released, his ankles still bound as the knife tumbled off the bed and hit the floor with a clang. He made no attempt to remove the blindfold. He wanted to feel what Chastity had felt when he had taken her in the dark.

Without the use of her hands, her body took him deep. Heavy breathing mingled with his. A soft moan echoed. Was it his expression of pleasure, or hers?

Featherlight touches were erotic in his lightless world, touches that caressed his body as if seeking to etch it into memory.

He felt cherished. He felt…loved.

"Touch me, Seth." Her plea was breathless.

It was amazing. Even without sight he knew exactly where her breasts were. There was no fumbling to locate them, only the knowledge of her body. But this time it was different. When his fingers closed around them they were firmer, laden with desire, smooth as velvet.

Seth's sense of smell was heightened, too. Her body's perfume teased and caressed him. Her taste lingered on his tongue.

She arched into his palms and panted the words, "*I love when you touch me.*" Surrender was in her tone, in her actions as she leaned forward and pressed her mouth to his. Her lips parted on a sigh, allowing him inside.

Ahhh, sweet and decadent.

"Seth," she whimpered against his mouth, breaking the kiss and pushing upward to brace her palms on his chest. Her movements quickened. She began to ride him hard, fast and urgent.

He grasped her hips, holding their bodies together tightly as they moved in the rhythm of two people joined as one. Light splintered the darkness behind his eyelids. Chastity began to tremble.

They were close, so close.

It was like an explosion. Total surrender as they rocked back and forth, tumbling into the place where ecstasy overpowered the senses and lifted lovers into a trancelike state of bliss.

Raw intimacy. The selfless act of giving ones body and soul.

Seth's cock jerked once, twice, content. Chastity's core rippled around him as the last of her orgasm subsided. He drew her closer. Their descent was effortless as they floated back to earth, sated in each other's arms.

Drifting off to sleep, Chastity nuzzled closer. "Seth…" She inhaled and slowly released a breath. "I love you."

Seth's body lay spooned against Chastity's as the sun peeked through the curtains. A flurry of dust motes danced upon the ray of light as he listened to her shallow breathing. The night had been astonishing. He had taken her in every way imaginable, but this time she had willingly offered herself to his exploration.

As she had drifted off to sleep she had uttered words of love. Words he had strived so hard to hear from her lips.

His plan was coming to fruition.

He could leave her at any moment, confident that the sting of rejection would be there. Last night she had revealed her hand. She cared for him. Somehow he didn't find comfort in the knowledge. He knew he didn't have the strength to let her go, to walk out that door, at least not right now. He needed more time.

Caught in a grip of unnamed emotion, his grasp around her waist tightened.

"Seth?" Her voice was drowsy.

He released her and she rolled to her back, then to her side, pressing her flesh to his. Heavy eyelids rose, revealing dark, aroused eyes.

A stray curl fell between them. He brushed it away, reveling in the touch of her skin, the beauty of her thoroughly fucked smile.

Chastity was a goddess, and she was all his.

Wrapping his arms around her, he pulled her atop him. "What do you want to do today?" He kissed the tip of her nose.

Her jaw dropped. Her palms braced against the bed, stiffening, raising her so that her nipples brushed his chest lightly. "What?" Confusion reigned in her eyes.

He jerked her hands from beneath her, and she yelped and fell against him. "Don't you want to spend the day with me?"

"Yes, b-but what about the game? You know, you Master...me slave." Her words vibrated against his skin.

He laughed and she relaxed, her body melting into his.

In truth, this whole arrangement was beginning to worry Seth. Chastity still had not confided in him. Unless she was a brilliant actress, she cared for him.

Then he remembered that she had confessed her love for him two years ago, even made it to the chapel and down the aisle before she had left him.

Had he done something to drive her away?

Had something else been the catalyst?

And what about Monty and Voyeur II?

The game wasn't over, at least not in their eyes.

* * * * *

Monty Jamison, the game host of the Voyeur II series, moved nervously around the plush room located in the center of the citadel of Ecstasy Island on Zygoman. He tugged at his blue designer jacket, and then flicked a piece of lint off his shoulder.

From the reports he had received, Seth's woman wasn't breaking. The producers of Voyeur II were getting excited. There were only three days left.

By the looks of things, Chastity Ambrose would walk off this planet one hundred million dollars richer.

He had to do something, and fast.

The stream of calls to Monty's office were increasing. His anchorwoman had reported that Seth and Chastity had looked pretty chummy in a secluded area of the planet. Clearly their little love nest wasn't as isolated as they had thought. From the tape Monty reviewed, Seth was making the most of this adventure.

The Master-slave dinner had gone unattended the night before, instead, they'd had one privately in their chambers. The reports of laughter and heavy breathing had brought Monty to see for himself how it was going.

To his regret, the stories were true. He brushed a trembling hand through his hair.

Seth was a friend, but money was money. Monty's job was at stake. Seth was a businessman. He would understand.

When Tor and his brothers entered the room, Monty's nervousness struck a new high. The three barbarians hovered over him, staring at him as if he were an insect about to be squashed.

Tor took his outstretched hand. "Mr. Jamison, what brings you to Zygoman?"

The other two men didn't bother to shake his hand in greeting. Like shadows, they disappeared to the back of the room. Monty turned so that his back faced the wall.

"Miss Ambrose. I hear she's not weakening."

"No, it appears that Mr. Allen and Miss Ambrose have come to a meeting of the minds. They are enjoying each other as they should."

Monty was sure there was a double meaning behind the large man's words, but his own livelihood was at stake.

"Voyeur II wants to raise the heat. What's left in your bag of goodies?"

Tor's brows rose with distaste at Monty's comment.

"The slave auction is tonight. I had scheduled a four-way for the last night. But I suggest that you cancel both of these events. Voyeur II has lost."

Monty took a brave step forward. "Wait a minute. I've paid you for the ultimate, the whole shebang."

"Yes, but the remaining events will not sit easy with Mr. Allen. He has real feelings for this woman. He is not a man to be toyed with."

"You leave Seth to me." Monty moved before the fireplace and gripped the mantel for support. "Now, I want you to push the four-way up for tonight. Hold the slave auction tomorrow."

The scowl on Tor's face sent a shiver up Monty's back. "You want us to rearrange our agenda to accommodate Voyeur II?"

"Yes," Monty's voice squeaked. He cleared his throat gaining back his composure. Money talked louder than words. "Just tell me how much."

What was a few more thousand dollars when one hundred million was at stake?

Tor's brothers moved out of the shadows to his side. The threesome was a formidable sight. Surely Miss Ambrose would crumble when faced with them in a four-way.

And Seth? Well, this would just be a bump in the road. Once it was over it would be over. His friend would understand.

Voyeur II had never had a winner. In all Monty's eight years of hosting the game show, he had ensured the contestant's failure. Chastity was a sure thing, Seth's revenge the catalyst. Yes, it was true the ratings were soaring. A major sports figure on a sex-themed game show was advertising gold. The fiery exchanges between Seth and Chastity were magical on screen. But something was going wrong. Seth's vengeance was cooling, and Chastity was becoming way too submissive for Monty's comfort.

"You'll speak to Mr. Allen?" It was Terrance that spoke. "He must concede to this before we proceed."

Monty moved toward the door, and as he passed through it, said, "Yeah, I said I would."

In the hallway Monty breathed a sigh of relief. Now if he could just make it to the transport without running into Seth, he would be home free. But luck wasn't on his side as he slithered around a corner, running smack-dab into the very person he had hoped to elude.

"Seth!" Their hands clasped in greeting.

"Monty. I've been trying to contact you." The unease in his friend's smile made Seth uncomfortable. "Why haven't you returned my calls?"

"Travel, bro. Hightailed my ass up here to see how things are going." Monty chuckled nervously. "Well? How're things going?"

Seth nodded his head in short multiple jerks. "Good, real good."

Monty crammed his hands into his pockets. "So, why the calls?"

"I want you to cancel anything else planned for Chastity."

Monty jerked his hands out of his pockets, palms outstretched. "Whoa, no can do, buddy. My hands are tied. Unless you can get her to willingly agree to quit, accept the loss."

Something in the man's tone troubled Seth. Whatever it was, it made the skin crawl across his arms.

Seth pinched the bridge of his nose. Something was driving Chastity. She wouldn't willingly concede, especially since she had come so far. He laughed inwardly. She had been run through the wringer. She deserved the money. Still, he wished she would confide in him, let him help her.

"Not a possibility in hell, Monty."

"Remember, anything you do to stop what Ecstasy Island has planned for her will jeopardize her chances for the money. If she truly needs the money, she'll hate you for interfering." A friendly arm snaked around Seth's shoulders. "Be tough, bro. No matter what occurs in the next couple days, you can forget everything that happened here. And then you and Chastity can pick up where you left off two years ago." A hefty pat on the back and Monty continued, "Unless, of course, she's playing you like a fiddle." The man shook his head. "Wouldn't want to see you go through that again."

Monty had voiced what Seth had been struggling with the last few days. He hated that his friend was cultivating the tiny seed of distrust that still lingered.

After they said their goodbyes, Seth wandered around the complex grounds. Chastity awaited him in their bungalow. He had left her behind to call Monty, only to find his friend heading toward the transport. Suspicion crept into his mind. Monty had been leaving, not arriving.

What was Monty up to?

From the corner of his eye, Seth caught a glimpse of Chastity and the dark-haired slave he had heard called Tatiana. Their stealthy movements made him wary. He decided to follow.

Through the halls of the citadel they glided on featherlight feet. Peering around corners, they made their way past one door and then the next until they disappeared into a conference room. Hidden behind a door, Seth watched. Within seconds Tatiana slipped from the room.

Seth moved closer so that he could see inside. Chastity moved nervously around the room. She stretched, long and lean, as if her muscles ached. She had good reason for them to, he thought, recalling their exotic aerobics the night before. She fidgeted with the chairs. Her eyes glanced restlessly toward the door and then to the tele-communicator centered on the large oak table.

No matter what emotion flowed through her body she was beautiful. He breathed in the sight.

When the tele-communicator rang Chastity lunged for the phone. Tears welled and streamed down her cheeks as she listened and spoke to the unknown caller.

Seth held his hand over the motion detector, allowing the door to slide open an inch at a time until he could hear what was being said.

"I know—I know, I love you, too. We're almost there. I'll have the money in three days."

Her words and the passion behind them hit Seth like a sledgehammer. Stunned disbelief and savage pain warred within him. He should have kept his heart locked up tight. His need for revenge, to understand *why* she'd left, moved him beyond obsession.

Man, the biggest mistake he'd ever made was letting her walk out that door two years ago without explaining why.

Or was it when he'd let her walk back into his life?

Chapter Eleven

Chastity was bursting with happiness as she slipped from the complex. The sky seemed bluer, the sun brighter, as she made her way back to the bungalow. Her mother was well. The money was within Chastity's reach. And Seth was hers once again.

Thankfully, Seth had just left to contact a friend when Tatiana had arrived. She had placed the call to Chastity's mother, directing it to a tele-communicator in a conference room that allowed such inter-planet calls.

Chastity had barely made it back before Seth entered the room.

He walked straight up to her and commanded, "Kneel."

She drifted to her knees, willing to play the game. But there was something different in his eyes when he looked at her. A vein ticked in his neck. His teeth were clenched, occasionally sawing back and forth.

"You're here for my pleasure, wench," he murmured. His hand trembled as he grabbed her hair and pulled back on it until she was staring up at him. "*My* pleasure," he repeated, pushing her from him. "Now get onto the bed and spread your legs."

Chastity scrambled to her feet. As she undressed, her pussy roared to life. The dampness between her legs renewed. God, she wanted this man.

But something was wrong. She sensed it in the grate of his voice, the edginess of his movements.

Naked, she slid under the covers, the cool, crisp sheets rasping against her heated skin. Her body ached to feel his cock buried within her. Her nipples tingled with anticipation.

He yanked back the bedding, tearing it from its corners and tossing it to the floor.

She smiled. He wanted it rough. Quickly, she inched her legs further apart.

"More." His hands capture her thighs and drew her open wide. A burning pain raced up her leg from the awkward position. For a moment he stared quietly. Then he released a growl from somewhere deep in his throat. His body covered hers.

Chastity felt the head of his erection part her pussy and then he thrust his hips, burying deep inside her. She moaned her satisfaction.

But it wasn't the gentle loving, or the rough play, she had anticipated. His body pounded hers as if he sought to punish her with his cock. Cruel fingers dug into her thighs as he spread her wider, beyond the limits of her muscles. His groans were guttural as he plunged deeper, harder.

His climax came fast and hard. He threw back his head and roared like a wounded animal. The sound was gut-wrenching, as if it tore from his very soul.

He was hurting.

Sometime between this morning and this moment something had happen. Chastity had no doubt that it involved her. His need to punish her was obvious.

Little by little, the barrier between them went up again, one brick at a time.

Seth lay silently atop her. His breathing ragged, heartbeat rapid. She wanted to hold him. Explain to him why she had left him, but fear of rejection, fear of alienating him, kept her from speaking.

"Seth," she whispered.

He rose, took one look at her and climbed off the mattress. "Get dressed. You're going home."

Chastity scrambled from the bed. Caught in the sheets she tripped, her knees hitting the floor as she struggled to reach him. "No, Seth. Please, I can't."

He turned toward her, his eyes shadowed and empty. "After today I don't want to ever see you again." The cold words hit her like a right to the cheek. She could almost hear the crack of bones, or was that the breaking of her heart?

Tears welled. "Seth, you can't mean it. Please...tell me you don't mean it."

A statue of indifference, he glared at her. "I do."

"Then please let me finish the game. I'll disappear out of your life and never return." She fell to her knees, her world crashing down around her. "Do to me whatever you wish. But please, please, don't ruin this for me. I *need* the money." Her sobs were humiliating, but she couldn't hold them back.

One moment she'd had everything, the next, nothing. How could things change so quickly?

This time she wouldn't just let him go. In a last ditch plea she cried, "Seth, tell me what changed. I thought that we... I-I love you."

Without a single word, he walked to the door, slid it open and was gone.

An hour passed. A knock at the door brought Chastity to her feet. "Seth!" But instead Passion Flower entered.

She bowed. "Slave Chastity, your presence is requested at the Temple of Worship."

Numb, she couldn't comprehend the woman's request. "What?"

She pressed a long, white toga in Chastity's hands. "You will dress in the gown of innocence and follow me." When Chastity made no effort to dress, the woman said, "Quickly, you mustn't keep them waiting."

"Them?"

"Your Master and the others."

Knowing that Seth would be there, that she would have another opportunity to talk to him, Chastity snatched the robe from the woman's hands.

Dressed and walking at a steady pace, Chastity followed Passion Flower through the gardens, past the citadel and into an area that she had never been to before.

A mountain of lush green rose majestically against an aquamarine sky. Glistening water sprung from multiple crevices to cascade into a surrounding moat. The imposing channel gave the illusion that it guarded secrets and hidden treasures within.

A swing bridge stretching across its width swayed with the light breeze. Crawling ivy intertwined with the rope handrails. A cobblestone walkway zigzagged up the steep face of the mountain and then vanished, as if it simply disappeared into the precipice.

The vista held an enchanting charm, a natural, almost spiritual feeling of vitality, of life.

Chastity took one look at the shifting overpass, the churning water, and hesitated.

"Hold tight to the handrails," Passion Flower instructed as she stepped upon the wooden walkway.

Chastity dared to place one foot upon the gently swaying bridge, quickly withdrawing. "Surely there's another way? Maybe a transport that can beam us up to the top?" she asked.

The dark-haired woman glanced over her shoulder. "The ruggedness gives it a natural quality, does it not?" She slid across the bridge like it was nothing.

"Natural is not the word I'd use… Maybe unsafe, perhaps treacherous." Chastity frowned and took a step, and then another. "Where are we going?"

"All will be known in good time. Now we must make haste."

It was slow going, but Chastity finally made it across the bridge. Seeing Seth was her motivation. Although she wondered if, after today, she'd ever see him again. Was he, as well as the money, lost to her?

Passion Flower pushed open a rugged oak door hidden behind layers and layers of ivy. No way would Chastity have found this entrance, if not for her guide.

A floor of gold and silver led the way. The hall was illuminated by sparkling gems, diamonds, rubies, sapphires and emeralds. The colors ricocheted off the walls, a kaleidoscope, forming rainbows everywhere she looked.

In awe, Chastity stared at her surroundings. "What is this place?"

"A temple of worship."

Chastity ran a hand along the cool wall. Then she stopped. How could she have forgotten about the night's scheduled activity? "Is this where the slave auction is to be held?"

"No, it has been rescheduled for tomorrow night."

The woman evasiveness made Chastity's brows dip. "Then what are you worshiping?"

Passion Flower stopped. "Today, *you* are to be worshipped." Then she picked up the pace, continuing on.

Passion Flower opened a door that seemed carved right into the stone and ushered Chastity in. Halfway into the room she became aware of the unnatural quiet. Slowly, she turned.

From behind a partition, Tor, Terrance and Shawn appeared. All three men were naked. Their erect cocks were rock-hard and growing larger by the minute. A sight to behold, if she didn't hold so much animosity toward them.

But all she could think about was Seth.

From behind the barrier, he appeared. If ever eyes were as cold as ice, his were. Empty of emotion, he stared through her as if she didn't exist. Quietly, he took a place inside an alcove that was designed as a sitting room with several chairs, a couch for lounging and a coffee table.

Tor approached her. "Chastity, do you want to suck my cock?"

"Huh?" Surely she'd heard the man wrong. She pivoted on the balls of her feet and stared in disbelief at Tor, and then glanced at Seth.

Seth turned away, closing himself off from her.

Chastity's heart plummeted.

Tor grasped her by the arm. "For your hesitation, you have earned a punishment."

Bewildered, she looked at the hand restraining her. Slowly her gaze moved from the hand, up the arm, to the face of her captor. "Punishment?" Chastity could hear the confusion in her tone.

"Have you not been instructed not to speak unless requested?" Tor didn't wait for her response. "You have earned a second punishment." He waved to the two men that followed him around like shadows.

Each of Tor's brothers took one of her arms and led her to a glacier formation with golden ivy growing out of deep fissures. Delicate purple flowers with red pollen-bearing stamens unfolding around a bright yellow pistil were scattered throughout the tawny leaves.

The iridescent crystal glimmered, creating an array of colors similar to the aurora borealis. In fact, the entire room was a luminous phenomenon. The air, water and land was alive with atomic particles striking and exciting atoms, to create an almost fairytale effect—as if fireworks continued to explode throughout the atmosphere.

"Disrobe," Tor commanded.

And wouldn't you know it, Chastity earned herself another punishment for not responding quickly enough to the beast's liking.

"For your three punishments I wish for you to suck Shawn's cock while Terrance fucks your ass, and I your pussy. Do you remember your safe word?"

Ohmygod! Somehow Chastity had fallen into an erotic version of Goldilocks and the Three Bears—er, Barbarians.

Afraid of Tor's retribution, and the fact that her infractions seem to be skyrocketing by the minute, she swiftly nodded.

Surely, Seth would not allow this violation. She looked at him, expecting to see outrage. Instead, his eyes were dark, hollow shells. Desperately, she held on to a thread of hope that Seth cared about her enough to stop this travesty.

Tor approached. "Do you agree to your punishment?"

A pregnant moment passed, and when Seth made no attempts to intervene, Chastity surrendered to her fate. As Seth had said previously, it was a just a game.

Yielding, she nodded.

If he didn't care what happened to her, why should she? The sooner this was over the sooner she could leave...and she was ready to leave now.

On Tor's command, Terrance took a seat on a protruding ledge. An icy blue glow created by the heat of his body radiated from beneath him. Florescent blue veins of color shot out from beneath him, arcing through the rock like lightning. Reaching behind him, he produced a mother-of-pearl shell and used its contents to lubricate his erection. Chastity watched the slow rise and fall of his hand. The motion made the man's cock lengthen even more.

And that thing's going up my ass!

Okay, she'd take this like a man, so to speak. As if any of the men in this room would willingly agree to insert that huge thing up his puckered anus.

Assholes...all of them!

With a wave of Tor's hand, Shawn began to climb the ice-like steps. Each footstep produced a similar effect as those created by Terrance's buttocks, but with a different colorimetric quality. His first step produced a red vein that zinged from his heat. The second, green, and finally yellow, as he stopped, his backside facing her.

When two strong arms whisked her off her feet Chastity couldn't restrain her squeal of surprise.

As she was cradled in Tor's strong arms, he spoke, "Terrance will slip his cock into your ass, Chastity. You are not to take Shawn into your mouth until after I have entered your pussy." She felt a finger probe her entrance as he whispered in her ear. "I want to hear your moans of pleasure as I fill you."

The man was stark-raving mad if he thought she would gain pleasure from this—this meaningless act.

No, this was her fault. She had agreed to endure anything that didn't physically harm her. In truth, she could end all of this with a single word. *Red*. Seth had given it to her on the first day.

Then Tor smiled. "One other thing, you are not to come until I give you permission."

Oh, like that was even a possibility. God, she wanted to smack the arrogant man.

Next thing she knew Terrance's large hands held her hips and slowly he entered her, inch by inch, gently…gradually…until he was buried deep in her ass.

She gasped and felt her eyes widen in disbelief.

Chastity was attempting to catch her breath when Tor moved between her thighs. With his hand he guided his cock to her pussy. Playfully, he rubbed the head of his erection along her folds. "Release your fluids, Chastity. Welcome me."

Never! She was horrified as her traitorous body did as he commanded.

He smiled. "I am pleased with you." Then he entered her.

Chastity cried out at the sensation of being stretched and filled beyond limits she thought humanly possible. And by two men she'd rather see hung by their balls than deep inside her.

Firmly, Tor lifted her chin. "Remember, Chastity, do not come until I give you permission." Slowly his hips began to pump. Terrance matched his rhythm.

Tor motioned with his hand. "Shawn."

Carefully Shawn straddled the ledge, wedging himself between Tor and Chastity. His dark, aroused gaze met hers as the head of his cock touched her lips. She couldn't think, and she couldn't seem to turn away.

Slowly, he slid his hands into her hair, nudging her closer, her lips open. She felt him tremble when her mouth closed around him.

"Watch me as I fuck your beautiful mouth," Shawn ground out through clenched teeth.

And she did. Every taut breath he struggled to inhale, and the pleasure-pain expression upon his face.

"You will drink from me." His voice was a throaty growl.

It was unlike anything she could have imagined. Three men fucking her at once? Her mind fought the erotic sensations that her body welcomed. Terrance sliding in and out of her ass, Tor fucking her pussy and Shawn's cock filling her mouth. She almost forgot the fourth man watching from the shadows.

Was Seth hot? Did he enjoy seeing three men fuck her?

The pace quickened.

Faster.

Harder.

Three firm cocks thrusting in and out her body, filling her with such intensity, driving her so close to orgasm that she wanted to scream.

Could she hold out? Who would reach fulfillment first? And what would be her punishment if she failed?

A rich musk of sex and sweat perfumed the air. The heady scent of testosterone and her pussy juices was an aphrodisiac to her senses. She felt as if she was standing on a cliff, begging to be thrown off. As her body began to tremble, Chastity cried out around Shawn's cock.

A rush of fire swept through her body and mind. It was all too much. She willed herself to gain control. Fought to go to that place where nothing existed.

It was Shawn's deep guttural groan that saved her and pulled her back from the edge. So violent was his release that he jerked her head back, slamming against her mouth, spilling his seed down her throat. She had to concentrate simply to breathe, to swallow.

Before drinking the last of his semen she felt Terrance's cock contract, his fingers digging into her hips.

"Now, Chastity," Tor shouted. "Come with us now."

Terrance grasped her nipples, clamping down hard.

Lightning bolts exploded in her head. Her body vibrated with the impact of three mind-blowing orgasms igniting at once. Sandwiched between two growling lions, she screamed as a blaze of fire burned through her.

Writhing, she fought to stop the convulsions. She could feel their fingertips, their skin rasping against hers. A sensitivity so intense it pushed her past pleasure into pain.

What was her fucking safe word?

"*Stop*!" she cried. "No more."

Immediately, her body was abandoned. Consciousness wavered. Strong arms embraced her, pressing her against a wall of tense muscle that shook with emotion. Next she was passed to another man. He trembled so badly she thought he'd break into a million pieces.

Then she felt herself float across the room, coming to rest on a cloud—or was it a bed? Did it matter?

A whiff of specter-dust appeared beneath her nose. She coughed as the sleep-inducing drug filtered through her nasal passages and began to take hold. A blanket of darkness was pulled over her as she slipped off into the night.

* * * * *

Seth's heart pulled tight in his chest, making it difficult to breathe. Watching the expression on her face when Terrance slid into her ass had him on his feet and moving, only to plow into an invisible force that had him falling back on his heels. He took another run and flung himself toward the group, bouncing off the invisible barrier with a *thud* as soon as he hit.

The sons of bitches had locked him into the alcove using a force field.

Desperately, he pounded on the barrier, shouting every threat he could think of in the process. He'd friggin' tear the place apart, if he only knew how.

One thing was for certain, when he got out of this damn prison Monty was a dead man.

They were *all* dead.

Blood boiling, he watched Chastity through a red haze. His world shifted around him. The very ground seemed to tilt, and then spin. She *needed* him and he had fed her to the wolves.

Control. He needed to find the place within that helped him through difficult situations.

Difficult? That was an understatement. This was a catastrophe.

He should never have left Chastity alone. They should have discussed what he had overheard earlier today. If he had only insisted two years ago that she explain herself, none of this would be happening now.

Palms against the invisible glass, Seth took a deep, calming breath, knowing he was on the verge of losing it. He forced his heart to slow to normal.

Chastity's face was lightly flushed, a sheen of sweat beading on her forehead. Her breath came in soft pants as Tor approached her. Then she was gone from Seth's sight, enveloped between the men that he swore would never touch her again.

Animalistic mating sounds, grunts and moans, floated into the air. Hers? Theirs? It was agony not knowing how Chastity was reacting. All he could see was the tense asses of Tor and Shawn as they pumped their cocks into his woman.

Through a sticky web of anger his own dick hardened. He wanted to be the only man between Chastity's ivory thighs, the only one exploring the treasures they hid. To be the only man to taste her hot pussy on his lips, his tongue. And the only man to make her scream in ecstasy as her body shattered beneath him.

Her cry of distress almost ripped his heart from his chest. Immediately the men stepped back from Chastity, gave her room to breathe.

The wall restraining Seth disintegrated and he rushed to her side. Terrance gently held her trembling body. Beside him, his brothers stood guard, their stances tense, ready for Seth.

"Your woman has not been harmed. She only needs to breathe." Tor raised his hand, restraining Shawn as Seth stepped forward.

Seth couldn't remember when he had felt so close to murder. He wanted to smash their faces in, tear them from limb to limb. His shaky hands itched to retaliate, but revenge would have to wait. Chastity was his main concern.

A growl surfaced as he tore Chastity out of Terrance's arms and pressed her possessively to his chest. The warmth of her skin was reassuring. He checked her pulse, her breathing. When he was satisfied that she was okay, he simply held her.

God, he loved this woman. But this time his realization didn't conjure the animosity it had before. It was time to face his emotions and deal with them.

Seth gazed down on her ashen face, her dark lashes resting on her flushed cheekbones. He kissed her brow. She was his, and he would do whatever it took to ensure it. After tonight, no man would ever touch her again.

A gentle tap on his shoulder had Seth spinning on his heels, ready to rip whoever it was a brand-new asshole. When he saw that it was Passion Flower he tried to relax, but he was strung tighter than an aerolite-bow. Even her peaked, naked breasts had no effect on him.

"Master Seth, a bed has been prepared for your slave in the adjoining quarters." She waved a hand. "Please follow me."

It was an atrium. Several varieties of palms—sago, queen and Mexican—were scattered among a verdant floor of grass, moss and ivy. Flowers of every shape, size and fragrance added to the aura of paradise as Seth lay Chastity upon a billowy cushion of white satin that blended in with the scenery. It was as if God had dropped a little slice of heaven on Zygoman.

From a rock table next to the futon, Passion Flower retrieved a petite bottle that seemed to glow with an inner light. She extracted the stopper and gently swept it beneath Chastity's nose. The woman upon the bed squirmed, her hand swiping through the air, fighting off the smell as if a fine powder tickled her nose.

Seth growled, his protective side bursting through. "What is that?"

Passion Flower's calm appearance made Seth uneasy. No one would even think of approaching him when he was this angry. However, she simply smiled and settled a small hand on his arm.

"Specter-dust, a sleeping aid, it will help her to relax. Would you like for me to bathe her?"

It was only then that he noticed Chastity reeked of sex. The smell of another man, several men, made his stomach churn. He wanted every trace of what had happened purged from her body—inside and out. If only he could purge it from his memory.

"Yes." He looked about for the men that had defiled her. "Where is your husband?"

Passion Flower dipped a cloth into a basin and gently began to cleanse Chastity. "Revenge is not what this woman would want."

"How do you know what she wants?" Seth snapped. The woman dared to condone what her husband and his brothers had done, and then tried to use Chastity's virtue in an attempt to save them from his wrath?

"Is it not the game both of you agreed to? Did you not know the terms of agreement with Ecstasy Island?" She looked up from her ministrations. "My husband and his brothers have fulfilled their bargain." She resumed bathing Chastity.

The last thing Seth needed was legalese thrown in his face. Yes, he knew the terms. And yes, he knew what this "four-way" *thing* entailed. He hadn't like the sounds of it then, and he sure as hell didn't like it now. Besides, hadn't the slave auction been slotted for tonight?

Passion Flower calmly faced him. "Master Seth, help her see this through to the end. Her reasons are honorable."

Stunned, Seth grabbed the woman by the shoulders. "You know why she's here?"

"I know many things. The walls have ears." Passion Flower shrugged out of his grip. "You two were meant for each other. And it will be so."

Great, all he needed was a walking fortune cookie sprouting off predictions. "Why is she here?"

"It is not for me to say. But know what has happened here today has been a celebration. Three powerful men have worshipped your woman and—"

"They used her." Like a bitter acid, Seth's rage surged anew through his veins. Fists clenched, his pulse and breathing in a race to see which one would fail first.

Replacing the stopper in the specter-dust bottle, she nodded her head knowingly. "*Aaah*, then you do not understand the ways of Zygoman and her men." With sedate hands she waved a path in front of herself. "Look around you. This is a place of reverence, of peace and serenity. Have you not wondered why this event took place here and not in the gardens or dungeons of the citadel?" A shadow passed before her eyes. "Do you not see the respect these men have for women? Do you not see that they honored her body through theirs?"

She gazed down at Chastity and then back at Seth. Envy brightened the Asian woman's eyes. "No man could take her body without touching the beauty of her soul. What you witnessed was not an act of the flesh, but a rebirth of life, an internal passion released from one spirit to another. Your woman lit each man's inner candle." A single tear fell. "Did you not see the glow, the harmony between them?"

The cool composure Passion Flower wore began to crack. She swallowed hard, her voice cracked. "*That* is why Tor will never join with her again." Without another word she turned and walked away.

Speechless, all he could do was blindly stare at the archway the woman passed through. Her insight had touched him like no other. He searched back, bringing the men's faces to the forefront. Yes, tranquility would describe their expressions.

Seth pivoted and looked at the sleeping woman before him. She was beauty and virtue incarnate. Why had he not seen it? Why had it taken another man—no, make that three—to open his eyes?

There was more, so much more, about Chastity that he wanted—needed—to know. If the detective he was to meet with tomorrow didn't have the answers, then Seth would drag it out of Chastity, one revelation at a time. She wouldn't escape him this time, not without revealing the truth.

"Master Seth." When Seth turned, he saw Tatiana in the doorway. The woman appeared hesitant to enter. "I have been asked to sit with Chastity."

Suspicion came alive within him. "Why?"

The petite woman bowed her head clasping her hands in front of her. "Chastity is my friend. And a call awaits you in the citadel."

Could it be the call he'd been waiting for? Reluctant to leave Chastity, but anxious to speak with Zac Lawrence, his detective, he waved the woman into the room. "You will allow no other to enter."

Tatiana gazed down on Chastity. A smile slid across her face as she brushed a lock of hair behind Chastity's ear. "If it is your wish."

"No one," he reiterated firmly.

Big brown eyes met his. "No one, Master Seth."

"If she wakes, you will escort her to our bungalow."

She nodded. "Yes, Master Seth."

Even with the woman's promise, Seth felt a sliver of unease crawl beneath his skin. As he exited the room he took care to look around for another presence. The room where the iridescent crystal glowed was empty. The hallway was empty. There were no signs of the Vikings lurking about.

Good.

If it was the last thing he ever did, he was going to find out Chastity's secrets. And win her back, if she would have him.

Chapter Twelve

The warmth of the afternoon flooded over Chastity as she sat by the pond. She hugged her knees and gazed at the tranquil scenery. The sky was a clear aquamarine. The smell of flowers and grass and water filled the air. She tilted her head back, in order to feel the light and heat on her face. For a moment she was at peace, refusing to let the previous night's events dim the beauty of the day.

But try as she might, yesterday kept rolling through her head. Seth had threatened to send her home. He was mad, but for what reason, she had no idea. Then she had been fucked by three men while Seth looked on.

Talk about a full day.

It had been an erotic experience. Pain and pleasure blurring the lines where one ended and the other began.

Her body ached, but pleasantly. It was hard to explain and even harder to understand. She should've been repulsed when Terrance slipped his cock into her ass, instead, the intrusion had excited her. The arrogant asshole…

Chastity chuckled, thinking it ironic that she referred to him by the same location on her body he chose to enter. Surprisingly, he had been gentle, even tender. Almost as if he'd morphed into another man, one unlike the domineering beast that had spent the last couple of days making her life a living hell.

Still, the warmth in Shawn's eyes, the sensuality in his voice flowing over her skin as she took him into her mouth was…

Well, there were no words, at least none she could come up with at the moment.

When Chastity had risen from her slumber in the Temple of Worship, her first thoughts had been of Seth. Tatiana had informed her that business had called him away. He had left on a transport early this morning.

A niggling of apprehension tugged on her heart. What if he didn't return?

What if she never got the chance to express how sorry she was? More importantly, how much she loved him.

And what would happen to the money, her mother? Would all be lost?

Emotion bubbled up, warring inside her. She placed a palm against her mouth holding back the despair that began to surface. Just then a couple entered the garden. Desperately, she blinked back unshed tears.

They were the same ardent pair she had seen on the first day she arrived. Their playful interaction, the love emanating off of them, their laughter as they reveled in each other, made Chastity burst into tears.

What a fool. Seth would never love her like that again. She had sealed her fate two years ago. He might take her body, but he would never trust or love her again.

She swiped at the rebellious tears. What did she expect? She had lied and betrayed him.

Chastity saw Shawn enter the garden. Her shoulders drooped, her head shaking side to side. She just didn't need this right now. A nervous twitch developed in one eye as she thought about last night's encounter. She had no doubt that running into any of the Thorenson brothers, not to mention Seth, would be awkward at best.

Determined steps headed in her direction. Her heart leaped into her throat. Unsure how to react, she began to rise.

Shawn held out a palm. "Please, don't get up." Like an imposing oak tree, he stood quiet for longer than was comfortable. He simply stared at her, as though trapped deep in thought.

When he spoke it was almost a whisper. "I only wish to thank you for last night."

Confused, Chastity could do no more than gawk at the man. "Thank me?"

His feet shuffled. An almost boyish expression graced his masculine features.

Well, I'll be damned! The man was nothing but a big teddy bear.

On the outside he was confidence personified. Yet Chastity could now see the air of shyness he hid behind the firm mask.

"You are a beautiful person. I desire only to thank you for sharing yourself with me."

Well, Chastity guessed that was one way of putting it. She wanted to hate this man and his brothers. Still, it was hard to be angry after such an eloquent expression of gratitude. She felt the heat of a blush fan across her cheeks.

He knelt and gently cupped her face in his palms. "You mustn't be embarrassed or ashamed of what transpired. You must celebrate the sensual experience, the giving of one to another." Abruptly, he released her.

It was amazing, the quiet giant that hadn't spoken more than a handful of words all week was now talking to her as if they were friends. As if they shared…an intimacy.

Whoa. After last night they did share a certain intimacy. Between him and his brothers, they had touched every place on her body, inside and out. She had tasted this man's essence. How much closer could you get?

There was something pleasant about Shawn's persona today that encouraged her to speak. "I don't know what to feel. I don't understand my feelings."

Soft, knowing laughter spilled from Shawn's full lips. "*Chastity*."

A shockwave filtered through her. He'd called her by name, not *slave*, not *slave Chastity*, but Chastity. And he was talking to her as if they were equals, not Master and slave.

Shawn took a seat beside her. "If we don't know the faces of good and evil, how are we to recognize them?"

Good...evil? *What the hell was the man talking about?* Bottom line, she just didn't know whether to feel dirty after last night's episode, or to stash it away into a closet as something out of her wildest dreams.

And what did Seth think? How would he feel about her now?

Shawn must've read the confusion she felt in her heart as he continued to explain, "Moral...immoral. Each of us wants to believe that we are good, while in the dark recesses of our minds we hunger for a taste of the bad. The dark side gives us strength, allows us to recognize the difference." He cocked his head, looking at her as if he sought confirmation that she understood, before he continued, "Fantasies are located in the dark side of our minds. Like day and night, one side is not whole without the other."

He slithered onto his side, lying eye-to-eye with Chastity. She knew it was an intentional move to put them on an equal level.

"To venture into the shadows where the seat of your power resides can be a scary thing. With the right partner your dark side can blossom into a beautiful garden of erotic fantasies—" he paused, "—just waiting to be picked and cherished."

Chastity laughed, truly laughed, for the first time since she arrived on Zygoman. His words were liberating. "Shawn." She tried out the newfound friendship, voicing his name without placing Master before it. "You make it sound, well, wonderful."

The wind blew an errant curl into her eyes. Gently, he brushed it away. "It is. You must find the beauty in everything and treasure it." He reached over and squeezed her hand. "Tonight is the slave auction. I wish to bid for your favors, if you are not opposed. In my bed you will be treated as a queen, never a slave."

Whoa! This was not what Chastity had expected. One part of her refused to lead Shawn on, while the other part of her brain remembered Dawson's threat. She shivered at the thought of the despicable man, or someone like him, touching her.

"Is it a given that I must participate?" The disappointment in his eyes was instantaneous.

"If you are to thwart Voyeur II, it is."

She forced a smile, "Then I would be honored and pleased to share the evening with you."

Shawn's features softened. She had seen that dreamy expression on other men's faces, including Josh, Seth's cousin. But like the others, Shawn was a handsome man, but he wasn't Seth.

As Shawn began to rise, she placed a hand over his. "You mustn't bid beyond your means." Dawson was a rich man. He meant to have her. As much as she detested the thought of a night with the cruel man, she didn't want Shawn to beggar himself.

He laughed, stood, and beamed down at her. "A night *alone* with you would be worth all the riches in the universe."

His words left her stunned, feeling beautiful and sad at the same time. As he walked away, she rose. How was she going to make it through the night, through the next couple of days?

Staring into the depths of the pool, a shiver raced up her spine. She turned to find Dawson beating a path toward her. She twisted her head, praying that Shawn was still in sight, that he would handle what she knew would be a distasteful encounter.

Stopping before her, Dawson slowly twisted the ring on his finger. He stood for a moment in silence, animosity dripping from his body. She half expected to see smoke rising from the fire in his eyes.

He leaned forward with a snarl and murmured, "Tonight, you're mine."

Chastity's knees almost buckled at the menacing tone of his voice. Her heart pounded against her chest. When a single fingertip slid down her bare arm, fear took shape and crawled across her skin. Her stomach pitched.

It would serve the man right if she spewed her lunch all over his designer shoes. Then again, paybacks could be a bitch, and there was already enough hostility between them.

Without another word he turned to leave. As she watched him disappear around a corner, Chastity wondered if Voyeur II would win after all.

* * * * *

One screen after another flickered in front of Seth's eyes. An older version of Chastity flashed on the screen. Quickly, he scanned the article beneath the picture. His jaw dropped open.

He couldn't believe what he read, what he saw. It was all there—another piece of the puzzle.

Chastity's mother was alive.

"She was exonerated?" Seth asked in disbelief, remembering Chastity's plea to contact her mom the day of the game show. He had called her a liar. Guilt tugged at him, weighing him down in his chair.

And what about the call she'd made from Ecstasy Island's conference room? Had she spoken to her mother or to a lover?

If it had been her mother, then all the signals Chastity was sending him were real. She'd even said she loved him. The revelation was an instant aphrodisiac.

His cock hardened. His need to hold her, to slip between her thighs and thrust into her wet core intensified with every tight breath he inhaled.

When he got back to Zygoman he was taking Chastity to bed and keeping her there until he made up for the two years he lost. There would be no doubt in her mind how he felt about her.

The beefy detective slid his feet off the desk. The thump brought Seth's attention back to the man in the room. Zac leaned forward, resting his elbows on his knees.

"Yes, only three months after she was incarcerated. It was self-defense. The man attacked her." He sat up and leaned back in his chair. "She was pretty messed up. It took a little time to get the facts straight."

Seth pushed a button and the screen went black. "Why hasn't she been released?"

Chunky fingers threaded through Zac's graying, brown hair. "That's the mystery. I've sent a retainer to the moon to investigate. Appears the lady might have pissed off someone with a little money. At least that's my guess."

Seth stood. "All this time, someone has been paying to block her release?"

The man across from Seth slowly nodded.

The palm of Seth's hand landed hard against his head. It all made sense now. Chastity needed money for the release of her mother.

Okay, so that piece of the mystery was solved.

Still, he had to wonder. Why had Chastity walked out on him two years ago, and what did this have to do with his cousin?

"Did you get anything more on Josh and Chastity?"

A crooked smile flashed across Zac's face. "As we speak, an associate of mine is at his house."

And where would Josh be while all this was taking place? Seth was sure his cousin wouldn't simply open his door, invite the investigator in, and then spill his guts.

"Where's Josh?"

"Out of town. Lucky break, he took a transport from Earth last night. Neighbors said he's on vacation, left his pooch with the old lady that lives next to him."

Although Zac Lawrence had discovered the whereabouts of Chastity's mother, Seth still didn't know how much to trust him. Seth needed more information and he needed it now.

"What do you hope to find?"

"Anything. Nothing. You never know." Zac pulled a toothpick out of his pocket, stuck it between his lips and began to chew. "Can't leave any stone unturned." He shifted his burly body in the chair. "Seems to reason that your cousin and Miss Ambrose are connected, if not intimately—" he pinched the bridge of his bulbous nose before he gazed back at Seth, " — perhaps their relationship has something to do with her mother."

Even the little ounce of hope the detective offered, that no affair existed between Chastity and Josh, made Seth feel better. But why hadn't Chastity told him about her mother? And why had she walked out on him without a single explanation?

Seth glanced at his watch, it glowed five o'clock. Three hours before the slave auction began. He had to stop Chastity from going through with it. The transport from Baccarac to Zygoman left in fifteen minutes. It took approximately two and half hours to travel from one planet to the other. He'd make it if he hurried.

"I've got to go." Seth raced for the door. "Call me as soon as you find out anything."

"You b—"

But the man's words were cut off as the door slid shut. Heart racing, Seth's feet pounded down the hall. Fortunately, he had met with Zac Lawrence in a conference room at the Transport Station. The loading platform was just around the corner.

Seth was pissed that he'd had to leave Zygoman, instead of Zac coming to him. But they both agreed that a central meeting place was for the best.

With a leap, Seth jumped aboard the conveyor. He barely took a seat in the lounge before the transport shifted into gear and lifted off.

The first beer went down with difficulty. His nerves were stretched tighter than the membrane on a drum. The second brewskie slid down easily as he began to relax. Seth wanted desperately to believe that Chastity loved him. Just the thought made his cock harden. He leaned back in his chair, closed his eyes, and released the pent-up breath in his lungs.

God, her long legs, lithe body, succulent breasts, and oh, the treasures that lay between her thighs.

His erection jerked. He cupped a hand over it in an effort to quiet the wild thing, succeeding only in dredging up memories of Chastity's hands caressing, her hot wet mouth licking and sucking, taking him deep between her cherry-ripe lips. His hips thrust and a breath caught in his throat.

His eyes popped open. "Ah, shit." The damn place was crawling with people and here he was seconds away from jacking off.

Seth squeezed his legs together and inhaled deeply, but it didn't help much. Because he knew once Chastity was in his arms again he would strip her naked, slowly, removing each article of clothing one piece at a time. He would speak of love with his eyes, his hands and his body. There would be no doubt in her mind after he branded her, drove his cock deep into her pussy, that she was his and his forever.

His erection stood at full-mast.

"Fuck." He leaped to his feet and began to pace. This was going to be the longest two and a half hours of his life.

A sonic boom exploded around him. The carrier bounced and Seth almost lost his footing as he grappled to stay upright. A couple of women began to scream, their husbands attempting to calm them. A small child, maybe two, was crying as his fearful mother gently soothed him.

Chaos reigned until a teleporter entered. The tall, lanky man cleared his throat, a small sign of his own unease with the situation. "We have run into a meteor shower. It's nothing to be concerned about. Please remain seated. If you need to move about the cabin, please be careful."

Meteor shower? That was all Seth needed. He took a seat next to a window and peered out. Flying sparks and fragments pelted the transport. The banging against the hull was unnerving. At least he didn't smell smoke or anything burning, and they *were* still in the air.

A yank on his sleeve brought Seth about. A small boy stared at him. "Are we going to die, mister?"

Seth scanned the room for a mother or father who might be looking for their son. Everyone seemed involved with someone else. It appeared the child was alone. Moisture glistened in the little boy's eyes, tugging at Seth's heart.

He patted his thigh and the kid smiled, crawling into his lap. Seth brushed his hand soothingly over the child's head. "Not today, little man. I've got something important to do."

A man next to them grinned. "Hey, aren't you—" he shook a long finger, "—uh...Seth Allen?" He snapped his fingers. "Yeah, you're Seth Allen." He slapped his knee, shaking his head as if he couldn't believe his luck. "Kid, do you know you're sitting on the lap of the 2104 Astral-ball Champion? Maybe even the greatest Astral-ball guard in the universe."

The boy beamed up at Seth. "Really?"

Seth nodded.

The child leaped from his lap. "I've gotta tell Nanna."

Seth's brows dipped. He scanned the room again for someone looking for the boy. "Where is your Nanna?"

"Bathroom." And in a split second the boy was off.

"Charles Lacker. It's an honor to meet you."

Seth accepted the outstretched hand of the short man.

"Where you headed?"

Before Seth could answer, his tele-communicator rang. "Excuse me. I've been waiting for this call." Seth lifted the receiver to his ear as the line crackled and popped.

"Zac, is that you?" Seth rose and on unsteady feet made his way from the lounge into the hallway, the ship's tilt increasing the difficulty of walking. "Zac?"

"Mr. Allen—" The static increased. Seth moved further down the aisle. "Mr. Allen."

"Go ahead, Zac, I can hear you now." There was a long pause. "Dammit, Zac, talk to me."

"Mr. Allen, I'm afraid you're not going to be happy with what I have to report."

Dumbstruck, Seth listened to the unbelievable story Zac began to unravel. Several times it felt like his heart jumped into his throat. When the man finished and hung up, Seth released the breath he didn't know he held.

Slowly, he snapped the tele-communicator closed, then quickly opened it and began to call Zygoman. Dead air greeted him.

This couldn't be happening. He burst into the lounge, locating the tele-communicator near the bar. Jerking the receiver from the receptacle, he pressed it to his ear.

Again nothing.

Desperately, Seth yelled, "Does anyone's tele-communicator work?" Immediately, phones were whipped out of pockets and purses, but each face staring back at him, each head shaking "no", sent a chill through his bones.

He had to stop the slave auction.

Chapter Thirteen

Tatiana held up a long evening gown that looked like it had been spun from gold. "It's a gift from Master Shawn." A gleam of interest shone in the woman's eyes.

Chastity's palm smoothed over its softness. "It's beautiful." She knew the clingy fabric would mold and caress every curve of her body. The long sleeves went past the wrists, ending in a point at the middle finger. Each sleeve had a small thread that would slip over a digit to keep it in place. With a high neckline, her body would be totally covered, except for the slit that traveled up her thigh, allowing a hint of skin to be displayed.

It was a dress of seduction. Show nothing—tell all.

"Apparently, since your Master isn't here to choose your wardrobe for tonight, Master Shawn took it upon himself to supply you with this." Tatiana held up heels that glistened. "And these."

Chastity's palm covered her mouth.

Glass slippers?

In this erotic fantasyland was she to be Cinderella? And if so, where was her Prince Charming?

She thought of Seth and the elation she had felt only moments ago disappeared.

Tatiana laid the articles on the bed. "What's wrong?"

Chastity shook her head and forced a weak smile. "Nothing. Will you help me into that exquisite gown?"

It would do Chastity no good to want what she couldn't have. Nor would it do any good to postpone the inevitable. Another man would share her bed tonight.

Mackenzie McKade

Dressed, Chastity couldn't remember when she'd felt more beautiful. Tatiana had pressed a special blend of lilac, henna and other unique ingredients that guaranteed to heighten arousal into her skin. The oil the woman had used made the dress slither across Chastity's flesh, an erotic caress that kept her ardor at a slow burn.

Chastity felt the flush of excitement between her thighs and shivered. Her skin felt stretched tight over her body, hypersensitive to every thread of fabric. This was almost as bad as Terrance's chastity bell.

For a brief moment Chastity thought of masturbating. Of slipping her fingers along her swollen lips, dipping them into her wet pussy and stroking her clit to a climax, just to prove that the dress couldn't withhold her orgasm like the bell had. Her breasts tingled. She cupped them in her hands, her eyelids closing as her fingers danced over her nipples, teasing and playing.

When her eyes opened Tatiana was smiling. "Are you ready? Or do you need a minute or two, or three…?"

Chastity groaned. "As ready as I'm ever going to be."

As she stepped out into the night, Chastity couldn't help but appreciate the stars and the two crescent moons that seemed to spoon each other like lovers in the ebony sky. This planet was indeed a paradise.

Click. Click. Click. She listened to her heels striking the cobblestone path.

Where was Seth? Had he left her for good? Would she never again feel his caress upon her breasts, his cock sliding in and out of her sex?

The dress was doing unusual things to Chastity. She swore she felt Seth's touch, his mouth upon her breasts, sucking, licking and biting. Moisture pooled between her thighs and she trembled. She needed his body pressed to hers like she needed air to breathe. Without him she wasn't whole, complete.

Passion Flower was standing at the entrance of the ballroom when Chastity arrived. The woman didn't appear to be her usual calm self. Instead, she gave Chastity an uneasy smile and pushed open the doors.

When Chastity entered, a hush fell over the room. Then Tor appeared before her. The man who had humiliated her, pinched her nipple on stage in front of thousands of people, bowed and extended her his arm in a display of gallantry that sent her heart racing.

Frozen in place, she snapped her slack jaw closed when he raised her hand and placed it in the fold of his arm. Then he escorted her to the platform where the individuals to be auctioned stood.

To say she stood out like a sore thumb would be an understatement. Most wore the clothing of a slave. Some even had rags and chains on, to denote their stage in life. Still others wore the black leather trappings of bondage. A couple of women were decked out in baby-doll pajamas.

Among all the servitude Chastity felt like a princess.

As she looked about, the crowd split like the red sea parting, and then Shawn emerged. He smiled and she felt heat fan her face.

The man had said she would be a queen in his bed. And to all present he staked his claim, approaching her and drawing her out of line, to his side.

In was a blatant act of possession. She was his. It was obvious to everyone in the room—except for Dawson.

Dawson slithered to their side. He pinned Shawn with a steely glare. "When does the bitch go up for bid?"

The smile faded from Shawn's face, and his fingers clenched into fists. Before he could react, his brothers appeared out of thin air, restraining his arms.

The low grating growl he released sent a shiver up Chastity's spine.

How could she have ever thought him a teddy bear? This man was as dangerous as either of his brothers. "Still waters," Tatiana had said, but "silent and deadly" seemed more apropos.

"Due to her contract with Voyeur II, Miss Ambrose will not be auctioned tonight, or any night." Shawn's statement stunned Chastity, as well as his brothers. Their blank stares revealed that this was the first they'd heard of the arrangement.

"You're fucking kidding," Dawson blurted. His face reddened with such speed Chastity thought he might have a stroke. "I want the bitch." Spittle sprayed from his mouth. "She's mine. I have plans for her."

In a slow deep voice, Shawn murmured, "Well, you can't have her."

Dawson took one more look at the three men before him. "We'll see." The avowal lingered on the air like a foul green cloud, before he spun on his toes. An eerie mien of danger and retaliation followed him out the door.

Breath gushed from Chastity's lungs. She struggled to inhale. Shawn's touch was gentle as he gave her arm a squeeze. "He can't hurt you."

Tor moved in between them. "I think we need to talk."

Chastity felt small, insignificant, surrounded by the three large men. It didn't help when Terrance frowned at her as if saying, *this is all your fault.*

"You've broken the contract with Voyeur II." Terrance glared at Shawn, before he refocused his scorn in her direction.

"I don't see it that way," Shawn calmly replied.

Tor's lashes swept his cheeks. He shook his head. "How do you see it, little brother?"

"If Dawson had won the bid, Miss Ambrose would be in danger. You know as well as I that the man is a son of a bitch. He already made one attempt to harm her."

Tor and Terrance exchanged glances.

"When?" Tor asked, looking at Chastity for affirmation.

"A couple of days ago. He attacked me. Shawn and Tatiana stopped him before…" Chastity's words drifted off.

"I should have banished the man from the island the night of orientation," Tor grumbled through gritted teeth. He exhaled making a whooshing sound. "What's done is done. But I want the bastard watched." He pinned both brothers with a glare. "Any more infractions I will personally toss his sorry ass out of here—no matter how influential he is."

Exasperated, Terrance ran a hand through his hair. "Fuck, little brother, you've got us in a heap of trouble with Dawson, Voyeur II, not to mention Allen when he returns."

"Voyeur II wants her paired with a different partner tonight." Shawn flashed Chastity a grin. "I'm just offering my services. We agreed to keep her safe. This way Voyeur II gets what they want…"

"And you get what you want," Tor added sarcastically.

Terrance raked Chastity from head to toe. "Did you have to dress her like royalty?" He frowned again. "Could you at least drag her out of the room by her hair? Or do something, so when this gets back to Voyeur II they'll know she didn't go willingly?"

With that Shawn raised Chastity into the air and threw her over his shoulder.

A grunt pushed from her lips. Dazed, she lay listless, and then she started to kick and scream. Fists pounded Shawn's back lightly before she raised her head and winked at Terrance.

The brawny man stumbled back. His blank face nearly made Chastity slip out of character and into hysterics. Instead she hollered louder, choking back her giggles until she felt the cool air of the outdoors brush her face. When Shawn set Chastity on her feet a stream of laughter flowed from her lips.

Shawn looked at her.

"I'm sorry, it's just your brothers. They almost shit their pants when you tossed me over your shoulder."

"So all that kicking and screaming was for show?" Shawn's hopeful expression brought home Chastity's situation.

The man before her had rescued her not once, but twice from Dawson. He expected a night of passion. Throw in a little bondage, erotic torture and whatever other fantasy he could think of, and you had hot, unadulterated sex.

Chastity's stomach pitched. Her hand rose to cup his jaw. "Of course."

Skeptical, he gazed into her eyes. Then his arms slipped around her waist. He pressed her body close. His lips met hers.

Featherlight, undemanding, he coaxed her mouth to open. When she surrendered he laid siege, tasting and exploring, delving into her as if he thirsted for her, hungered for her.

There was something sad, almost lonely, about the man in her arms. It made Chastity want to weep.

Whack! The blow came out of nowhere. Shawn crumpled in her arms, blood seeping from an open wound on the back of his head. A scream tore from her throat as she cradled the heavy man to her chest, sliding slowly to the ground under his weight. A hand reached out from behind the injured man and tossed Shawn off her.

* * * * *

As soon as Seth's foot landed on Ecstasy Island's platform he burst into a run. The looks of astonishment and agitation he received while pushing past the other passengers didn't faze him. He had one thing and one thing only on his mind.

He had to find Chastity.

The night was dark, so when Seth tumbled over something big lying in the walkway he shouldn't have been surprised. However, the sudden attack that came from two different directions did surprise him. He was jerked to his feet before being slammed from one looming shadow to the next.

Running on adrenaline, Seth's fist connected with a muscular stomach, only to take one hard to the jaw. For some reason he'd been dropped right in the center of a boxing ring with two angry bulls.

Seth lunged forward only to have his foot hit something slippery. His body pitched backwards and before he hit the ground the two mammoths landed atop him. He struggled to move, but the big lugs bearing down on him held him in place.

"Tor, Shawn's moving."

"Terrance, is that you?" The weight on Seth's chest grew heavier. "Why the hell did you attack me?" Seth was angry. "Get the fuck off me."

"Fuck you." Terrance threw the obscenity back in Seth's face.

"What's got into the two of you? And where's Chastity?" No one answered Seth. The bulky shape in the walkway began to groan.

Tor released his hold on Seth. Terrance tightened his.

"Shawn, are you okay?" Tor asked his brother as he helped him to his feet.

"Shawn?" Seth was confused. Why was Shawn lying on the sidewalk?

Tor knelt by Shawn and proceeded to help him rise. "Tatiana heard Chastity scream. We came as quickly as we could."

Fear slithered into Seth's veins. "Chastity, scream?" But nobody was paying attention to him.

"Got...to...find...her." Shawn swayed. Tor grasped him around the waist.

"What happened?" Tor helped Shawn to a bench nearby.

"Kissing...wham!" Shawn's fingers touched his head coming back with sticky red blood. "Ah, shit."

Terrance's breath was hot as it flooded over Seth's face. "Where is she?"

"Get off me, you son of a bitch. I should be asking you the same question. Or maybe I should be asking Shawn. What did he mean kissing? And where is Chastity?" If someone didn't answer him soon he'd kill the whole bunch of them.

Yeah, right. Wasn't he the one pinned to the ground?

"Let him go." Tor took a cloth from his pocket and dabbed at the wound on the back of Shawn's head.

"What?" Terrance dug his knee into Seth's side.

"Stands to reason if Seth was at fault he'd be with Chastity, not wrestling on the ground with an unconscious Shawn." Tor's logic made sense. Terrance released him, stood, and extended his hand to help Seth to his feet.

Seth shrugged off the courtesy, wiping the blood from his mouth as he rose on his own accord. "Where is she?"

The brothers looked from one to the other. In unison they said, "Dawson."

"Dawson? What the hell's been going on here?" Seth had reached his limit. His gut clenched, half afraid to learn what had taken place in his absence.

Terrance moved toward Seth.

"Dawson wanted Cha—umm, your slave." Terrance stumbled over his words.

"You fucking sold her to that scum?" Seth's fingers itched to feel Terrance's neck beneath them, but he needed more information from him before he killed the man.

Seth listened to their explanations, growing madder by the minute. When Terrance finished, Seth's voice dropped to a dangerous low. "Where's Dawson?"

His feet were in motion before Terrance finished saying Bungalow Seven.

The door wasn't locked. It slid open freely at Seth's approach. When he saw Dawson's ass in the air driving wildly between spread legs, Seth's heart stopped.

"What the fuck," growled Dawson, glancing over his shoulder. The woman beneath him started to rise and he sharply backhanded her. A whimper floated from beneath him.

A red haze formed in front of Seth's eyes as he lunged for the bastard. He hit Dawson with enough impact to toss him off the bed, both of them rolling on the ground, fists flying.

Then Seth felt strong hands pulling at him. He fought to retain the stranglehold he had on Dawson's throat. Through a cloud of madness he heard, "It's not Chastity, Allen. It's not Chastity." Another set of hands grabbed him, and he felt himself pulled from his nemesis.

Dawson grasped his neck, wheezing as he attempted to breathe.

Seth looked toward the bed, where the young girl that had been dressed as a concubine at orientation wept quietly. A sheet hid most of her body, but her arms and legs were battered and bruised.

Tor took one look at the woman and turned to Terrance. "Throw his ass out of here. I never want to see his face on Zygoman again."

Terrance tossed the man a robe that was lying across a chair. It whacked Dawson in the face. "Pack your bags. You're out of here."

Seth tensed. "*Wait*! Where's Chastity?"

Smack! A palm lashed out, landing against the side of Chastity's head. She fell hard, the breath knocked from her lungs. She lay motionless, afraid to move—afraid not to. As she scrambled to her feet her gaze scanned the room. An abandoned building, old, dirty. Her feet hastened toward the door, only to come up short. A burst of pain exploded down each nerve ending as a rough hand grabbed her by the hair. Another palm slammed down over her mouth. She struggled, but she was no match for his strength.

Josh's eyes were wild, red and swollen like he hadn't slept for days. "Now you listen to me and don't say a word."

Chastity couldn't talk, much less breathe. If he didn't move his fingers away from her nostrils, she would suffocate. Just as darkness fringed the edges of her consciousness he released her mouth, only to force his lips on hers.

His kiss was a brutal rape of her senses. She struggled, but the hold on her head made it impossible to escape. Teeth grated against teeth, his tongue plunged deeply. Her stomach heaved and the taste of vomit burned up her throat.

And then suddenly it was over.

She sucked in a ragged breath.

Josh gently rested his head on her shoulder. "Why'd you do it, Chastity?" He sounded so lost, so young. His black hair fell forward, veiling his sharp features.

Chastity's voice trembled. "W-what, Josh? I-I don't understand. Why are you doing this?"

"Me?" His tone rose sharply, and then plummeted. "*Me?*" He lifted his head and glared at her. "You let him fuck you, didn't you?"

Bewildered, Chastity shook her head. "Who?"

"Seth. He shoved his cock in here." Josh drove his fingers roughly between her legs.

Chastity cried out in pain and fear. "I don't understand, Josh."

The hand that assaulted her fell to his side. Then he smiled, madness tugging at the corners of his mouth. The fist in her hair tightened. Without a word, he began to drag her through an opened door and into another room.

Chastity limped on one glass slipper, the other lost in her struggle as she attempted to follow him, reducing the pressure his hold had on her head. When she looked up, saw the chains attached to the wall, she gasped.

His laugh was cynical. "You wanted to experience bondage. Well, baby, I'm going to give it to you before we leave this planet."

Fear crawled across Chastity's skin. "Josh! Please, Josh, tell me what this is about." She pulled away, only to be yanked back toward the foreboding wall. She heard the first shackle close around her wrist, felt the cold steel against her skin. And then the second clanked around her other wrist.

Josh stood back and gazed at her. "I love you."

Chastity pulled against her bindings. She had to think of something, had to find out what was wrong with Josh. "I love you, too. But I don't understand."

"You're *my* girl."

She cocked her head confused. "Josh, we're friends. You're helping me with my mother."

His snicker made her flinch. "Helping you. God, Chastity, you're so stupid. Who do you think ensured that your mother remained incarcerated all this time? Who do you think paid for it?"

"You?"

"*Buzzzz!*" The obnoxious sound blared from between his lips. "Wrong. Try again."

She paused, remembering how much money she had given Josh. He had arranged for her to leave Earth, isolating her from news, her friends, Seth. He'd even provided her with a new identity and a job to ensure that Seth couldn't find her.

Before she asked the question she knew the answer. "Me?"

"Ding, ding, ding, give the woman a prize."

His confirmation hit her with a force that knocked the breath from her lungs. "You used *my* money to keep my mother locked up?"

Josh shrugged. "Seth's. Yours. A little here, a little there." He pinched her chin between his fingers. "But you had to ruin it, didn't you? You had to enter this contest. You had to fuck Seth."

Chastity couldn't speak. She couldn't think. All this time, Josh had manipulated her. He had ruined her mother's life. He had taken Seth from her.

And for what? Jealousy? A twisted sense of love?

When Josh's hand skimmed her neck Chastity allowed her anger to replace fear. She jerked her head away. "Don't touch me."

"Oh, baby, I'm going to do more than touch you. I promise."

When Josh moved to the door, then passed through it, Chastity breathed a sigh of relief. But it was short-lived as her eyes scanned the room. Whips, paddles, chains…she'd fallen back into a torture chamber.

But what really set her heart racing was the old-fashioned branding iron that glowed red in the fireplace. He couldn't possibly be planning to *brand* her…could he?

Chastity shuffled her unrestrained feet. She could coldcock him in the balls. But when he revived he'd be livid.

She felt helpless, hopeless.

Josh was mad. He would never allow her to leave alive. He couldn't. She would die here. Her mother would remain incarcerated on the moon. And Seth would think that she'd disappeared yet again.

The sound of footsteps sent goose bumps skittering across Chastity's skin. She gasped as Josh entered. He was naked, his cock rigid.

Her heart slammed against her rib cage as he approached. The touch of his hand on her face made her sick. She steeled herself not to flinch, but couldn't help it.

Josh hissed at her reaction, backing away. Then he reached for a strip of cloth and a red rubber ball with straps. Before she knew what was happening he forced her jaws apart and pressed the ball into her mouth, securing the ties. Then the silk sash was placed over her eyes.

Chastity began to salivate as she listened to Josh move around the room. Fluid accumulated, dripping from the corners of her lips and down her chin.

Josh moved in front of her. She felt his warm breath on her face as his fingernails dug into her chest and pulled, ripping her dress. In a last-ditch effort, her knee rose and she nailed him in the balls.

Josh shrieked. Chastity felt her gown go down with him as he hit the floor. For a moment she heard groans as he thrashed about, and then there was silence.

He rose and padded across the room. Chastity listened to his movements and prayed that he'd leave.

Instead she heard the rustling of coals. Her body went numb. The thought of her flesh burning, searing beneath the brand crashed down on her.

She couldn't do this. She wasn't strong enough.

Quietly she slipped into her safe zone, pulling the blanket of unconsciousness over her head.

Chapter Fourteen

Chaos reigned on the planet of Zygoman. Seth, with the help of the Thorenson brothers, was tearing the place apart looking for Chastity. She had been gone about an hour, every minute that passed more precious than the last.

Guards had been set up at the transport platform. Every one of the guests had volunteered to search. Yet Chastity was nowhere to be found.

Torches and light sticks lit the way as they searched the bungalows, the citadel, the Temple of Worship, the Forest of Immortality and the gardens, with no success.

It was as if she had simply vanished.

Seth was at his wit's end. Exasperated, he turned to Tor. "Is there any other way off the island?"

"Only a small platform at the southwest side of the planet. It hasn't been used in ages."

"But it's there." Seth pinched the bridge of his nose and then rubbed his forehead, attempting to ease the throb of a headache he didn't need. Time was slipping away. "Any buildings that haven't been searched?"

Shawn moved next to his brother. "Tor, there's that outbuilding located just off the old platform."

Tor's brows dipped. He shook his head. "Hasn't been used in forever."

"She's got to be there."

Seth agreed with Shawn. They'd searched everywhere else.

Without hesitation, Seth said, "Lead the way, Shawn."

* * * * *

In the distance a light flickered and the pounding in Seth's head increased. His gait quickened. The vegetation in this part of Zygoman was wild, unattended. It was mere luck that he didn't trip on the maze of tree roots zigzagging above ground. As Seth weaved in and out, the ground shifted, or did it?

A nervous laugh surfaced. "Ridiculous," he whispered. Yet he could have sworn that the gnarled roots moved. Any moment he expected one of them to snake out and grab his ankle.

Instead, Seth's heart stopped as a strong hand folded around his biceps. Sharply, he was jerked back. He clenched his fist and drew it back, then stopped in mid-swing.

"Fuck, Allen, you want to announce our presence?" Tor bent at the waist to catch his breath.

Shit! The pounding that Seth had heard wasn't his heart, but his feet striking hard against the ground. He'd been running, leaving everyone behind. A tight breath wheezed in his chest. He looked past Tor's stooped body. The guiding light didn't look any closer than it had a minute ago. How could that be?

He wanted—no, needed—to run, to beat a path straight to Chastity. The heaviness in his chest screamed that time was of the essence.

The thundering of more footsteps brought Seth about. When Terrance and Shawn appeared around a bend, Tor motioned for them to slow their pace, pointing to the growth around them. "Watch your step and douse the damn light sticks."

Seth, too, twisted the bottom of his luminary, and darkness spilled around them. He widened his eyes, pupils dilating. At first he couldn't see anything. Then, slowly, the two crescents hanging in the sky produced enough brightness to see the shapes of objects, but not their identity.

"Move it," barked Seth, a lack of patience in his edgy voice. A wary hand rubbed the back of his neck, feet moving. He had to get to Chastity and fast.

When the form of a small building, a warehouse of sorts, became visible, a chill slithered up Seth's spine and froze him in place. The dense vegetation and the blue-gray moonlight gave the structure an eerie, almost dissolute, effect.

Then a plethora of goose bumps alerted him that Chastity was near. His body could sense her, his cock tightened. Even with the current precarious situation, the thought of being near her—holding her in his arms, his erection sliding in and out of her wet pussy—excited him, warring with the possible danger that lay ahead.

Drawing closer, approximately a hundred feet away, Seth strained to see inside the building. The windows were intact, crusted with layers of dirt that obscured his view. The centuries-old structure showed its neglected state, as the siding—warped and rusted in some places—made a God-awful screech that grated against his nerves. From the chimney a thin cloud of smoke rose, swirling as it climbed into the sky before dissipating.

A dark image slipped past a window. Icy fear cut through Seth's veins like razor blades. He hadn't known fear had a taste, but it was there, acid upon his tongue. And he'd never remembered a time when he was so anxious. Afraid of what he might find, afraid of what he wouldn't.

"Tor and I will take the front." Seth waved Terrance and Shawn forward. "You two the back. We go silent from here on." The men acknowledged his order as they activated the ear and mouth receptors that would allow them to talk to one another. Then they moved out.

Standing out of sight, Tor used the palm of his hand to wipe away a patch of the grime from the window where they had seen the figure. He stepped forward and something crunched beneath his feet. The snap sounded like it was amplified. The man flinched, and then looked over his shoulder. Even in the dark Seth could see worry furrow his brows.

"She's in the back room. There appears to be only one man." Tor paused, but only briefly. "We'd better hurry," was all he added before addressing his brothers with apprehension in his voice. "Terrance, Shawn, get in place. We're going in."

From one end of the house to the other, the outbuilding shook as doors crashed inward, making it appear as if a tornado slammed into it. Like lightning racing across the sky, Seth and Tor darted through the narrow passageways, meeting Terrance just as the big man's shoulder hit the ancient door, splintering wood.

Charging in, Tor followed Seth.

What Seth saw drew him to an abrupt halt. He couldn't breathe. It was like walking into a nightmare.

Chastity's body was slumped, her chin listless upon her chest, her wrists outstretched, bound to the wall by medieval shackles. She wore a blindfold and a red rubber ball was wedged into her mouth. The front of her evening gown was ripped down the center, exposing her breasts, the smoothness of her belly, the small patch of dark curls at the apex of her thighs and her beautiful long legs. Even beneath the stretchy material of what was left of her gown, the muscles and tendons in her arms bulged, revealing the stress of hanging languid by her limbs.

She made no sound — no movement.

Beside Chastity, a naked man held an ancient red-hot branding iron poised and ready to press against the tender flesh of one of her breasts.

The man jerked around.

Seth's heart slammed into his chest.

"Josh." Seth's voice was weak with disbelief.

The shock surfacing on his cousin's face faded. Then he grinned, a smirk that made Seth's stomach pitch. Josh's lips curled up maliciously, baring his teeth. Ebony hair, normally picture-perfect, was tousled and tangled. His red-rimmed eyes were wide — madness haunted them.

This was not the boy Seth had grown up with. Seth struggled to put the pieces of what he was seeing together.

The report Seth's detective had given him had explained Josh's involvement in Chastity's disappearance. The retainer on the moon had met with her mother. Seth knew why Chastity had left him at the altar two years ago, knew Josh had instigated her flight. But never had he thought his cousin's connections were sinister, or that he was capable of harming Chastity.

Or had Seth just not wanted to believe it? Seth looked at the man before him through different eyes. Jealousy. Envy. Rage. Had the signs been there all their lives?

But why Chastity? Why here...now?

Josh gazed adoringly at Chastity. Slowly, he threaded his fingers through her hair. "She's beautiful, don't you think, Cousin?" He leaned forward and pressed his dry and chapped lips to Chastity's ashen cheek. She remained listless as his tongue flicked out and licked a path from her chin to cheekbone. "And she's mine." The back of his hand grazed lightly along her slack jawline.

Seth took a step forward. "Josh —"

Josh jumped back. The iron in his hand wavered, halting Seth's words. Even in the dimly lit room Seth saw the brightness of the red-hot steel reflecting a pink shadow off of Chastity's alabaster skin.

Josh pivoted and glared at Seth. "She doesn't love you." He tilted his head as if listening to an inaudible sound. Then he answered with a quick nod. "She wants you to leave now."

Something was dreadfully wrong with Josh. Seth took another step, but stopped when he saw his cousin bristle and the wavering iron come dangerously close to burning Chastity.

"Chastity asked me to come and rescue her." Josh began to caress a path down between her breasts rising slightly with each sedated breath.

Heat raced up Seth's neck, scorching his ears and cheeks. Fingers tensed, and then clenched, itching to tear his cousin's hand away. But through the grace of God, Seth remained still, afraid of what Josh would do if the men stormed him.

"I'm always rescuing her…from you. Always from you… She's mine — gone — " He rapidly shook his head. "Now — then — " he rambled incoherently before adding, " — she needs me, you know?"

Seth cast a glance toward Tor and Terrance, and then he took another step forward. Both men followed his cautious movements, remaining silent in the shadows, waiting for the moment to act.

Chastity's breaths appeared to be slowing, becoming shallower by the moment. Had Josh overdosed her, or had she escaped too deeply into her safe zone? Anxious to put an end to this and to verify that she was okay, Seth held out his arms in invitation to try to tempt Josh away from her.

"We both need you, Josh. We're family, bro."

As Josh's head shook wildly the branding iron swung away from Chastity's flesh.

Seth breathed a sigh of relief. Still, he prayed that a brilliant plan would come to mind before his cousin snapped.

Like a child, Josh's bottom lip puffed out. "No, you don't."

What had happened to the man he'd grown up with?

Without warning, his cousin's mood switched from pouty to sober. Again, his attention was drawn to the almost lifeless woman beside him. His body slackened. "But Chastity loves me."

Josh's fingers closed brutally around a breast. "See? She doesn't flinch when I touch her. She wants me to touch her — not you." Five angry red impressions marked Chastity's tender skin as he released her.

Seth's fists clenched. Rage curled through his body like a wildfire. His cousin was a dead man.

Josh lifted the branding iron in front of him jabbing it toward Seth like a saber. Seth took a cautious step backwards out of the slashing iron's path.

"I'm going to brand her with my initials." The fiery letters "JA" glowed brightly, sending a wave of fear through Seth. Then Josh grasped his cock in his free hand. "Before I brand her with this."

Josh's shaky hand slipped up and down the length of his dick, a bead of moisture glistening from its tip. His face hardened, his brows pulling together into a lustful expression as he continued to pump his erection. With a blissful sigh his eyelids drifted closed.

All three men lunged at once.

Immediately, the air grew heavy and musty as heavy boots struck the dust-strewn floor.

At the sound of their pounding footsteps, Josh's eyes shot wide. He barely skirted them, moving quickly to a table near a window. Before Seth knew it, Josh had a gun aimed at him.

Josh's hand shook. His features mellowed into a semblance of regret. "Don't make me kill you, Seth." The man's voice again turned childlike. "Take your friends and leave us."

There was a loud *crash* as glass shattered, showering Josh and the floor. Like an avenging angel, Shawn soared through the window as if on wings. His aim was true as he slammed into Josh's back.

Josh pitched forward. A grunt wedged from his lungs.

Seth charged him.

As Josh fell, he squeezed the trigger.

The gun discharged.

Seth heard a cry. Felt searing pain.

Through a haze he realized the cry was his own. He attempted to move, to help the three men who had tackled Josh, but his knees buckled. He crumpled to the floor.

More intense pain slammed Seth's body. From a distance, he heard a scuffle, smelled the pungent scent of blood. Bone met bone. The crunch was sickening. Josh screamed.

Everything went deathly silent.

"Allen?" Tor's large hands shook Seth. "Allen, can you hear me?"

Seth attempted to rise, but his left arm wouldn't hold him. "Chastity." Seth's voice sounded weak even to him.

"You've been shot. Stay still, buddy, you're bleeding pretty bad."

"No," insisted Seth. "Chastity must wake...lose her...too deeply under."

Pain lanced Seth's chest as Tor brought him into a sitting position. "Tell me what to do."

Already Terrance and Shawn were taking Chastity's listless body from the wall. When the handcuffs opened, she crumpled. Shawn caught her beneath her armpits, then swept her up, cradling her in his arms.

Against Tor's warnings to remain immobile, Seth fought to get to Chastity, crawling, dragging his body across the floor using his good arm. "Bring her to me," he groaned. The intensity of his injury made the lights fade in and out. Seth fought to stay conscious, leaving a path of blood behind him.

Tor's hand halted Seth. "Allen, you can't move. Shit, the bleeding is getting worse. Dammit, Shawn, get her over here, *now!*"

Seth coughed, and the result was excruciating. He felt the pressure of Tor's hand against his shoulder, felt ice rip through his veins.

"Lay her next to me," Seth managed to say. Tor was gentle as he rolled Seth onto his uninjured side.

Shawn positioned Chastity so that she and Seth were face-to-face.

"Beautiful," Seth murmured, bringing his hand to her cold cheek. His tongue slid over parched lips, his mouth even drier. He leaned forward with Tor's assistance. "Wake up, angel," Seth whispered. "Baby," he swallowed hard, "I-I need you to wake up."

Nothing. Chastity's breathing remained shallow. Her pasty skin was haggard, lifeless.

"Baby, please wake up." It was a struggle for Seth to speak, but he went on, "I...love...you..."

When she didn't respond, he touched his lips to hers. His caress had awoken her before. He prayed it would again.

He'd give his life for Chastity. He loved her that much.

"Hold on, Allen, help's coming." Tor offered support, as he continued to exert pressure on Seth's wound.

Seth was too weak to speak. His limbs were numb. He barely had enough energy to keep his eyelids open. There wasn't much left of his kiss, just the pressure of his mouth resting against hers.

Then Chastity's eyelids flickered. He felt her breath tease his. Relief filtered through his tattered body.

Her eyes were still closed when she whimpered his name. Seth tried to respond. But it was no use. His fight to stay conscious had come to an end.

Chapter Fifteen

Chastity awoke with a jolt. She flung herself off the bed so quickly that her stomach churned. Acid beat against her abdomen like waves crashing over jagged rocks. She tried to suck in a breath to ease her dizziness, but it was hell going from slumber to panic in less than a nanosecond.

Memories assailed her mind. Where was Josh?

Without a moment wasted, Chastity spun on her heels. *Smack*! She hit a hard wall of muscle. Terror-stricken, her fists swung out. But strong arms pulled her naked body close, sending her resistance into a whirlpool that spun around and around.

With each spin of Chastity's stomach she felt her hope sucked away. A whimper of defeat slipped past her quivering lips. She was going to be sick.

"Chastity." A familiar voice whispered her name. A fresh musky scent tickled her nose. Panting, she inhaled and released a raspy breath. "Seth."

Chastity's chin rose and Seth smiled down at her.

Confused, she looked around. Taking in the comforting sight of their bungalow and Seth, a feeling of safety flooded her.

Overwhelmed, she flung her arms around Seth. He groaned, not in ecstasy but in pain. She quickly stepped back, tearing herself from his arms and eliciting another groan from him.

"Seth?"

"It's nothing." But the agony etched into his handsome features said differently. She raised her brow in question.

"Josh left me with a little souvenir."

Her feet drew her closer to him. "Souvenir?"

Seth's one-shoulder shrug brought another grimace. "A gunshot wound."

Chastity's jaw fell, her hand rose to rest on his uninjured arm. "*Oh my god.* Do you need to sit, lie down, o-or something?"

A roguish grin lifted the corners of his mouth. "I'll take 'or something'." Then he opened his arms wide. "Come here, baby."

Chastity flew into his embrace, this time more gently. Face buried against his chest she felt the heat of tears sting her eyes. Emotion choked her. She swallowed the apprehension sticking in her throat and prayed she could finish her sordid tale before he walked out on her. Either way, she was coming away from this experience with a clear conscience.

"Seth, I need to explain why I left two years ago." She wasn't going to waste a single minute. Not when time was so precious.

Seth set her from him. The absence of his embrace and the cool breeze of a fan overhead made her shiver. He pinned her with a glare and frowned.

Chastity's heart stopped.

"I don't need an explanation. I only need to know if you love me."

Breath stolen by Seth's words, Chastity struggled to respond. A single word tickled her throat begging to be released. When a simple "yes" finally squeezed from her lips she watched in dismay as Seth turned his back on her and walked away.

Confusion reigned as his footsteps padded across the room. With his good hand, he reached for a paddle from the wall of erotic torture toys.

Chastity's chest tightened, her heart's palpitations quickened. After all she'd been through, he was going to spank her? She had confessed her love and he was still playing the game. Or was getting her to confess her love part of the game?

Seth pivoted and faced Chastity. When he graced her with a playful smile her heart soared. He wasn't mad. He was in the mood to play. And this was a game she didn't mind playing.

Smack! The paddle resonated off his thigh. "Yes?" He raised an arrogant brow.

Excitement filtered through Chastity's body. Her nipples tingled. Her pussy wept. God, she loved this man. But above that, she needed to feel his cock between her thighs. She needed him to fill her, complete her.

Chastity drifted to her knees, head bowed, pulse racing. Through feathered lashes she peered up at him. "Yes, Master?"

Seth nodded to the right. "Lean against that mirror."

Chastity rose, her ass swaying as she approached the full-length mirror. Slowly, she bent over, placing her palms against the cool glass and gifting him with a view of her swollen lips, already dripping wet.

He groaned.

She grinned.

In the reflection of the mirror she saw the bulge in his pants take a firmer form. He licked his lips. "Spread your legs." The gravelly tone of his voice made her quiver.

Deliberately, she hesitated, teasing him as she arched her back and raised her ass. His growl of discontent reminded her of a tiger being refused a meal. Like a predator, he stalked across the floor.

The vision of Seth the hunter—and she his prey—flooded her mind.

The second growl was a warning that made her quickly scoot her limbs apart. Better safe than sorry. She didn't know how this game was going to play out. Would she end up on the table taking it in the ass, or in bed with Seth in her arms? Then again, did it matter?

The lustful expression on his face sent heat waves coursing through Chastity.

In a taxing tone he barked, "Not fast enough, *wench.*"

The paddle grazed lightly over one cheek and then the other. Chastity's skin tingled, blood rushing to the surface of her ass as a gush of warmth slid down her thighs. She was so hot, so aroused. Her breasts ached with a fullness that needed to feel his touch, his mouth suckling, pulling, biting. She whimpered, squirming against the leather like a cat in heat. The torment was unbearable.

"Please, Master," she begged.

Dark eyes beamed in the mirror. "Please what, slave?"

Chastity's tongue made a slow sensuous path along her lips. "Spank me," she breathed.

When leather met skin, Chastity thought she'd died and gone to heaven. Between pain and pleasure was ecstasy. Overwhelming emotions pushed a cry from her mouth. It was a unique blend of femininity and masculinity, of submission and power.

Again, the paddle bounced off Chastity's ass. Tears filled her eyes from the exquisite release. Seth's lips pressed against one heated cheek and then the other.

As the burn subsided, he leaned over Chastity's back. His hand caressed the soft area between her breasts. In the reflection of the mirror she observed Seth as he watched his fingers move achingly slow across each nipple, tweaking them before weighing each breast in his palm. Then he continued smoothing down her stomach, playing at her navel, before running his digits through her tight curls. When they disappeared into her wet pussy Chastity felt like sobbing.

As Seth thrust his fingers in and out of her sex, he kneeled and nipped her ass.

She yelped, enjoying the sting of his teeth, the intimacy.

He laughed. "Slave, what do you want me to do to you now?"

Chastity inhaled deeply. "Please, Master, fuck me."

Seth removed his hands from between her thighs. "I've got a better idea." He pulled his shirt gingerly over his head. Next to go were socks, shoes, pants and finally his briefs.

Like a Greek god, he stood before her, his sex long and hard, arching against his firm belly. With ease, he slid onto the bed and held out a hand. "Make love to *me*, Chastity."

A shaky palm covered her mouth. *Oh my god*, he'd used the "L" word. She blinked, forcing back the emotion stinging her eyes. "I love you," she choked.

"I know, baby, and I love you, too."

Chastity climbed atop Seth, her naked body sliding seductively over his. Just the touch of her skin against his set him afire, making his cock harden, his balls ache. Purring laughter vibrated his length. He moaned, afraid he'd wake from the delicious dream. Hips rocked against his, the smallest movements massaging and squeezing his cock. Then he heard Chastity laugh again, a sweet, beautiful sound that rocked him down to his core.

Seth opened his eyes and gazed at the angel atop him. He smiled as he tried to lift his arms to embrace her. Fire ripped through his left shoulder. He groaned.

"Be still or I'm going to stop," Chastity threatened softly before lifting her hips and then grinding them against his, taking him deeper.

His right hand brushed a curl behind her ear. "You, okay, baby?"

Chastity rose on her palms, separating their chests. Two heavenly breasts swayed back and forth with the rhythm of her body.

"I don't know." She wiggled her brows. "You tell me how I feel." The inner muscles of her pussy flexed, caressing and sucking him further into her heat. Then she pulled back so that the head of his erection stood poised at her entrance, drawing out the anticipation of plunging again into her swollen heat.

Flinging his right arm back, a hand over his eyes, Seth released a deep breath. "Heavenly. You feel heavenly."

Slowly and deliberately, she glided her wet desire across his. She anointed him with the expertise of a temptress. Sharp fingernails grazed his chest, sending a path of fire in their wake. When she dragged her nails across his nipples, he moaned, his hands reaching for her breasts.

Man, the woman was good. Between the sounds of flesh pounding and her pussy wrapping around him like a second skin, Seth's blood churned. Her body took what he offered, his cock beating against her vaginal walls.

Tiny goose bumps rose across Chastity's body before she gasped, and the first wave of climax hit. Seth reveled in her deep, orgasmic moans, the soft whimpers as sweet spasms milked his rod. The woman made him so hot, so hungry. He thrust his hips again and again, pace increasing.

Chastity flung her head back. She cried out, riding him harder, faster. Then she grasped his nipples and twisted as another summit hit.

Bittersweet pain rushed Seth toward his own pinnacle. His balls drew up tight, he strained, and his climax went over the top. His body jerked, his dick twitching as it pumped a final jet of come deep inside Chastity's core.

Sated, Seth pressed her to his chest, knowing how she liked to be held after their loving. But he wasn't prepared when her rapid breathing became ragged. Then he felt the first tear fall as she began to cry.

Seth kissed the top her head, inhaling the light, floral scent in her hair. "What's wrong, baby?"

Between sobs she struggled to speak. "So much to t-t-tell you."

Gently, he flipped her on her back and wedged his hips over hers so that she couldn't move. He stared into bright eyes that shimmered with anxiety.

"Chastity, I know about your mother. I know why you left me. Nothing matters any more."

A stream of tears trickled from her eyes. He laughed and wiped them away, but new ones appeared.

"Josh?"

Seth kissed her lips. "Locked up tight. He can't hurt either of us again."

Chastity's eyes closed and an expression of relief softened her features. But still, tears seeped from between her lids.

"Stop crying, baby." Seth ran the back of his hand across her soft cheek. "We'll work through this. The only thing I want to know is, will you marry me?"

Chastity's eyes popped open in disbelief. "Marry?" She sniffed and delicately wiped a finger beneath her running nose.

Well, that had certainly stopped the tears. He squeezed her tightly, deliberately pushing away any doubt. "Yes. Will you finish what you promised me two years ago?"

Loving arms closed around his neck. "Oh, Seth." She planted little kisses along his jawline. But it was her answer — "Yes, yes, yes!" — that made him laugh with elation.

Seth lunged from the bed. "Then get dressed — I have a wedding gift for you. You've got thirty minutes. Tatiana will come for you." He bent over and kissed her lightly before adding, "And don't be late."

Chapter Sixteen

Strange didn't begin to describe how Chastity felt. The last couple of days had been a whirlwind of emotions. After Seth quickly dressed and left, she pushed back the covers and rose from the bed. Arms extended, she stretched, and then rolled her shoulders. From the throbbing ache in her arms to the stiffness in her neck, every pain reminded her of the devastating night with Josh.

God, she'd never been so scared.

This morning's activities had taken her soreness to a different level. Her skin hummed with heightened sensitivity. Her lips were swollen from Seth's kisses. The warmth of his spanking lingered, marking her. And the delicious twinge between her thighs…she sighed…was the sweetest of all.

"Seth loves me." Happiness bubbled inside Chastity like effervescent champagne, or the sparklers burning with bright, colorful sparks during a Fourth of July celebration back home. She blinked and searched through tears of joy for clothing she knew awaited her.

On the chair that usually held her ensemble laid a white bustier trimmed in silver lace. Next to it, lay a matching pair of bikini panties cut high on the thigh with sheer baby-doll ruffles on the buttocks. Chastity touched the silky material and knew immediately that it would glide over her skin seductively, stroking her pussy with each step she took. The mere thought made her breasts tingle and lit a smoldering fire between her legs.

Yet it was the golden choker-necklace dotted with sparkling diamonds that made her breath catch. "Oh my." In awe, she raised the jewels to her neck. Coolness slithered around her throat, sending chills racing up her spine as she fastened it.

What wonderfully wicked thing did Seth have planned for today?

As Chastity wiggled into the bustier, plucking the laces tight, the decadent material caressed her breasts, lifting them upward and outward. The sensual panties were next. When she slipped her feet into matching white heels she couldn't help admiring the picture of naughty innocence she portrayed.

Chastity took a long, hard look at the woman in the mirror. Seth had asked her to marry him. She had accepted. In the recesses of her mind a niggling of doubt surfaced. Stubbornly she fought it back into the shadows. She squared her shoulders and headed for the door.

The fairytale would come true this time. It just had to.

Chastity squinted against the radiance of the afternoon sun as she heard the bungalow door slide shut behind her. As her gaze absorbed the exquisite gardens of Ecstasy Island, she could've sworn the grass was greener, the flowers brighter and the clouds fluffier in the aquamarine sky.

Fact was, everything looked better through the eyes of a woman in love.

"Chastity." She started at Tatiana's sudden appearance. The woman's face beamed. "I've been asked to escort you to the Temple of Worship."

Chastity felt the blood rush from her face. She couldn't believe that Seth would allow his future bride to be fucked by another man, not to mention by three at the same time. Like a knife pressed deep into her heart, it hurt to remember their morning, to recall their words of love and to know it meant so little, if anything, to Seth.

Then Chastity remembered Voyeur II, the game, and that as far as everyone on this planet was concerned she was still Seth's slave. Apparently Seth felt the same way.

Disheartened, she followed Tatiana through the gardens and past the citadel, and over the creaky wooden bridge that swayed with a rhythm that had Chastity's stomach somersaulting.

As they entered the room where the iridescent crystals glowed, Chastity gazed about. The room was empty except for the flood of colors and lights dancing within the crystal. In the air, tiny starbursts ignited. The energy level was so high that she could feel electricity brush her skin. She shivered, sensing something big was about to happen.

Spellbound, Chastity stood motionless as Seth entered the room. Her anger vanished with his appearance. He was dressed in an elegant tuxedo, black with satin lapels, and a pristine white shirt. With a flick of his head, waves of ebony hair floated on the air, drawing her eyes to the matching bowtie around his muscular neck.

Seth's presence was bigger than life, filling the archway to the beautiful atrium she had awakened in the previous day. Piercing eyes raked her frame coolly, as he stroked his mustache, running his fingers over his goatee. Then with a wave of his hand, he motioned her to him.

Chastity couldn't move.

What kind of man confessed his love then allowed this to happen?

Seth quickly moved to her side. He frowned. "Are you okay?"

Through a wall of emotion she breathed, "Is this your surprise?"

"Well—" he looked around at the room, "—part of it."

Chastity snapped her jaws together to resist the urge to respond. Heat singed her cheeks. It took a massive willpower not to reach out and bitch-slap the man.

Then as if it couldn't get worse, Seth threw back his head and roared. Full-bodied laughter spilled from his mouth. In a quick move he reached out and brought her rigid body into his arms.

His warm breath caressed her ear. "Do you trust me?

Trust? She gazed deep into his blue eyes, and then she saw it… Love. Could she return his love and give him unconditional surrender? As she melted into his arms she knew the answer was… "Yes."

Seth stepped away and held her at arms length. "Do you love me?"

"With all my heart," tumbled helplessly from her mouth.

His tongue moistened his dry lips. "Will you marry me, here? Now?"

Chastity's eyes widened. A tremble rocked her down to her soul. "What?"

Passion Flower approached with a large white box, a red bow wrapped around it. She placed it in Seth's open hands.

"It only just arrived." His outstretched hands presented the gift to Chastity. "I'll hold the box, while you open it."

Chastity gripped the ribbon and pulled, allowing it to uncurl and float to the ground as she raised the lid. The cover slipped from her grasp and tumbled next to the ribbon.

Her eyes widened with wonder. One palm covered her mouth, while the other one brushed the tissue paper back.

Inside was a wedding dress.

"For me?" she gasped, extracting the gown.

Seth laughed. "Yes, for you." He set the box on the floor. "Passion Flower, will you assist Chastity?" The Asian woman took the dress from Chastity's trembling hands and slipped it over her head, careful not to disturb her hair. The strapless gown slid down her body, conforming to her shape, until it floated gently to brush the floor. It was satin and lace, and exactly like the one she had worn on their first wedding day.

"How?" she asked.

"It's not the same one." Seth took a step back. He stroked her with a tender gaze. "But how I remember—" his words seem to stick in his throat, " — how I remembered you that day. Our wedding day."

Chastity had not forgotten that day, and evidently, neither had Seth.

Tatiana stepped forward and placed a lacy coronet weaved with blue forget-me-nots and baby's breath on Chastity's head. The airy veil slid over her naked shoulders, sending goose bumps across her skin as it settled at her elbows. Then the woman pressed a bouquet of matching flowers into her hands. Its sweet delicate scent rose to surround her.

Seth meant to marry her this very moment.

Seth held out his arm. Chastity was bursting with emotions as she weaved her arm around his. Together they entered the adjacent chamber.

Her steps faltered. Tatiana, the Thorenson brothers and Passion Flower were in attendance.

Chastity stared at the smiling faces before her. Emotion gathered tight and heavy in her chest. She swallowed hard, choking back stinging tears. Should she pinch herself? Surely this couldn't be happening. Was her dream finally becoming reality?

Seth drew her close. "Before we begin, I have another gift for you."

He disappeared behind a large boulder. When he appeared again, a woman in a gauzy blue gown held his hand. Immediate jealousy stung Chastity's heart. Then the air in her lungs seized. She took one blurry look and then another. A tremor racked her body.

"Mom!"

The frail woman released Seth's hand and fled into Chastity's open arms. They embraced.

Through a haze of tears Chastity murmured, "How? When?"

Celeste Ambrose wiped at her daughter's tears. She smiled at Seth. "Your young man made it happen."

Chastity looked at Seth standing apart from them. He had done this for her. She remembered the game, the money, the years of work to obtain her mother's release. How much had it cost Seth?

Chastity's arms tightened around her mother. "But how? When?"

"Does it matter, sweetie?" Celeste eased herself from Chastity's embrace. "Now, daughter, I believe this man has waited two long years to wed you." Her lips curled into a smile. "Now go to him. Make him happy."

Chastity didn't need any more encouragement as she released her mother and flew into Seth's awaiting arms.

"Thank y—" Chastity's words of appreciation were smothered by a kiss.

"If the two of you can come up for air, I'll start the ceremony." Tor moved in front of them.

Chastity's obvious confusion spurred Seth to explain that Tor was, in essence, the captain of Zygoman, and therefore ordained to perform marital rites.

Chastity couldn't help the blush that surfaced as she stood before the man who had thoroughly fucked her, and was now performing her wedding ceremony. Was life strange, or what?

* * * * *

"…I now pronounce you Master and slave." Passion Flower gave her husband a sharp elbow to his side that elicited a chuckle from the audience. He cleared his throat. "Husband and wife," he corrected, before frowning at his spouse. "You may kiss your bride."

Seth stole Chastity's breath away as he pressed his lips to hers. Tender, yet masterful, he branded her with his affection, leaving no doubt that she belonged to him. When they parted, their love was reflected in each others eyes. He grinned and swept her off her feet, into his arms.

Chastity inhaled a blissful breath as Seth nuzzled her hair.

"You're mine." It was a growl of possession that sent chills slithering up her spine. Arms tightened around her, reinforcing his words.

Everyone else in the room ceased to exist as far as she was concerned.

Seth's racing heart and heavy breathing matched hers. If he was as hard as she was wet, they would climax as soon as naked flesh slid across flesh. She fought the desire to wedge her hand between them to verify the condition of his cock.

It wasn't necessary.

The dark hunger in Seth's blue eyes told Chastity that she had guessed right. Seth wanted her as much as she did him. Without a word, he headed toward the exit.

As they reached the door Tor's strong hand folded around Seth's biceps, halting their escape. "That can wait, Allen. A celebration feast awaits you and your bride in the citadel."

Chastity's pulse faltered. Another test of willpower came as her heated body slithered down Seth's. And, yep, his cock was rock-hard as he paused, settling it between her thighs, pressing his hips against hers before setting her on her feet.

A featherlight kiss and then Seth whispered, "Later."

Chastity nodded, barely able to stand on the rubbery legs perched beneath her. But a secure arm linked with hers, helped guide her through the door and the rest of the way out of the temple.

Above the chatter that filled her head as the small group of people headed back to the citadel, Chastity beamed. *I'm Mrs. Seth Allen.*

Seth grinned, placing an arm around her waist and drawing her closer. "And don't you forget it."

Embarrassment burned her face. She had spoken aloud.

"Has a nice ring to it, doesn't it?" Seth squeezed her. Then he frowned. "I didn't have time to send for your ring."

"I don't need a ring." And Chastity didn't. All she needed was Seth's love, and her mother, who had walked up next to her.

"Mom, the house is gone. Everything is gone." Chastity hung her head. The weight of her actions was heavy on her shoulders as she told her mother about the sale of their belongings. Even harder was admitting that she had given the proceeds to Josh. Monies used to retain Celeste instead of release her.

A loving hand settled on Chastity's arm. "Honey, that's water under the bridge. It's over." Celeste's voice firmed. "I don't want to hear mention of this nasty incident again." Her fingers shook slightly as they tightened around Chastity's arm. "Today is your wedding day. It's a day of celebration."

Chastity's mother wasn't fooling anyone. The deeply etched lines on the woman's face screamed of her trials. Only time would heal her wounds, and those that Josh had inflicted on all of them.

With that, they entered the beautifully decorated ballroom. A lavish spread of Egorian breads, Baccarac fowl and meats, exotic native desserts from Zygoman and an array of fruits and vegetables from Earth, covered the richly adorned tables. Above them, a million sparkling lights twinkled like stars in the heavens, illuminating the great hall. Flowers and greenery appeared as if they had sprung from the drywall and floor.

Passion Flower led Chastity and Seth to the head of the table. Two large, intricately carved chairs—thrones—awaited them. Passion Flower perched on her tiptoes and brushed a kiss across Seth's cheek.

Next, she did the same to Chastity, pressing her cheek to her, saying, "The dark has been lifted. Follow the sunshine in his eyes. It will show you the way into the abode of bliss."

Then the woman bowed and took her place next to Tor, who sat at Seth's left. Terrance was on the other side of Passion

Flower, and Shawn was strangely absent. Tatiana escorted Celeste to Chastity's side. Then as a group they sat.

Immediately, servants swarmed them with wine and drink. Laughter filled the air. Yet Chastity couldn't forget Passion Flower's words. Chastity looked over at her husband. He turned and their gazes locked. Passion Flower was right. Sunshine brightened his eyes, brightened her life.

A warm hand lifted her gown and traced a path from her knee to the apex of her thighs. She cocked a brow, meeting her husband's mischievous grin. Quietly, she parted her legs, offering the seeking fingers free passage. But the dark expression of hunger on Seth's face was not appeased with the grape Chastity popped into his mouth.

Slowly, Seth bit down on the juicy fruit. Then his hand pushed past her panties. He chewed once, twice. His fingers gently probed. He chewed again and hit pay dirt as his digit sunk into her heat.

Chastity's nipples tingled, her clit swelled beneath Seth's exquisite touch as he caressed her folds. Her hips lifted from the chair to meet his thrusts, eager to reach the summit that was building inside her. When he extracted his hands from her pussy, Chastity whimpered.

"*Seth*?"

"Hush, my love."

Chastity's eyes grew wide as Seth plucked a grape off the platter and pushed it into her mouth, along with the finger that had been buried to the hilt inside her. The purple grape blended with her essence was a heady combination as she sucked gently, pulling him deeper into her hot mouth.

Suddenly, a racket from outside drew their attention. Seth's finger slipped from Chastity's mouth as a barrage of cameras and Voyeur II personnel clattered through the doors. Beyond them was Monty Jamison, with Shawn Thorenson close behind.

The wary expression on the game show host's face made Chastity wonder if he was here of his own accord, or if the brawny man behind him was the reason for his unexpected appearance.

A rough shove against the man's back answered her question.

Then, like a true professional, a smile lit Monty's face. "Cameras." The lights showered him, following his every step, then swooped in on Chastity and Seth, blinding them. Both of them brought a hand up, squinting as they adjusted to the glare.

Slowly, Chastity brought her hand back down. As Monty padded closer, Chastity could see that he looked a little green around the gills.

Monty stopped and grinned impishly into the cameras. "And so we end this competition with a surprise marriage." A hearty pat to Seth's back pushed him forward. "Miss Ambro— uh, Mrs. Allen—it appears that you have won both the money and the man."

With exaggerated effort, Monty extracted a slip of paper from his pocket and extended it to a stunned Chastity.

She blinked and gazed down at the blurry numbers on the check.

So many zeros. She trembled, remembering why she had entered the contest, the reason for it sitting safely next to her. Chastity closed her eyes for a moment, recalling her anxiety when Seth appeared on stage. Seven days, six nights as slave to the only man she ever loved. The ups and downs she had experienced.

Slowly, her chin rose and she opened her eyes. Seth smiled, his head nodding toward the check in encouragement. "Go ahead—take it. You won, baby, it's yours."

Won? Little goose bumps rose all over Chastity's body as her fingers closed around the cool paper. *Won?*

It was true, Voyeur II had lost and Chastity had won. She glanced up at Seth. Without a second thought, she passed the draft to her mother.

Tears glistened in Celeste's eyes as she stared down at the check in her hand. Then her eyes rose. "Chastity?"

Chastity swallowed hard. "It's yours, Mom." She clasped Seth's hand and weaved her fingers through his. She turned and gazed deep into his bright eyes. "I gained something more precious than money, Mom. I won a second chance at love."

About the author:

Arizona is the place Mackenzie McKade calls home along with her husband, three daughters, and grandson. If she isn't at the computer writing or buried nose deep in a book, you'll find her on a four-wheeler, or a jet ski, or being pulled behind her family's 26' Monterey boat on an oblong tube called a 'hot dog'. As writing is a passion with many—it's an obsession with her. Who knew that the wild things going on in her head someone would actually buy? But she's thankful you do and hopes you find joy and entertainment in her sometimes—okay most of the time—risqué ramblings.

Mackenzie welcomes mail from readers. You can write to her c/o Ellora's Cave Publishing at 1056 Home Avenue, Akron OH 44310-3502.

Why an electronic book?

We live in the Information Age—an exciting time in the history of human civilization in which technology rules supreme and continues to progress in leaps and bounds every minute of every hour of every day. For a multitude of reasons, more and more avid literary fans are opting to purchase e-books instead of paperbacks. The question to those not yet initiated to the world of electronic reading is simply: *why?*

1. *Price*. An electronic title at Ellora's Cave Publishing and Cerridwen Press runs anywhere from 40-75% less than the cover price of the <u>exact same title</u> in paperback format. Why? Cold mathematics. It is less expensive to publish an e-book than it is to publish a paperback, so the savings are passed along to the consumer.

2. *Space*. Running out of room to house your paperback books? That is one worry you will never have with electronic novels. For a low one-time cost, you can purchase a handheld computer designed specifically for e-reading purposes. Many e-readers are larger than the average handheld, giving you plenty of screen room. Better yet, hundreds of titles can be stored within your new library—a single microchip. (Please note that Ellora's Cave and Cerridwen Press does not endorse any specific brands. You can check our website at www.ellorascave.com or

www.cerridwenpress.com for customer recommendations we make available to new consumers.)

3. *Mobility.* Because your new library now consists of only a microchip, your entire cache of books can be taken with you wherever you go.

4. *Personal preferences are accounted for.* Are the words you are currently reading too small? Too large? Too...**ANNOYING**? Paperback books cannot be modified according to personal preferences, but e-books can.

5. *Instant gratification.* Is it the middle of the night and all the bookstores are closed? Are you tired of waiting days—sometimes weeks—for online and offline bookstores to ship the novels you bought? Ellora's Cave Publishing sells instantaneous downloads 24 hours a day, 7 days a week, 365 days a year. Our e-book delivery system is 100% automated, meaning your order is filled as soon as you pay for it.

Those are a few of the top reasons why electronic novels are displacing paperbacks for many an avid reader. As always, Ellora's Cave and Cerridwen Press welcomes your questions and comments. We invite you to email us at service@ellorascave.com, service@cerridwenpress.com or write to us directly at: 1056 Home Ave. Akron OH 44310-3502.